BLOWN

BLOWN

NOLON KING

STERLING & STONE

To YOU, the reader.
Thank you for your support.
Thank you for the wonderful emails.
Thank you for the thoughtful reviews.
Thank you for reading and loving our stories.

Chapter One

TUESDAY ...

ALISON DESPERATELY NEEDED something to take the edge off, but unlike most of her so-called friends, she refused to treat her every emotional swing with a pill.

Even pulling into a parking space at the Rolling Knolls Country Club (never too near the clubhouse) made Alison want to start grinding her teeth. Actually walking into the place and then carrying on long-winded yet entirely vacuous conversations with a rotating gaggle of wealthy housewives and overly indulged soccer moms was enough to put her in a cold sweat. *Every time.*

Even after all these years — nearly twenty of them now, if Alison included the time before she and Tom finally traded *I dos*, back when she was working so furiously to earn a hint of affection from a soon-to-be mother-in-law who Alison now understood had zero capacity to offer it.

She would never step foot inside the country club

again, if were up to her. Sure, plenty of people in Las Orillas aspired to be like the Botox-infused fembots that littered the grounds like so many lost balls in all those sprawling acres of manicured lawn.

High school had made Alison miserable. All the cool kids with too much cash spending four years making her feel terrible about herself. To her mind they were the scariest breed of people. Even with everything, they wanted those below them to feel like they had nothing.

Now, as a good wife worthy of the blessed life her husband had given to her, fostering relationships and remaining pleasant with those very same people was just another part of her job.

The women here were Tom's bread and butter, which meant she had to spread herself emotionally thin in order to keep him happy. And for Eleanor to orbit the *idea* that she *might* be a worthy match for her son. To make sure that Sarah thought she was a good mom who could get along with her friends' parents when she needed to.

Not that there were any parents in this particular crowd. Tiffany had made it clear on numerous occasions that if she was ever "forced to be a mom," she would pay a surrogate because "to hell with that shit ruining her body."

Alison was at the country club to help Tiffany and her little cadre of sycophants "plan" their annual charity drive. She was helping at Tom's insistence, even though Alison knew from both instinct and experience that she would end up doing most of the work.

She wished the meeting was on the weekend instead of during the school day. At least then Sarah would be with her, and Alison wouldn't have to go through this all alone like she'd had to more and more all the time.

"I have a great idea!" Tiffany crowed.

Alison didn't need to hear whatever her frenemy was thinking to know it was something she would have to smile through. Same as she could already imagine Jenna and Belinda's ass-licking responses.

"I can't wait to hear it." Alison forced a smile.

Tiffany wasn't just gorgeous, she was actually a former model, now married to a sugar daddy in his sixties. She availed herself of every cutting-edge beauty treatment money can buy. At just twenty-four years old, Tiffany was *already* sweating the mounting years and her ability to keep Richard's interest. A reasonable concern considering she was already wife number three.

Though Tiffany wasn't the first person she'd ever met who had apparently grown up with ambitions of one day becoming a trophy wife — Rolling Knolls seemed to stock them like bottles of wine in a cellar — she was certainly the most obnoxious about it. Tiffany had always acted rich, but Alison knew a fellow survivor of impoverishment when she saw one.

Jenna was engaged to an actual billionaire, but even her fiancé's majority stake in HealthyHome wasn't enough. She had always *wanted* to be a model, and figured if she kept her perfectly shaped nose far enough up Tiffany's butt, the queen bee might throw a few former contacts her way. In the meantime, Jenna would have to settle for an endless array of selfies and scheduled photoshoots detailing her "everyday life."

She was always copying Tiffany *just enough* to highlight her obsession without making the imitation (or downright mimicry) her defining characteristic. Jenna was always dieting, dipping into the latest fad or toying with slang she couldn't quite pull off, even though at twenty-four she hadn't actually aged out of the language. Jenna was always offering Alison fashion or diet tips that she didn't want or need, and never had any intention of following. She always seemed to be working to impress Tiffany without ever realizing how little the queen bee actually cared.

Belinda was a sort of odd woman out in Rolling Knolls in that her husband had married Belinda for *her* money. They played deeply-in-love better than most, but Alison could see right through it. Able was born into an absurdly wealthy family that had lost all of their money thanks to a series of bad real estate investments in the early 2000s. Belinda was quite the party girl; drugs, especially coke, plus a teenage arrest for possession she was actually proud of, for the 'street cred' it apparently gave her. But when her family passed, the will stated in no uncertain terms that she had to settle down and marry someone respectable before she could access any of her waiting offshore accounts.

But the will said nothing about that husband needing to be straight.

Maybe Alison was wrong, and Belinda's gorgeous, sophisticated, George Clooney lookalike really didn't give a shit if his smokey-eyed and raven-haired bride was grabbing her ankles for any willing gentleman outside of their country club circle. Members specifically. Cabana boys and massage therapists were apparently both on the table, since Alison had heard a few stories about both. Belinda loved to brag, but odds were strong that Able had shared a few such dalliances with the occasional cabana boy himself.

So yes, Alison wanted to be anywhere else in the world right now, but she took tremendous pride in being the very best wife she could possibly be, and if Tom needed her to hear all about Tiffany's "great idea," then that's exactly what she was going to do.

"I've been thinking about how you and Sarah are volunteering to help all those poor little puppies that can't be adopted … *that's* what inspired my idea." Typical Tiffany, needing to give her idea an origin story instead of just saying it.

"They're not 'puppies,'" Alison corrected, despite knowing that was a fruitless exercise.

"You know what I mean," Tiffany laughed. "*Puppies* equals *little dogs.*"

Even if that was how the word worked, it wasn't like the shelters were only filled with smaller dogs. But it did make sense that Tiffany would see the world through the lens of her dog, Dickens, an absurdly spoiled Pomapoo she carried everywhere, and was peeking out of her ridiculous little "puppy purse" now.

"So what's the idea?" Jenna asked.

Belinda was barely paying attention, her wandering eyes now gazing out the clubhouse windows, onto the golf course where she was probably looking for a caddy to sit on.

"I'm going to raise money so that we can give those unwanted doggies a makeover!" Tiffany clapped for herself.

"*A makeover?*" Alison repeated, because that was so much less confrontational than *You've gotta be kidding me.*

"Right! Just think: we can create some character costumes and give those poor, ugly little puppies some full-on makeovers. That ought to give them a chance at finding a home!"

"So … makeup on dogs?" Alison nodded, buying a moment to conjure her rebuttal.

"Exactly!" Tiffany basked in her self-anointed brilliance.

"That's a great idea!" Jenna said.

"How old do you think he is?" Belinda nodded at a

passing server, who didn't look old enough to buy himself a drink. "I bet he has a big dick."

"Rescue dogs need help with socialization more than anything else. A lot of the … puppies … that end up in shelters have had some sort of traumatic experience, and they need to be trained out of bad habits. They don't really need … makeup."

"Oh my gawd, Alison." Tiffany laughed at her. "You're so nuts and bolts."

"I'm not sure what you mean." The smile was getting harder to hold.

"She means you're a stick-in-the-mud," Jenna explained.

"I'll be back," Belinda muttered, already walking away, on her way to a "chance encounter" with the server.

Tiffany continued. "Of course they need training and whatever, but isn't that really like step two? I guess your 'all dogs are equal' stand is admirable, but it's hardly realistic. No one wants an ugly dog. That's why the shelters are full of them. My idea solves that problem."

Alison shook her head. "I'm not sure that makeup and costumes are really going to solve—"

"Oh my gawd," she said again, "you're not even listening. Think about the facts here."

"I would love to. Do you have any?" Alison laughed, making light of their moment before it escalated into something else.

"Like, imagine one of those ugly dogs is missing an eye. Do you really think that anyone is ever really going to adopt a dog that reminds them of a pirate?"

"Um …" Alison wasn't sure where to go with that.

"Of course not!" Jenna answered for her.

"Or, you know how some of the ugliest mongrels have messed-up teeth?" As if on cue, Dickens bared his perfect teeth. Tiffany and her Pomapoo probably shared a dentist. "No one wants a dog with Steve Buscemi teeth."

"I didn't know—"

"But imagine that dog is wearing an adorable little mask. No one will even know they have a mongrel with Mississippi mouth until *after* they get the thing home. You see what I'm saying?"

Unfortunately, she did.

"We could call it Mongrel Mardi Gras!" Jenna suggested.

Alison's phone started ringing, saving her from having to decide which of the two insulting ideas required her attention most, or at least first.

"If you'll just excuse me for a moment." She turned away with a hard-working smile and answered her call. "This is Alison."

"Good afternoon, Mrs. Tanner. This is Lucinda Washington, the principal at—"

"Of course, Mrs. Washington, I know who you are." Alison's heart was already pounding. "Is everything okay with Sarah?"

"Unfortunately not."

"Is she hurt?" Alison swallowed a knot.

Jenna appeared curious, and Tiffany agitated by the interruption.

"No, Mrs. Tanner. It's nothing like that. But I am going to need you to come and pick her up. And we will need to have a conversation when you get here."

"Can you tell me what the problem is?"

"Sarah has been caught smoking marijuana on campus with two other students."

Alison gasped, hand to her mouth like a cartoon. She was tempted to say something like, *Are you sure there hasn't been some mistake?* But of course there hadn't been any mistake. Now she was going to have to kill Sarah, if Tom didn't murder Alison first for allowing something like this to happen.

"I'm so sorry." She shook her head to herself, glad that her back was to Tiffany and Jenna so they couldn't bear witness to her blooming embarrassment. "I'll be right there."

She ended the call, got a glimpse of Belinda touching her potential conquest on his arm, then turned back to the pair of socialites awaiting a fresh serving of still-steaming gossip.

"What is it?" Tiffany asked. "Did Sarah do something terrible?"

"I'll see you girls later. I need to go and pick her up from school."

Tiffany giggled, clearly delighted by Alison's misfortune. "You're not really planning on jetting out of here without telling us what she did, are you?"

"Apparently a couple of her friends were smoking pot and she happened to be with them when they got caught."

"But she didn't inhale, is that it?" Jenna looked at Tiffany, waiting for her pat on the head.

"Ooooh … Tom is going to spank you." Tiffany giggled again. "Don't worry, sweetheart, quitting is easy. I've done it a bunch of times!"

Alison didn't know whether she was more furious, or humiliated.

Either way, right now she felt like the worst mother ever.

"I've gotta go," she told them again, ignoring their comments and questions to leave the pair standing with open mouths.

Belinda turned from her prey to look at Alison curiously on her way to the door.

She left the clubhouse, walked to her faraway spot, shaking her head and wondering who was responsible for this mess on the way.

And then she realized:

It had to be Miguel.

Chapter Two

"I JUST WANT to make sure that we're all on the same page here," the principal said.

"Of course." Alison nodded again.

"With all due respect, Mrs. Tanner, I'd like to hear the same thing from your daughter."

"Sure," Sarah said, sounding indifferent.

"We all know you can do better than that!" Alison snapped at her daughter, before turning back to the principal. "She's just embarrassed. Nothing like this has ever happened to her before."

"You mean the drug use, or the getting caught?" Lucinda gave her a dry smile.

"Either one." Alison kept her hands in her lap. She wanted them to stay folded but couldn't help clenching and unclenching her fists. "This is new territory for both of us. I really am very sorry."

"I don't think you're the one who should be apologizing," Lucinda said.

Alison turned to her daughter. "Sarah?"

"I'm very sorry … for doing something that's already legal in this state."

"Legality has nothing to do with it, Miss Tanner. You are sixteen years old and were caught with a controlled substance on school property. Worse, you don't seem to be taking this situation seriously at all."

"She is taking it seriously," Alison said.

"I'm taking it super seriously," Sarah agreed, in words if not in tone.

"We will deal with this at home. But in the meantime, what is her consequence for this first-time offense, Mrs. Washington?"

She leaned forward. "You seem to be placing a lot of emphasis on this being Sarah's first time. You do understand that doesn't diminish the severity of what has happened?"

"I understand the seriousness of this situation." Alison nodded. "And like I said, her father and I will deal with this in a way that fully supports what you're working to accomplish here at school. But there is a big difference between a habitual drug user, and someone who has clearly made a mistake by hanging out with the wrong crowd and—"

"Right, Mom. Because I'm not capable of making any decisions for myself."

Alison turned to Sarah. "Is this a decision you're proud of?"

Her daughter grunted without answering.

Sarah wasn't the type of kid to use drugs. But as much as it saddened Alison, her daughter *was* the kind of kid who had a deep need to fit in with her friends, even if doing so came at the expense of her own character. She had obviously lost a battle with peer pressure, and surely that first shot had been fired by her new friend, Miguel.

"Again, I feel like we're focusing on the wrong elements

here," Lucinda replied, before returning to Alison's question. "Sarah is facing a mandatory three-day suspension, and I need you *both* to understand that she is getting off easy."

"Absolutely." Alison hated that answer, already imagining Tom's response, but she vigorously nodded while Sarah sat like a statue beside her.

"In LA County, students can be arrested for possession of marijuana on school property under California law."

"Arrested?" Alison repeated. "But it's legal."

"Marijuana is still a controlled substance. And again, it isn't legal on campus. Adults can still be arrested for an ounce or less, assuming classes or school activities are underway. You may think this is nothing—"

"I certainly don't think that!" Alison exclaimed.

"—but it's a misdemeanor charge punishable by a maximum fine of $500, or ten days in a county jail."

"Jail!" It was getting harder to breathe.

And still Sarah seemed like she couldn't care less.

"While we still must adhere to Health and Safety Code, Section 11357, Sarah is a juvenile, and we can afford some leniency. However, if Sarah is ever caught with drugs on campus again, she will be expelled immediately." Lucinda shook her head. "No exceptions."

"I can assure you, this was a lapse in my daughter's judgment. Nothing like this has ever happened before, and I promise it will never happen again."

Lucinda narrowed her dark eyes on Alison, making her want to shrink back in the chair. "Let's hope that's the case, for all of our sakes."

Alison was muttering more apologies as she stood, trying to ignore the amusement that appeared to brighten her daughter's eyes. Not a word until they were both in the car and Alison was pulling her Porsche

Cayenne out of the school parking lot and onto Appian Avenue.

Then, finally: "What do you have to say for yourself?"

"Um … how about, weed is legal and less dangerous than the wine you drink every night?"

"Really, Sarah? You want to get smart with me about this right now?"

"I'm not sure what you're hoping to hear, Mom. Do you want me to agree with you?" She shook her head. "Because that's not going to happen."

"Where is this coming from?" Alison had to keep her eyes on the road, infuriated by the garbage coming out of her daughter's mouth. "Since when do you think it's acceptable to skip class and do drugs with—"

"Cannabis is a plant."

"That's what you have to say?" Alison could only spare a moment of glaring at Sarah before she returned her disappointed gaze to the road. "We'll just see what your father has to say about this when he gets home."

Alison had every intention of leaving it at that, and did manage to stay silent for another seven seconds or so, but then the tirade came before she could stop it.

"There is *nothing* worse for you than drugs, young lady. If you were planning to throw your entire future away on one terrible decision, you're doing a great job. Insist that marijuana isn't a drug all you want — believe me, I've heard all the arguments. But cannabis wouldn't be a controlled substance if it wasn't dangerous. You have a beautiful brain. Do you really want to destroy it like this?"

Alison shook her head, juggling too many thoughts at once as a past she wanted to forget collided with a present she would do anything to protect. "Weed *is* a drug, Sarah. It messes with your brain *and* it's addictive. The stuff destroys your memory." Another shake of her head. "I seriously can't imagine you getting called into the principal's office for anything worse."

Instead of apologizing, Sarah laughed in her mother's face and made everything worse. "Well then, I find your lack of imagination seriously embarrassing."

"Are you really being smart with me right now?"

"It's amazing that I can be, you know, considering all those brain cells I've been killing."

Alison kept driving, refusing to dignify that with a response, chewing on her bottom lip while gripping the steering wheel.

Kids were *way* too lax about drugs these days. It was even worse now than when Alison had been Sarah's age. The cause was obvious. With the recent wave of legalization sweeping the nation, of course people were going to disregard the dangers. But *legal* didn't equal *safe*, and it never had.

Alison was proud that she had never taken anything stronger than Advil ... and that epidural the doctor had finally talked her into after the screaming started, going into her ninth hour of labor. But she did understand what her daughter was going through.

Maybe she should try to be more understanding.

Maybe she shouldn't be handling this like her own mother had.

Maybe this wasn't the end of the world, and Tom wouldn't be furious like she kept imagining.

What happened to her in high school had been his fault, after all.

Alison didn't exactly have a dirt floor childhood, but her parents had watched every dollar, and used way more of them than they could afford sending her to Constellation, an absurdly priced private school where they felt certain that a steep investment in their daughter would ultimately afford her a much better life than the one they could provide.

Living an off-the-rack life amid a bespoke student body was hard, and Alison had spent a disproportionate part of her high school career trying to fit in. Only after making friends with Leanne Graham her senior year did she come anywhere close. Thank to Leanne, Alison got invited to a senior party. The cool kids were all drinking and smoking — cigarettes and weed. She didn't partake even then, and felt guilty just being around the illegal activity, perpetually scared of getting caught and disappointing (and embarrassing) her parents. Paranoid as she usually was back then, Alison had practically expected police to raid that party, and was barely surprised when they did.

Her shock came when one of the party-goers rushed to flee the scene and shoved a bag of contraband into her hand. Alison had grabbed the bag before she knew what was happening. Officers on the scene had a hard time believing that sack full of pills and weed didn't belong to her like she tried to insist.

That experience was both the best and worst thing that had ever happened to Alison.

She got arrested, despite her insistence that she'd never seen the bag until a minute or so before the police were questioning her about it. But she did earn the respect of everyone at the party for keeping her mouth shut, especially from the bag's owner — Tom Tanner, quarterback and MVP of Constellation's championship-winning football team. She got expelled, but ended up on a first date with her future husband just two weeks later.

"You have nothing to say?" Alison asked, a mile from home, after several minutes of heavy silence.

"What do you want from me, Mom?"

"I don't know, Sarah. How about we start with an apology?"

"Okay. I'm sorry you don't know the first thing about weed."

"That's not what—"

"Seriously, your *Reefer Madness* stance is embarrassing. Weed isn't addictive."

"Yes it is."

"Weed is like chocolate. Most people who smoke would rather have it than not, but that's not the same. And even if marijuana does mess with your short-term memory, it's not like smoking gives you Alzheimer's."

"Are you saying that your short-term memory isn't important?"

"If it helps me forget this conversation, then I figure it's a bonus."

"I seriously can't believe you right now. Your father is going to—" Alison stopped, her heart back to pounding at the sight of the police car parked in front of their house. "Great. Now we have to deal with the cops."

"Like the cops would really waste their time with this," Sarah said.

"Like usual, you have no idea what you're talking about."

"Okay."

Alison wanted to say, *Don't you okay me, young lady!*, but she kept chewing her bottom lip instead.

She pulled into the driveway, then killed then engine and got out of her SUV. A pair of men stood on her porch — an officer in uniform and a gentleman wearing a suit.

"Mrs. Tanner?"

She nodded at the man in the suit. "May I help you?"

"I'm Detective Ian Banks. I'm afraid that there's been

an accident." Then he cleared his throat and delivered the rest. "We need you to come down to the station with us."

Her heart stopped. A second later she stuttered, "Why?"

"To identify your husband's body."

Alison was staring at the detective as he said something else, but all she could hear was Sarah screaming bloody murder behind her.

Chapter Three

Alison drew a deep breath before entering the downtown precinct, adjacent to the Las Orillas courthouse. But that deep breath did little for her; she was still sweating out of her skin.

The station was only seven miles from their home on Cedar, but she had spent them all scared, bordering terrified, alone in her Cayenne as she followed the detective with her hands at ten and two on the wheel.

She had sent Sarah to stay with her best friend, Brooke. Alison couldn't stand the thought of dealing with Tom's mother right now, or any time, really. And whether the body belonged to her father or not, that wasn't anything a sixteen-year-old girl ever needed to see.

Alison admonished herself. She had to stop doing that, considering the worst as if it were possible. Of course Tom wasn't dead and this was all a big misunderstanding.

That's what Alison had told herself when Detective Banks delivered fake news on her porch, it's what she told herself on the way downtown, and what she had to keep telling herself now.

He led her to a small room with mirrored windows on two of the four sides. It looked like every interrogation room she'd seen on all those crime shows, but felt far more cold and sterile than she would've thought.

She sat opposite him at a metal table where a closed manila folder was sitting. "We're not going to the morgue?"

"Not necessary." He shook his head. "Usually this is done with photos, unless there's doubt or you really want to see him in person."

"I … I don't know." Alison swallowed a thick lump in her throat.

"It's okay," said Detective Banks. "Take your time."

She stared at the closed folder, her heart racing, her chest feeling tighter.

There was no way to prepare for something like this. A part of her was grieving already, even though she'd yet to see his body. She wasn't ready to say goodbye.

She needed to be a big girl and get this over with.

She steeled herself and nodded. "Okay, show me."

"I need to warn you—"

"I don't want to know anything." If the detective finished his sentence Alison might run from the room. "Just … show me what you need to show me."

He opened the folder and slid one of several photos to her.

She should have waited for his warning.

Yes, it *was* her husband. No doubt about it. Tom no longer looked handsome. His strong jawline still balanced an almost effeminate nose, and the three-day beard he'd left with this morning would have perfectly accented his face. But his throat was cut wide open and there were gashes all over his body. Alison was desperate to believe that this was some lookalike, but the Army tattoo on his left shoulder wasn't a lie.

She swallowed her vomit, barely managing to keep her whimper inside. She braced herself, breathing to keep the tears from coming in a flood.

Her eyes moved from the photo to her shaking hands, staring in disbelief and nodding to herself. "That's him," she muttered.

"Thank you." Banks took the photo from Alison and returned it to the folder before closing it, thus sparing her the rest of the images.

"What happened?" she finally blurted.

"Where were you this morning?"

"I brought my daughter to school, I had errands to run, and then I went to the club for lunch with friends. Why?"

"Your husband's body was found in the restroom at This is Sparta. Do you know what he was doing there?"

"Working out? Meeting a client? Working out with a client?" Every word made her feel even more frantic. "What happened?"

"What do you know about your husband's activities on April 11 of this year?"

"I'm sorry?" Alison wasn't sure what she expected to hear, but it certainly wasn't that.

"How about on May 8? Does that date ring any bells?"

"I have no idea what you're talking about." Alison shook her head, inches from losing it. "What happened to my husband, Officer—"

"Detective." He offered her a well-polished smile and introduced himself again. "Ian Banks."

"Okay, Detective Banks" — his name tasted bitter on her tongue — "can you please tell me what happened to my husband?"

A slight nod followed by an unexpected answer. "Your

husband was involved in a murder. His body was discovered late this morning."

"*Involved,*" Alison repeated. "You mean he was a victim."

"Your husband was in Las Vegas for two days in January. Any idea what he was doing there?"

"He was at a convention. Why are—"

"What kind of convention … if you don't mind my asking, Mrs. Tanner."

"Some consumer electronics show or something. He was hoping to pick up a few clients."

"What kind of clients?"

"For his consulting business."

He nodded, but gave her a curious look. "And that makes sense to you? That a man with a successful Southern California consulting business would be in Vegas trolling for clients?"

"I wouldn't say he was 'trolling for clients.' He was—"

"Did he have any scheduled meetings that you know of?"

"Tom didn't really tell me much about his business."

"Are you sure about that?" The detective stared at her hard.

Alison shifted in her seat. "I'm happy to answer your questions, but I deserve to know what's going on here first. My husband's been murdered and I'm in here getting interrogated by a homicide detective about random things that have nothing to do with anything."

"I apologize for the misunderstanding." Banks shook his head. "The questions have everything to do with the case. We've been looking into Tom for some time now."

"What? Why?"

He leaned forward, seeming to assess her for a long moment before delivering his answer. The man seemed calm and methodical. The exact personality type Alison got along with best. Under normal circumstances. These were anything but.

"Your husband's death wasn't random, Mrs. Tanner. His body was mutilated in a way that matches the MO of a local drug gang."

"Why would my husband have anything to do with — a local drug gang?"

"That's what I was hoping you could tell me." His smile was friendly enough, but Alison didn't believe him. Cops were always playing nice. "Who did your husband sell drugs for?"

She had fallen asleep while watching a thriller. She would wake up any second now, as soon as Tom rolled over and pressed his hardness against her.

"WHO DID HE SELL DRUGS FOR?" Alison was surprised by her own yell, and downright shocked when she started laughing hysterically. "This has to be some sort of misunderstanding."

"Cooperate with us and you can plea bargain for a reduced sentence."

"I don't know what you expect from me ..." Alison was still laughing, hard enough that she needed to stop for a few deep breaths before she could get anything else out. "My husband was a successful consultant. Why would he even *need* to sell drugs?"

"Has it ever occurred to you that your husband's business might have been a front?"

"Of course it hasn't." She laughed again. "I want to speak with someone in homicide."

"I'm afraid that's not possible."

"OF COURSE IT'S POSSIBLE!" Then more hysterical laughter.

The detective stared at her, maybe even *through* her, saying nothing.

"This is outrageous," Alison added.

But still nothing from Ian Banks.

"What is it you're expecting from me?" She swallowed hard to keep the rest from slipping out: *My husband was just murdered, you animal!*

"We've been after this organization for a long time. If you're willing to cooperate by turning on the dealer that you and your husband were working for—"

"ME AND MY HUSBAND?"

"I understand you're upset, but all the yelling really isn't—"

"I want to call my lawyer." Words Alison never imagined coming out of her mouth. At least not from the inside of an interrogation room.

"You're sure you want to do that?"

"I've never been more sure of anything in my life," she replied, sounding several degrees braver than she felt.

"Do you have their number handy, or is that something I can help you to get?"

"I'm fine. Thank you." Alison took out her phone, wanting to hurl it at the detective's forehead. Then she opened her contacts, found *Jarod Harris,* and pressed *Call.*

Four rings, then right to voicemail.

"Hi there, Jarod ... this is Alison ... Tanner ..." She swallowed, wishing she was alone without Detective Ian Banks staring right through her. "There's been a terrible accident ... with Tom. I'm at the police station right now and need you to call me as soon as you get this."

She hung up the phone and returned it to her purse.

Banks kept staring at her.

Again, she shifted in her seat. "How long do I have to stay here?"

"You're welcome to go right now."

"So now you don't think I'm in cahoots with my drug-dealing husband?"

"I apologize if this is all coming as a shock to you," said the detective, sounding surprisingly sincere — not that she believed him. "I just want the truth. If you're genuinely innocent, then you have my word that I'll do everything in my power to make sure you're cleared of your husband's criminal activities."

"*Alleged criminal activities*," Alison corrected.

"If you're lying, then I will make sure you end up in jail."

The confidence in his threat was chilling.

"I swear, whatever this is, I don't know anything." She shook her head, vehemently, as if that might help to underscore her point.

"Even if that's true, I'm sure you'll find the next few days illuminating. And I assure you, Mrs. Tanner, your life will be much easier if you cooperate with—"

"Are we done here?"

The detective stood. "You are free to go at any time."

She stood and started toward the door.

"One moment, Mrs. Tanner."

"What is it?" Alison snapped as she turned back around.

He slowly approached, showing her his open palm. "I'm going to have to ask for your phone."

"Of course you are." She pulled it out of her purse and shoved it into his hand.

"I'll give you a call on your home line if I have any questions."

Alison tried not to growl. "If you have any questions, you can talk to my lawyer."

Banks handed her his card. "You might want to have him give me a call directly."

She took it, then he opened the door for her.

Alison left the station without another word, climbed into her Cayenne, and made it three long blocks before she turned the corner onto Ocean and started to scream.

Chapter Four

"Just tell me what I need to do next." Alison hated that it sounded like she was begging.

Jarod sighed with a shake of his head. "It's not that simple. There isn't one path here."

Alison had been at her lawyer's office for two hours now and felt even more lost than she'd felt on the way over. Her husband had been murdered, then she'd been interrogated by some know-it-all detective, only to have her lawyer act like he was granting a big favor by fitting her in.

All that time in the waiting area while he finished up with his client, feeling like the receptionist was judging her, followed by even more anxiety while Jarod called Detective Banks.

Most infuriatingly, not only did he not have any answers, it felt to Alison like Jarod might not believe her. Everything about this situation was unacceptable.

"Can we sue them? The police department, I mean?"

Jarod shook his head, bemused, like he wanted to laugh. "No. I'm sorry, but that wouldn't get us anywhere.

First things first, we need to figure out your money situation."

"You mean for your retainer?" Alison asked, growing more insulted by the minute. "Isn't that—"

"No." He shook his head again, sobriety now alight in his eyes. "Your assets have all been frozen."

"You're kidding me. How can they do that? Just because they suspect that—"

"Not only have your assets been frozen, the police searched your house while you were being interrogated, so—"

"How can they do that?"

"With a warrant, Alison. But the search means that if you had any cash stashed at the house, you can consider it gone."

"I keep a few hundred dollars in a Pringles can in the pantry, just in case, but that's it."

"You're sure?"

"Why wouldn't I be sure?"

"Well then, it looks like you're effectively broke. Except for whatever you might have in your wallet. So like I said, we'll need to figure out your money situation."

"I don't understand why this is happening to me. There must be some mistake." Then, after her lawyer left her without an answer: "RIGHT?"

Jarod took a long moment to look at her, but still didn't answer Alison's question. A habit he'd adopted early in their conversation and hadn't yet managed to shed.

"I don't want you talking to anyone about anything."

"What would I even say?" Alison asked.

"Absolutely nothing."

"How long do you think it will take to clear this up?"

Again he gave her a curious look, as if trying to solve a

puzzle. "You're not exactly making this easy on me, Alison."

"What do you mean?"

"I think you know what I mean."

"Really, I don't."

"I've already spoken with Detective Banks."

"I'm well aware of that. I gave you the number, and was waiting while you talked to him. *Remember?*" Alison was feeling agitated enough to break something.

"There's more than enough evidence here. It sure looks like Tom was—"

"Guilty? Of course *the detective* thinks that! Otherwise he wouldn't have been interrogating me! But you're my lawyer, Jarod — isn't it your job to believe me?"

"Absolutely not." He shook his head. "My job is to keep you out of jail. I'm sorry about what happened to Tom, and I do understand that this is all a big shock. But even if you didn't know … the depth of things … I have a hard time believing that you had *no idea* what was happening or what your husband was doing. So, please, if you want my help, then I need you to start telling me everything you know."

The tears finally started to fall. "But I don't know anything!"

"Detective Banks did seem to have a hard-on for catching Tom, but he doesn't necessarily think that you're involved. If you are innocent here, I suggest you cooperate completely. Then I can do my best to make sure the investigation focuses on—"

"You've gotta be kidding me." Alison left her seat and started pacing the office. "Why aren't you helping me to prove his innocence — YOU'RE OUR LAWYER!"

Jarod shook his head. "I'm *your* lawyer, Alison. With all

due respect, Tom is dead. And given the circumstances of his passing I think it's safe to assume he was involved with some dangerous people. My job right now isn't to prove that his murder was an accident, it's to prove that Tom was acting in isolation and that you had little — or even better, *zero* knowledge of his wrongdoing. Then I can keep you out of prison."

"Why would *I* go to prison?" But Alison didn't need to ask; she had seen all those shows. "What are the best and worst case scenarios here?"

"Best case, we prove you had nothing to do with your husband's criminal activities, and no prior knowledge of his activities. Failing to prove that, we would focus on getting you off with the minimum penalty. That means covering your tracks."

"What do you mean 'failing to prove that'? I'm telling you, Jarod, I had nothing to do with any of this. And no idea. There are no tracks to cover."

"So far you've only dealt with one detective. I've dealt with enough of them in my time to get a decent read. This guy seems fair. But soon the DEA is going to get involved, and those agents tend to be … more aggressive. I suggest telling both the police and the DEA everything you know so—"

"I DON'T KNOW ANYTHING!" Alison sat back down and drew a deep breath to reset herself. "Why won't you believe me?"

Jarod sighed and finally gave Alison her first truly compassionate look of the day. "You'll have to forgive me. I've been a lawyer for nearly thirty years. I've seen this cycle too many times — I don't know how to ignore it."

"And what cycle is that?" Alison asked through clenched teeth.

"The one where a client comes in here claiming their innocence. Then a month later the truth is out there like a cancer in my life. At this point, it doesn't really make any difference, *as long as my clients are honest with me.*"

"So, if you can get away with it, then good for you?" It was getting harder and harder to throttle her fury.

"Not exactly." He shrugged. "But honestly, at this point I'm a lot more concerned with my clients making me look like an asshole in court. Guess how many times that's happened." Jarod insulted her with a laugh. "So maybe you don't know anything, and just *maybe* Tom was actually innocent here, but that's awfully hard to swallow considering—"

"How dare you!" Alison was back out of her seat. But this time she wasn't pacing. She planted both of her palms on Jarod's desk, then leaned into his face and finished her thought. "How dare you sit there and talk about Tom like that. He was your client, and you were his. I have no idea what's actually happening here, but isn't it *possible* that my husband wasn't a drug dealer? Isn't it *possible* that Tom has been framed?"

"Of course it's possible." Jarod offered her a conciliatory nod.

"But you'd rather not believe that. It's easier to assume he was guilty."

"I would very much *rather* believe in his innocence, Alison." Now Jarod had an almost icy serenity. "But there is a big difference between making an assumption and drawing a conclusion based on the available evidence."

"You mean whatever it is that cop told you."

"Yes. But it's not like that's all I have to go on. You just said that Tom was my client just as much as I was his, correct?"

Alison swallowed and nodded, her nerves on fire.

"Tom rather abruptly quit his consulting a few years back. Our last meeting was 'on the house.' His way of apologizing for walking away without any warning. He referred me to Druer & Beck. They've done a great job for me, so everything ended up working out for the best. But whatever Tom was doing for money, I'm quite sure that 'consulting' has nothing to do with it."

Yet another brick on her toe. But still, that was hardly proof that her murdered husband had been dealing drugs. "So as far as you're concerned, he's guilty."

"Until proven innocent."

"Isn't it supposed to be the other way around?"

Jarod shook his head. "Not in this office."

"Fine. If you won't help defend Tom, I'll hire a private investigator."

"Great idea. May I ask how you plan to pay for services rendered?"

"Are you asking about you or the investigator?"

"Either one," Jarod answered, holding her angry gaze.

And in that moment she suffered a pair of realizations in unison.

For the first time since marrying Tom, Alison understood exactly how much she depended on her husband for everything when it came to their money, alongside the bone-hollowing knowledge that even if he hadn't been lying to her, that misplaced over-reliance on Tom might have been the biggest mistake of her life.

"I know it might not feel like it right now, Alison, but I promise, I am on your side. Go home. Take some inventory of the situation, then give me a call back and we'll figure out what's next."

Home. The word should have made her feel better, but it turned her stomach instead.

She left the office after a mumbled goodbye, then drove to the first and last place that she wanted to go, clutching her stomach with one hand while steering with the other, crying the entire way.

Chapter Five

Alison pulled into the driveway, then sat in the cabin of her Cayenne, finally out of tears.

Jarod had told her that the cops searched her place while she was downtown. Now she thought about all those crime shows and imagined the chaos inside her home.

She needed to get out and confront her new reality. But it was all too much, and without a couple of minutes spent cradling her still-churning stomach Alison felt sure she would vomit all over her entryway rug before she could close the front door.

She turned on the radio, curious to see if the local news had anything to say about the event that had so suddenly destroyed her life. But she heard only commercials, and each one felt like a slap in the face, reminding her of a life that had been stolen away without any warning.

You can do this, Alison told herself.

Then she finally got out of the car and walked up to her front porch.

The door was unlocked, which struck her as almost brutally rude.

She went inside, grateful that her tear ducts were dry as she surveyed the mess left behind by a team of uncaring cops. The scene looked mostly like she had imagined, with their family belongings turned topsy-turvy in search of any evidence that might prove what her husband had been up to. And, apparently, that Alison had been involved in whatever it was.

They had pulled all of her pictures off the wall, emptied every one of her drawers out onto the floor, and yanked all the clothes and shoes from her closets. The shows had taught her to expect as much, but she hadn't anticipated all the unscrewed light switch plates, electrical socket and vent covers now littering both the hardwood and her carpet. Same as she had no way to anticipate the wallpaper in Tom's den hanging low like the peel of a mostly eaten banana.

It looked like a pack of wild animals had found their way inside her family's once well-appointed and lovingly cared for home. Alison had a hard time determining what was missing, and figured it would take days of cleanup before she could make a proper inventory. The Pringles can had been opened, but they had left the three $100 bills of "just in case money" with a receipt that let her know the cash had been catalogued in some way.

Sarah's laptop was the only item that seemed to be missing from her room, and even that wasn't a certainty. She rarely took the thing to school, but that rule was far from absolute. Her shoes and clothes all appeared to be there. After a quick glance in her own closet, Alison determined that the same seemed to be true for her and Tom. Despite the disarray, their clothes and shoes appeared largely untouched.

Alison passed in front of the living room window several times before she realized there was a Chevy Tahoe outside with two men sitting in it, watching her house.

Fueled by fear and rage and confusion, she broke from her usual character and marched back out of the house, down her porch, across the street, right up to the Tahoe's window.

She knocked hard on the glass, and didn't even wait for the window to lower all the way before she snapped at the men inside. "Haven't you invaded my privacy enough by going through all of my things? Do you really need to sit out here staring at me, too?"

The driver looked at Alison without responding.

But the man sitting in the passenger seat had compassionate eyes. He gave her a friendly nod and said, "I'm sorry, ma'am, but we're just here to keep you safe."

"Safe from what? I'd feel a lot safer without a couple of strangers staring at me."

He nodded again. "I'm Officer Clark, and this is my partner, Officer Fulton. It looks like your husband might have been murdered after some money went missing. The same folks who took care of him might either assume you know where that money is, or that you're somehow responsible."

"Ah, now I understand!" Alison offered the cops an excited nod. "You're here for me. Thank you … I didn't realize this was a favor. In that case, can I get you anything? Maybe some coffee? It'll just take me a couple of hours, seeing as I need to clean the giant mess in my kitchen first."

Alison turned on her heel, stomped across the street, then went inside and slammed the door.

Again she thought back to all those TV shows. Of course the cops weren't here to protect her. Those two officers were staking out her house right now because they wrongly believed that her husband was guilty, and assumed her involvement in whatever they wrongly believed he'd been doing.

And yet, one phrase in that little story felt like a hangnail in her thoughts. *Wrongly believed.*

As much as Alison was loath to believe it, the possibility introduced by Detective Banks after he'd sat her down on the other side of a cold metal table in a claustrophobic interrogation room kept expanding inside her.

Because Banks hadn't been picking on Alison, he'd been doing his job.

And as cynical as Jarod might be, he was an intelligent man who had known her husband better than most.

So as much as Alison wanted to lock the thought away, wasn't it possible that the man she had loved and trusted more than anyone else in the world was in reality a criminal?

Like everyone she had spoken to since learning of the tragedy believed him to be.

The gravity of her situation suddenly felt like an approaching tsunami. She might as well have been drowning already, with all that speculation and conjecture like a thousand pounds on her head.

Her budding embarrassment felt bottomless, and yet it kept getting deeper as she cycled through her mental Rolodex, imagining how each person might respond, picturing all the whispering behind slightly covered mouths, hearing all the snickers as she passed.

Humiliation turned to fury at Tom. Perhaps Alison would find her way back to his side, but for the moment she felt just as sure as Detective Banks and Jarod.

How could he do this to me?

She went to the kitchen, considering a cup of coffee

like she'd offered the cops, but walked across the tile floor and into the dining room instead.

She was too upset for coffee; the acid would eat through her stomach.

She wasn't just fretting for herself, she was worried about Sarah. Sarah had suffered from a relatively minor run-in with the law compared to this, and even still that could have easily ruined her life. This disaster had the potential to obliterate Sarah's chances at getting into a good college or …

Alison couldn't even finish the thought, suddenly wondering how she would pay next month's mortgage if their accounts were all frozen.

Could they actually end up homeless?

She heard Jarod in her head: *Well then, it looks like you're effectively broke. Except for whatever you might have in your wallet.*

She might have fifty dollars, plus the two Benjamins she kept tucked behind her driver's license for emergencies. And the Pringles cash. But nine out of ten purchases went straight on her debit card.

She went back into Tom's office, digging through several piles until she found all the paperwork required to start making calls. On the hard line, of course.

Sure enough, Jarod was right. The police had claimed every account. Not just the household checking and savings, Tom's retirement was also gone. And most horrifying for its implications, the secret savings account that Alison hadn't even told him about was frozen as well. She had been slowly squirreling money away for a trip to Tahiti, wanting to surprise him on their anniversary this coming summer.

And *dammit* … even Sarah's college fund was frozen.

Alison would have felt like a monster raiding that

particular account, but emptying it out would still be better than homelessness.

Was that really a possibility?

No, she supposed not, though avoiding it might mean throwing herself at her mother-in-law's mercy. Alison didn't think Eleanor would ever help, unless it meant taking Sarah for herself. Any assistance coming from her would be a devil's bargain for sure.

A chilling thought, knowing she had the worst call of her life to make, and that she would have to do it soon. Eleanor had never been shy about letting Alison know how little she liked her, and just how far out of her league he had always been. But even all the times Alison had wanted to hurt Eleanor the way Eleanor always went to great efforts to injure her didn't make it easier to inform the harpy that her Tommy was dead.

Alison went back to wandering through her broken home, this time ignoring everything that had been ransacked and focusing on what she might possibly salvage to sell.

The TVs were all there, but their computers were gone, and her phone had been confiscated at the station. Alison was surprised to find that, like the cash, they had left her jewelry alone. Buying her precious metals and gemstones had always been one of the ways Tom had shown his love, so after a decade and a half her collection was relatively impressive.

But even if she were to pawn everything in the box, Alison probably wouldn't have enough to cover more than a few months of an absurdly priced Southern California lifestyle that covered everything from a sky-high mortgage to all the organic food from Provisions that Tom "couldn't live without."

She felt lost, with no idea who to call.

Surely not her bitch of a mother-in-law. Eleanor would end up blaming Alison for turning her perfect son into a criminal.

Alison's parents were dead, and probably wouldn't have been able to help even if they had survived the cancer that killed them both too early. Their collars were so blue, they were practically cobalt, both of them bringing home such miserly wages from a plant that moved to Asia after it was proven that their chemicals had been slowly killing its workers. Just like her parents. They died deep in debt, their house auctioned to pay it all off, leaving Alison with only an aching heart and twenty-seven hundred dollars.

It hurt to admit, but she had no close friends. Alison had lost touch with all of her high school and college crew after moving to Las Orillas with Tom. His needs came first, including their social circle.

She couldn't count on any of the people she regularly associated with at the club. Alison didn't like them and they didn't like her. She had always been marked as someone who didn't really belong in their circle, no matter how hard she'd tried to fit in.

Interactions had lived behind an unspoken facade. Even when things were at their best, it was social kabuki, with Alison sucking up to women she could barely stand for the sake of her husband's consulting career.

Except, if Banks was right, Tom's "career" was something else entirely.

She walked to the mantle, where a row of pictures was askew, though at least they were still standing upright, unlike all the framed photos littering Alison's living room floor.

She picked up her wedding photo, stared at it for several seconds before deciding that the picture was a lie and smashing it against the wall.

She collapsed to the floor, crying as she wondered what she'd done in her life to deserve this tragedy. She was surrounded by terrible people, including many who had made their fortunes by exploiting others, and yet her and Sarah's lives had been turned upside down?

This wasn't how karma was supposed to work.

After enough self-pity, Alison forced herself to stand.

Then she went to the utility closet in the kitchen, almost amused at how orderly it was inside. Apparently that wasn't a place worthy of hiding evidence, so it looked like the cops had left the area mostly alone.

She grabbed a broom and the dustpan, then went to sweep up the glass.

Once done, she collapsed on the couch, a tiny part of her convinced that this nightmare would be over by the time she woke up.

Assuming she could sleep on the couch.

She was exhausted, but also wired. And right now, she didn't want to be anywhere near her bedroom. The place where she had rested next to her husband every night now felt like the brutal lie that it probably was.

To her relief and surprise, sleep came as Alison closed her eyes.

But then she opened them hours later to find that the nightmare was only beginning.

Chapter Six

Alison circled the block for the second time.

Once more, then she would park. Or so she promised herself, even though she had made that same promise already after rounding the corner her first time.

She probably should have walked. Brooke only lived a half mile away. She could have used the time to think. And on foot, the Tahoe officers might have left her alone. It would be hard to keep pace a half block behind her, impeding traffic at two miles per hour.

Now they were hanging back, acting like they weren't following, even though they were rounding Grover for the second time behind her.

Alison knew she couldn't, or at least *shouldn't*, stall any longer. So she finally parked in front of Brooke's house and got out of the Cayenne, glancing over to see the Tahoe pulling up next to the stop sign a half block up.

She raised her fist to knock, but Brooke's mom, Tamara, opened the door before she could.

"Alison … I'm so sorry." Despite Brooke being Sarah's best friend, she and Tamara weren't close. Alison saw her as stuck-up, same as anyone else who frequented the club. But Brooke's mother pulled her into a hug and even seemed to mean it. "If there's anything I can do …"

Alison wondered what she knew. Sarah came over to Brooke's when her mother was on the way to *potentially* identify the body, as Detective Banks had put it. But Tamara was acting like that death was a foregone conclusion.

She opened the front door all the way and waved Alison inside.

Sarah looked up from the couch. Her eyes were blood-shot and wet. Her hair was matted, and though of course it was impossible, it looked like she had lost weight since Alison had last seen her a few hours ago. She jumped to her feet and started toward the door.

"Are you—" Alison started.

But that's all that was out of her mouth before Sarah stomped past her and Tamara, then out the still-open door. She was already in the Cayenne before her mother made it back out onto the porch.

"I'm so sorry." Alison shook her head — why was she the one apologizing? — then scurried after her daughter.

"Sarah … honey?" Alison asked as she climbed into her seat.

She was always on her daughter for assuming the worst, but this time Sarah was right, even without having any idea just how bad things truly were.

Sarah didn't respond, and flinched back when Alison tried to hug her.

Without knowing what else to do, and not wanting to push her when she seemed one raw nerve away from a total breakdown, Alison started the SUV and drove toward their freshly ransacked home.

Sarah didn't seem to notice the Tahoe keeping pace

behind them, and Alison sure as hell wasn't about to point it out. But she did finally break the painfully awkward silence as she swung into their driveway and put the car in park.

"Sweetheart. I can't even imagine what you're going through right now … even though I'm going through my own version of the same thing. *Please*, let me help you."

"Where's Dad? Never mind." Sarah shook her head. "You would have already told me if he wasn't really dead. How did he die?"

"Sarah, honey, let's go inside."

"Don't honey, sweetheart me, Mom! Tell me what happened! Where is Dad?"

"He's no longer with us—"

"DON'T FUCKING DO THAT, MOM! IS HE DEAD OR NOT?"

"Yes." All the air seemed to leave her, and Alison needed another long moment before she could get the rest out. "Something terrible happened … your father was apparently caught in the crossfire."

"All my friends are on LiveLyfe saying that there was some sort of a drug bust, and that Dad was involved …" Sarah choked hard on her feelings and words. "Why are they lying like that?"

Alison was gobsmacked, and temporarily at a total loss for words. She had barely managed to prepare herself for the impossible conversation of telling Sarah the surface-level story, she couldn't believe that her baby girl already knew about its rotten core.

"Let's go inside. We can—"

"Answer the question, Mom!" At least she had stopped screaming loudly enough to shatter the windshield.

Alison sank back into her seat and delivered her best version of the truth as she knew it. "According to police, there was nothing random about your father's death. It was a hit, the result of a drug deal … or something gone south."

"Why would they say that?" she blubbered.

Lying now wouldn't serve either of them, so as hard as it was to deliver this next bit, she had to stay strong. "They have a lot of evidence suggesting he was involved in some things he shouldn't have been."

"*Involved in some things that he shouldn't have been?* What are you saying, Mom? Do you really think Dad was a drug dealer?"

Alison shook her head. "Right now, I don't know what to think."

"HOW CAN YOU NOT THINK HE WAS INNOCENT?"

"Come on, please, let's get inside." Alison looked nervously around. "The neighbors …"

"FUCK THE NEIGHBORS!"

She turned on the engine and began to reverse, stopping halfway down the driveway when Sarah screamed at her again, slightly softer than the ear-splitting bellow from a moment before.

"Where are we going?"

"I'm taking you to Aunt Trudy's."

"I don't want to go to Aunt Trudy's."

"It's the best place for you right now." Alison began to reverse again.

But Sarah opened her door, jumped out of the SUV, stumbling as she hit the concrete, before recovering her balance and running toward the front porch of the only home she'd ever known.

She fumbled with her keys as Alison finished parking, and was already inside before her feet hit the driveway. She glanced up the street, noting the Tahoe before she closed and locked the front door behind her.

Sarah was already in her room.

Alison knocked three times on her locked door, gently at first.

No response so she tried again, hard and then harder, finally pounding with the side of her fist.

Instead of answering, the hallway was suddenly filled with the deafening sound of what Alison thought might be Ed Sheeran, though she wasn't well-versed in his music enough to know for sure. She thought that was Sarah giving the finger to her mother at first, since she always listened to music with her AirPods. But then she heard the muffled sobbing in a current under the melody and recognized the move for what it was.

Alison made a final attempt — one last trio of hard knocks with the side of her fist — before she finally surrendered, trading the hallway outside Sarah's bedroom for the kitchen and a better-than-decent selection of wines.

She ran her hands along the bottles, deciding that a pinot grigio would probably pair best with the uncontrollable sobbing she was about to embark on.

She went to the silverware drawer, laughed bitterly to herself when she saw it still hanging open like a tongue giving her the raspberries, then rooted inside for a bottle opener.

She popped the bottle and went to get a glass, but that only got her laughing harder. Even though that particular cabinet was mostly undisturbed and she could easily pour herself some wine if she wanted, Alison wondered why she should even bother. No use lying to herself, she would be drinking every drop in the bottle. The only thing keeping her from guzzling the whole thing outright was that Sarah might eventually stop weeping in the other room, and if that happened she might need a mother who wasn't cork high and bottle deep on the sofa.

So she poured herself a glass, all the way to the top, and started sipping as she walked from the kitchen to the living room. Her full glass was already significantly diminished as she looked out the window to see if the Tahoe was still there.

And yep, of course it was. A pair of officers watching her house.

Like she was a common criminal.

Alison started to cry, grieving and furious, hating herself for all the doubt that was already creeping deep into her pores, desperate to believe that this was all somehow a big misunderstanding. Tom was an innocent man, caught in something awful that had nothing to do with him. The police were grasping at straws.

She finished the glass, cursed herself for not drinking straight from the bottle, then turned around and started walking back toward the kitchen to correct her mistake, making a plan on her way.

Alison had told Jarod she was going to hire a private investigator, and that's exactly what she was going to do. She could sell some of her jewelry to cover the cost. Proving that her husband had somehow been framed was more important than paying the mortgage.

She should give their accountant a call. Maybe he could tell her how to unfreeze their accounts, if such a thing were even possible. And if not, then at least he might be able to answer some questions about Tom's supposed business.

She couldn't just give up. She had to keep looking. The cops might have missed something. Maybe she could find something in the house to prove his innocence.

Or his guilt.

At least then she would know either way.

Alison traded her glass for the bottle and started wandering the house, starting outside Sarah's door again. The musician who might have been Ed Sheeran was gone, and she didn't recognize the singer who had taken his place. But he had a softer voice, or the music was lower. Either way, Sarah's sobbing sounded even louder than before.

And still she ignored her mother's knocking.

Now that she really thought about it, Alison wasn't in the best shape to have a conversation with a private investigator, or her accountant. Really, she wasn't in the best shape to be conducting business with anyone. She should probably spend the night gathering evidence, then make her calls in the morning. Once she was fresh.

Like she would ever be fresh again.

Alison laughed, feeling half insane as she went through her house, same as the police had just hours before, sifting through all of Tom's stuff. His closest. His drawers. His desk.

But of course she found nothing.

And worse, she had no idea what to look for.

She was in over her head. What did a country club mother like her know about proving a person's innocence?

Alison finally gave up her search, collapsed on the sofa, and crashed harder than she ever had in her life.

Chapter Seven

Someone was pounding a rail spike through the base of Alison's skull while loudly clanging a gong and honking a series of vintage car horns.

Or she had a screaming hangover and somebody was on her front porch repeatedly ringing the doorbell.

Alison opened her eyes and sat up on the couch, working to wipe the gauze from in front of her eyes and clear the fog from her mind. The gong and the car horns had settled into a consistent ringing, but the rail spike to her skull had gone nowhere.

She looked around the living room, and the ugliest truth of her life came flooding back like a backed-up toilet gurgling shit onto the floor. She saw an acre of mess left by the police who had torn her home apart, all the missing photos that once hung over her mantle, and the empty bottle of pinot grigio lying on its side by the sofa.

At least that explained the rail spike.

She stood from the sofa and walked over to the front door, wondering why the ringing was so insistent. Whoever was jabbing their finger on that button over and over like that must really hate her guts. Was it the police? One of their neighbors? A "friend" from Rolling Knolls looking for gossip?

Is it really true? Alison imagined the trio of Tiffany, Jenna, and Belinda all abuzz, standing on her front porch, sculpted fingernails perched above their perfectly puckered lips.

Was Sarah still home? If so, why hadn't she answered the door? And if not, then where the hell was she? Though really, maybe that was for the best. Alison wouldn't have wanted Sarah to see her mother crashed out on the couch like that.

She peeked out the eyehole, feeling like an idiot when she saw the angry-looking woman still jabbing her finger on the doorbell. The first person Alison should have suspected, and the last one she wanted to see.

She opened the door in a flurry, before her mother-in-law could ring the doorbell again. Though Alison suddenly wondered, was she still her mother-in-law if her husband was dead?

"Hello, Eleanor."

The harpy shoved her way past Alison, storming inside and looking around the living room in disgust. Without replying to her greeting, or really acknowledging Alison at all beyond a lone curdled glance, she yelled for her grand-daughter.

"Sarah!"

"What are you doing here?" Alison asked her, wondering how drunk she still was, or at least how evident her inebriation might be, making her way to the sofa so she could kick the bottle beneath it.

Eleanor reeled around on Alison, spittle flying from her lips. "What do you mean, *What am I doing here?* My son is killed and I find out on the news!"

Her rage was barely in check, but for what might have been the first time in their relationship, the bitch had a point. Alison *should* have made that call, and was a coward for her avoidance.

"I'm so sorry, Eleanor. I—"

"I don't want to hear it. Where is she?"

"Where is who?" But, of course, Alison knew who she meant.

"I'm taking her with me. Living here with you is the last place she should be right now." Eleanor walked past Alison and started toward Sarah's bedroom.

Alison scrambled ahead, cutting her off before she reached the hallway. "I'm really sorry I didn't call you, Eleanor. Between identifying the body, talking to the police, going to see our lawyer, then coming home to this" — she waved her hand around the living room — "I just—"

"Couldn't stop drinking?" Eleanor sneered at her. "SARAH!"

Was she being obstinate by refusing to come out of her bedroom? Sleeping? Buried in her music? Or was it possible that she wasn't even home right now? Alison sure as hell hoped that wasn't the case, not just because she feared for Sarah's safety, but because Eleanor would really have her ass then.

"Can you please stop yelling? Sarah is sleeping. I'm sure you can imagine how upsetting this all was. The last thing she needs is—"

"Don't you *dare* tell me what my granddaughter needs."

She's MY DAUGHTER, you bitch. "I'm sorry, Eleanor. About all of this. But can we please talk like two—"

"SARAH!"

Alison finally found her voice. "You either need to stop screaming, or you need to leave."

"I'm not going anywhere."

"That's fine. Then please stop screaming."

"Why? Because you have a headache after drinking an entire bottle of wine?"

"No, Eleanor. Because it's obnoxious." Alison sighed. "Now, can we please talk?"

Eleanor stayed silent, replying only with her furious glare.

"I need to hire a private investigator, to help sort this all out and clear Tom's name. But our accounts have all been frozen, and so I have no way of paying him. Can you please help me?"

"That won't be necessary."

She drew another deep breath and tried again. "If we can just—"

"I've already hired one!" Eleanor snapped, narrowing her accusatory eyes on Alison. "So rest assured, I'm going to know *exactly what happened here.*"

"Are you suggesting that—"

"Not yet I'm not. But I am suggesting that you get a lawyer."

"I have a lawyer."

Eleanor gave her a derisive laugh. "You're going to need someone better than Jarod Harris." Then she laughed again. "I'll give you a name."

Sarcastically: "That's very kind of you."

"What's going on?" Sarah suddenly appeared in the living room.

Eleanor turned from Alison to Sarah. "Pack your things. We're leaving."

"Where are we going?" She both looked and sounded confused.

"I'm taking you with me."

"Why?" Sarah asked, her eyes wide and frightened.

"Because your grandmother doesn't think I'm capable of taking care of you right now."

"Damn right I don't."

Sarah shook her head. "I want to stay here."

"It's for the best, sweetheart. Your mother is going to—"

Sarah didn't wait for Eleanor to finish, turning around and retreating back down the hallway instead. Seconds later, they heard the sound of her loudly slamming door, followed by Ed Sheeran or whoever, all before Eleanor could close her mouth, let alone finish her tirade.

She turned back to Alison, no longer screaming. Her icy voice now held an eerie calm instead. "I'll be back soon. With a court order and some nice police officers to make sure the handoff goes smoothly. Make sure to have her things ready."

"You're not taking my daughter anywhere, Eleanor."

"She's *my granddaughter.* And you are clearly incapable of taking care of her."

"Based on what?"

"Just look at this place!"

"You mean the place that was ransacked by the police? Because of what *your son* allegedly did."

"Allegedly is right." Eleanor scoffed. "Maybe it's time that Sarah learns which one of her parents has a documented history with drugs, and getting into trouble with the law."

"You have to be kidding me. That was in high school!"

"Once a junkie, always a junkie."

"I was never a junkie!" Then, because Alison no longer had any reason to keep her husband's secrets now that he was dead, or willingness to keep getting bullied by his mother, "And those drugs were Tom's, anyway."

"Oh, that's rich." Eleanor rolled her eyes.

"It's the truth."

"Awfully convenient, this 'truth' coming out now."

"There's nothing convenient about any of this," Alison said.

"Any judge will clearly be able to see that you have a history with drug abuse and that I have Sarah's best interests at heart. And I'm sure my P.I. can clear up any remaining misconceptions."

"Why are you threatening me, Eleanor? This tragedy is happening to all of us right now. We're supposed to be family. Why—"

"No, Alison. Whatever you were involved with got my Tommy murdered, so don't ever use that word in relation to us again. *Sarah* is my family, and I will do everything in my power to protect *her*."

"You are delusional." Alison shook her head. "You don't have a clue who your son really was."

Eleanor laughed in her face. "I know *exactly* who he was, and *exactly* how much you took from him."

"How much I *took* from him?"

"Like you don't know he settled for you," Eleanor growled. "I'm sure you cried yourself to sleep plenty of nights thinking about it."

The ugly, unspoken truth that had festered between them forever was now finally rotting out in the open.

"Get out of my house," Alison said.

Eleanor laughed in her face again. "You better pack your shit, honey. Because it won't be your house much longer."

"Get out right now, or I'll call the police." Alison wondered if the cops were still parked across the street. And if so, could she go and ask them to drag this bitch out of her living room right now?

"You do that and see what happens," Eleanor said.

But then she turned around, walked toward the front door, and left without another word.

Alison took a moment to calm her breathing before collapsing back down onto the couch. She was staring at the floor when the sound of Sarah entering the living room surprised her. She looked up and Sarah surprised her again.

"Thanks, Mom."

"For what?"

"For not making me leave with that cunt."

"Sarah! Language, please. That is an ugly, ugly word." Still, homely as it might be, Alison was smiling inside. "But you're welcome."

Sarah came over, sat next to her mother on the sofa, and leaned her head on Alison's shoulder.

They shared a comfortable silence. There was no play-book for this. No app to guide her through the misery. No handouts with step-by-step instructions to follow.

She hugged her daughter harder, slowly rocking back and forth as they softly cried together.

The only thing more important to Alison than being a great wife for Tom was being an excellent mother to Sarah. Now the life she knew had been struck by a thunderbolt and her world was on fire.

"What are we going to do?" Sarah asked, finally pulling away.

Alison looked around at the mess. "Why don't we start by cleaning this place up."

Sarah's body language instantly changed. So did her tone. "Are you kidding me right now?"

"No, Sarah. I'm not kidding. Our home is a disaster zone and I need help cleaning things up."

"Dad is dead and you want to *clean*?"

"Your father is gone, but yes, life goes on. I'm sure I

don't need to remind you of everything your grandmother just said. She will be back, and the best thing we can do to avoid—"

"Can't you call someone?"

"To do what?"

"To clean this place!" Sarah said, with a tone suggesting that old Mom was being an idiot again.

Alison could tell her that they didn't have a dime in which to pay a cleaning crew, but that wasn't even remotely close to the point.

"Sweetheart, I need your help right now."

"That's not all you need!" Sarah launched herself up from the sofa and started marching toward her room.

"Sarah! Please …"

But she was already gone.

Adolescence had been gradually chewing at her daughter's cheerful disposition for a few years, but this devastating tragedy now threatened to swallow Sarah whole. More than just another one of her typical teenage fits, this time her daughter seemed to be falling apart.

Alison stood from the sofa and finally started to straighten the living room, thinking about the state of things. Not just what had happened, but the consequences of the happening.

She was a single mom, and would be for the rest of her life.

Right now she was 114 pounds of pure fury.

If Tom wasn't already dead, then Alison would have to kill him herself.

Chapter Eight

WEDNESDAY ...

"*PLEASE,*" Alison begged her daughter, "this is already hard enough without you and I being at odds ... no one will blame you for staying home from school."

"I've already told you a hundred million times that I'm going."

"You were *just suspended*!" Alison couldn't believe they were having this conversation.

"Right. I was suspended the day my dad died. There is like *zero chance* Mrs. Washington will stick to it."

"You don't know that."

"I *do* know that." Sarah played her ace. "I already called her."

"You can't go to school."

"I'm telling you that this is what's best for me."

"Fine," Alison surrendered with a grudge. "But I have a lot to handle today. So if you're going to school, then—"

"Brooke is giving me a ride, and I can walk to her house all by myself."

"I'm happy to—"

"Don't worry about me, Mom. You can go ahead and start on your super busy day or whatever."

Alison was much too exhausted to stay engaged in a battle she had no interest in waging, and zero chance of winning. "Tell Tamara I said thank you and—"

"I said Brooke is taking me, not her mom."

Great. Alison had told Sarah "a hundred million times" that she wasn't allowed to have Brooke drive her anywhere. It wasn't just that she'd only had her license for an hour and a half; Sarah had made the mistake of detailing a few of Brooke's misadventures behind the wheel. Nothing calamitous yet, but she had run up on two separate lawns and plowed into a trash can. Alison worried that it was only a matter of time before Sarah's bestie got into a more serious accident, and she didn't want her daughter anywhere near the passenger seat when that happened.

But again, that wasn't a battle she would win, or was even willing to fight this morning.

"Can you at least promise to pull the trashcan out to the curb so we don't miss pickup?" *Again.*

"Sure, Mom."

"Stay safe," Alison said, shaking her head as she walked away from the door.

It was hard arguing with Sarah under the best of circumstances, but after a few hours of alcohol-infused tossing and turning on the couch after what would surely go down as the worst day of her life, their back-and-forth felt especially miserable.

Alison turned on her shower to scalding, then got undressed and stepped under the stream, letting the water lightly burn her scalp and skin, helping her to wake the hell up for what promised to be another miserable day.

She had an eight o'clock meeting with their accountant, Louis. She had waited until daylight to text him, worried that he might be the kind of person who slept with their phone on the nightstand. Alison felt unreasonably guilty even from the thought of possibly waking him, despite her catastrophe. She had his number, but never a reason to text him before.

Good morning, Louis. I'm having a sort of emergency. Is it possible for us to meet sometime today? Or maybe talk on the phone?

Then she'd sat on her bed, holding the phone, wondering how long it might take him to answer.

He returned her text in seconds: *Of course. I was wondering when you would call. Can you come in at 8:00? Before the office opens?*

Now she was showered, dressed, caffeinated, and on her way, daring to hope that there might be something Louis could do to help the situation.

He shattered her illusion immediately.

"I'm sorry, Alison, but there's nothing I can do. Frozen is frozen."

"What does that mean? This can't be permanent … the government can't just keep all of my money … right?"

Louis shifted in his seat, clearly loath to deliver the bad news. "It's not *your* money. You and Tom were married, which means that all funds were and are community property. If the government believes that even a dime of that money came from the drug trade … well, in that case they have every legal right to hold it throughout the entirety of their investigation."

"How long will that take?"

He shook his head, shrugging. "There's not really a timetable for things like that. Could be years before things get cleared up. And if Tom is guilty, the money's gone for good."

"Of course he's not guilty!" Alison found that harder to believe every time she said it.

By the look on his face, Louis wasn't buying it either.

"You were tracking our money … isn't there anything you know that could possibly help me bargain with the police, or get them to unfreeze the accounts? Or clear *my* name, even if they can't clear Tom's?"

Louis turned away from her and toward his monitor. Then he started clacking away at the keyboard for several seconds before tilting the screen so Alison could easily see it.

"If Tom was doing something illegal, then he was also smart enough to make everything consistent, and keep it that way."

"What does that mean?"

"That I had no idea any of this was going on until the cops showed up with a warrant asking for copies of your records."

"What about Caliber Consulting?"

"That's what I want to show you." He pointed at the screen. "Here are all the invoices I used to 'bill' your husband's clients." Louis jabbed his finger at a separate column. "And here are the matching deposits into his business account. Bank transfers, PayPal payments, Venmo — however each of his individual clients decided to pay, everything lines up."

"Lines up with what?"

"With a very normal assortment of transactions. In other words, on paper, it looks as though Caliber Consulting was a legitimate business."

"*On paper* … So, you don't really believe that Tom had a legitimate business."

Louis leaned back in his seat and crossed one leg over the other, taking what felt like an almost exaggeratedly long moment before he responded. "I admit to having my doubts."

"Be straight with me, Louis. You think he was guilty."

"I'm deeply concerned that he was, yes. But I am cooperating fully with law enforcement right now, to prove that I had no knowledge of Tom's illegal activity, and that I've done absolutely nothing to cover for him, at least not knowingly. I strongly suggest you do the same thing."

"How can I cooperate when I don't know the first thing about what happened?"

"Just be honest with every question they ask, no matter how uncomfortable those answers might be."

"But I have been, and they don't believe me."

"Who is *they*?" Louis asked.

"The police. Some detective named Ian Banks—"

"We're acquainted, as of yesterday."

"—and the two cops who are apparently now living outside my house. Hell, my lawyer doesn't even believe me."

"That might tell you something right there," Louis said.

She shook her head. "I don't know, I think he assumes that all his clients are guilty."

"Most of them probably are."

"When did you get so cynical?"

"Inside every cynical person lives a disappointed idealist." Another shrug. "You handle money for a living, you see plenty of things you wish that you hadn't."

"Could you give me one of those invoices? I'd like to call one of the companies Tom claimed to consult for and see if that leads me anywhere."

"I'll do you one better." Louis offered her an understanding smile, and in the moment it felt like a rope that would keep her from falling off the cliff. "How about I call for you."

Alison returned his smile, again working overtime not to cry.

Louis pointed at a long column of possible clients. "Do you want to pick who we call?"

She leaned back in her seat with a shake of her head. "Surprise me."

"How about Impact Industries?"

"Sure … why that one?"

"Because it's a name that means nothing." Louis tapped a few keys, then the printer whirred as it spit Caliber Consulting's latest invoice into the paper tray.

He rolled over a few feet from his chair, snatched the invoice, then rolled back to his desk and dialed the phone while looking down at the number.

"Yes, accounts payable please," Louis said a few seconds later, raising his eyebrows at Alison. "Yes, of course." He covered the receiver and leaned toward her. "I honestly didn't think there would really be an Impact Industries."

That gave her a moment of hope. But it died just seconds later as she listened to Louis shuffle through a series of questions and redirections before he finally looked Alison square in her eyes.

"Impact Industries has no record of ever paying Caliber Consulting or Thomas Tanner anything."

Alison slowly nodded, for the first time accepting a pair of bloodthirsty truths.

Her husband had been lying to her about his business. Apparently for years.

And if he had lied about that, then of course he could be lying about anything.

She was already out of her seat and storming toward the door.

"Are you going to be alright?" Louis called out behind her.

"No," she answered without looking back.

Because now Alison knew the indisputable truth that she would never be alright ever again.

Chapter Nine

Alison was humiliated.

And not just with Tom, but with herself.

There were eight miles between her accountant's office on Anaheim and her home on Cedar, and yet Alison had considered wrenching her steering wheel to the left and plowing into the opposite side of traffic a half-dozen times.

None of those thoughts were serious. Of course she wouldn't actually kill herself. And yet, it was still mortifying that the idea had crossed her mind. Suicide had never been a part of her intellectual DNA, and yet Alison knew deep in her soul that such destructive thoughts would now be claiming permanent residence inside her now.

Alison would never leave Sarah all alone, especially knowing that she'd end up with Tom's sister in a best-case scenario, and would much more likely end up with the Wicked Witch of Las Orillas. Not to mention all the trauma of losing both parents in short succession. But the thought had nonetheless been there, and that felt like a cold blade piercing her overheated skin.

She pulled into her driveway, surprised to note that the Tahoe was now missing.

Alison was even more surprised by the box on her doorstep — she could immediately see that it had no markings and therefore couldn't have been left by any official entity such as UPS or the post office. Not that any of her regular delivery people ever made drop-offs this early.

Her heart pounded as she looked down at the box, wondering if there might be a bomb inside. If Tom had crossed people who were willing to kill him, then there was no reason to believe they wouldn't also target her.

That was why the officers in the Tahoe had been there, after all.

The officers who weren't there now, and could therefore no longer protect her.

She gathered her courage, kneeled down to retrieve the box, then glanced up and down the street as she opened her door and took it into the house.

She lifted the lid and found a cheap phone inside. A burner, as she had seen it called on all those shows. She held the phone for a minute, her heart still beating too fast and too hard, still wondering what she should do.

She turned it on and saw that the burner had a voicemail waiting.

Of course it had to be for her. She swallowed hard, pressing play as she pressed the phone to her ear. A scratchy, sinister voice darkened the other side of the line.

"Hello there, Alison Leslie Tanner, of 4832 Cedar Drive, mother to one Sarah Tanner, at least for now. Your recently deceased husband owed my organization a substantial sum. His debt has now been passed onto you. It is my duty to collect that debt, and your inherited obligation to make sure that I can. I'd like for us to have a little chat to sort this issue out, in person of course. I will be at the Rainbow Lagoon at five p.m. You'll know who I am because I'll be the one looking for you. You're a smart lady from what I can see, and believe me," he chuckled, "I can see plenty. So I am sure you don't need the reminder, but seeing as me and your now ex-husband were amigos — do they still call it an *ex* if he's full of bullets? I guess it doesn't matter. Point is, don't do anything stupid like handing this phone over to the cops, or anything else that might invite a machete to another branch on your family tree." After a short pause and some indecipherable background noise, the dangerous voice finally finished. "We have both lost enough already. You a husband, and me an excellent earner who did a very stupid thing."

Alison realized that she was still staring at the phone a full minute or more after the voicemail had ended. Too many conflicting thoughts ordered her around.

She was beyond terrified. For herself, but mostly for Sarah.

Maybe she should call the number back, rather than suffering through a day full of terror and anxiety while waiting to meet the killer at Rainbow Lagoon. But what would she say? And what if that only pissed him off?

She should probably just throw the phone away and do her best to ignore the call.

Except that the caller knew where she lived, and apparently everything else about her.

The Tahoe was gone and it might not come back.

Tom was dead, so it wasn't like Alison could pretend that this threat wasn't serious.

Did burner phones have GPS? The police would be able to tell that she had taken it inside even if she wiped her prints off of the plastic if so. And Alison had no way to look up the answer. Even if the cops hadn't confiscated every computer in the house, they could be monitoring her usage and tracking every search, just waiting for her to make a mistake.

Alison scoured her memory banks, frantically searching through whatever she could recall from every show she had ever watched with Tom, from all those episodes of *CSI* to that show with Selena something or other, where she profiled serial killers and the various ways they got caught.

But Alison wasn't being tracked by a serial killer, even if she was being threatened by a homicidal drug dealer working for some mysterious cartel.

Whatever she ultimately decided to do, right now the phone felt like a hot potato burning her fingers. She started toward her bedroom, figuring she would hide it inside one of her shoes for now, but she paused at the sound of her doorbell ringing halfway through the living room.

Her heart stopped. Alison was suddenly convinced that one of two things was happening: either the killer who had left that voicemail was standing on her porch ready to finish her off, or the police were onto her and there to confiscate her phone.

The first option was clearly ridiculous. Murderers probably weren't inclined to ring the doorbell. But the alternative filled her with chills and sent her scampering into the bedroom as planned — right to the closet where she found the closest shoe, which happened to be one of Tom's.

She tucked the burner inside and pushed it toward the hollow where his toes would never go again.

The doorbell was on its third ring by the time she was peeking out to see who it was.

"Detective Banks," Alison said as she opened the door, cool as she could possibly manage. "What can I do for you?"

"Mind if I come in?" He nodded toward her living room.

Alison gestured for him to come inside.

He looked around. "My apologies for all the mess."

"Just doing your job, I guess." Sometimes she hated her own sense of decorum. A different version of the same question: "Now how can I help you?"

"Mind if I sit?" This time he tipped his chin toward the couch.

Alison nodded and the detective sat.

Then she did the same, occupying an armchair a few feet away.

"I just wanted to check in, and give you an update," he said.

"About what?"

"About your husband's body, for one."

"What about it?"

"I thought you might want to know when it would be released after the autopsy. So you could make funeral arrangements."

Alison shook her head. "That's not why you're here."

"It's part of the reason."

"Please, Detective Banks. I've been insulted enough already."

"It's Ian." He offered her what felt like a genuine smile.

"Okay, *Ian*. Why are you *really* here?"

"I was wondering if you thought of anything you wanted to share since our last conversation?"

"You mean you were wondering if I'd had a sudden change of heart and was now willing to make a confession? Tell you all about how my husband was actually The Godfather of Las Orillas, and how I was his consigliere?"

He gave her another smile, this one seeming designed to prove his patience. "I was thinking more like something that might help us to track down your husband's business associates."

"You mean *former associates*," Alison corrected. Then, in case he needed the reminder: "My husband is dead."

"Perhaps something that might help us to prove your innocence," he further clarified.

"You mean besides the fact that I had nothing to do with any of this, and no knowledge that my husband was involved in anything illegal."

Ian raised his eyebrows. "Does that mean you now believe that he might have been?"

"What's that saying about anything I say could be used against me in a court of law?"

"Has anyone contacted you?"

Alison was happy giving the detective dick to go on, but that question stopped her cold. "My mother-in-law was here last night. Does that count?"

"I think we both know that it doesn't."

"So who do you mean?" Not that she needed to ask.

"Have any of your husband's *former associates* tried to contact you?"

"It would be hard to have any idea what they have or haven't tried considering I don't even know who they are."

"Fair enough." Ian nodded, but he was clearly assessing her.

Alison wondered if he could tell she was lying like all those detectives on TV. "What happens if someone does contact me?"

He straightened on the couch, obviously happy to hear that she might be playing along. But his voice and tone both turned sober. "You should let me know immediately. These are dangerous people that you don't want to mess with. If you are innocent, then you'll want that protection, and I'll want to make sure that you have it."

"So if I can figure out who my husband was working with, then you'll believe that I had nothing to do with this?"

"I promise you, Mrs. Tanner, nothing would make me happier. But ultimately it isn't my job to decide one way or the other."

"Then what is your job, if it's not to prove who's guilty and who's not?"

"That's up to a jury. My job is to figure out who did what, then pass my evidence on to prosecution."

"How am I supposed to prove that I didn't know?"

"A lot of juries respond well to honest tears on the witness stand."

"*Honest* tears?"

"They are the best kind."

That wasn't nearly enough. So no, for now she would not be giving him the burner phone. "I'll let you know if I hear anything."

He nodded, still seeming to assess her. "You're sure that—"

"I'm sure," Alison said, cutting him off.

The conversation was dead and he knew it. So after another brief exchange that included a few pertinent details about the release of Tom's body, Ian gave her another business card, identical to the one he'd handed her less than twenty-four hours ago.

"Please call if you hear anything." He offered her a final nod.

"You know I will." Alison gave him the same smile she'd worked so hard to perfect at the country club before closing the door.

Then she rushed to her closet, withdrew the burner from Tom's shoe, wiped it off with a paper towel, buried it at the bottom of the kitchen trashcan, then carried the bag out to the mini-dumpster outside that was still waiting for Sarah to do her job.

So Alison did the job herself, muttering under her breath all the way to the curb.

On her way back inside Alison noticed a midnight blue Crown Vic up the street that she hadn't noticed before. It might have been the bad guys, but instinct said it was a fresh shift in place of the Tahoe.

So what if they were watching.

She was just taking out the trash. Being a mom.

Proving that she was a victim in all of this.

Alison went back inside and closed the door behind her.

Then she started to clean the house, leaving Sarah a share for when she came home.

But by 4:30, an hour after she should be home — at the latest — Sarah still wasn't there. And Alison's calls were all going to voicemail.

After another quarter hour of frantic calling and escalating panic, Alison could no longer shed what she knew in her heart.

Tom had been stolen away from her.

And now their daughter was probably dead.

Chapter Ten

ALISON WAS PACING the house and going out of her mind.

It was now after five and Sarah *still* wasn't home.

She should have called the school sooner. Now her calls were going directly to voicemail. There were no messages on the house phone, but she couldn't even check to see if the office had left any messages or texts on her mobile, informing Alison of her daughter missing class. Attendance calls were sent out automatically, and usually arrived around four in the afternoon, even when Sarah's absences were excused. But without her smart phone, Alison got dumb about her daughter's whereabouts.

Brooke wasn't home, and Tamara either didn't know where the girls were, or she was playing it cool with her silence. Alison *thought* she was telling the truth. Even if she was stuck-up, it was hard to believe that one mom would lie to another when they were looking for her daughter. Especially considering what their household was currently, and rather publicly, going through.

Unless … their crisis was the reason for her lie?

Alison considered going out to that blue Crown Vic

up the street and seeing if they would help her, but she wouldn't know where to start. It wasn't like they could get a hold of someone in the attendance office on her behalf.

When Alison's brain refused to stop delivering the worst possible images to the front of her mind, she went into the kitchen, put her head in the sink, and turned on the faucet until a full blast of cold water snapped her back out of it.

Sarah was fine. This had nothing to do with the man (or men) who had murdered her husband. This was Sarah being a brat, trying to prove a point, worrying her mother because she knew it would get to her.

But what if she *had* been kidnapped to ensure Alison's compliance?

And what if the kidnappers were trying to contact her right now? On the burner she had carelessly thrown away.

What had she been thinking?

Alison could no longer take it, finally certain that her daughter had been accosted on the way home, possibly with Brooke. Representatives of some drug cartel were probably trying to call right now, and thanks to her failure to answer, Alison would have the blood of two girls on her hands.

She peeked outside, saw the blue Crown Vic, hesitated for several excruciating seconds, then bolted out of the house and over to the large can by the curb, hoping that what she was worrying about most right this second wouldn't be true.

But it was.

The garbage had already been collected.

She lifted the lid and looked inside anyway. Sure enough, Alison was staring down into ninety-six gallons of freshly emptied space.

She closed the lid and dragged the trash can back into their side yard.

Nothing to see here. Just another frazzled mother, doing her daughter's chores.

Alison was being stupid and knew it. She should have told Ian about the burner when he asked if she had been contacted. Now the bad guys were probably peeling the nails off of her daughter's fingers one at a time, punishing Sarah for having a mother who didn't know how to follow simple directions.

She pulled Ian's card out of her pocket, already on the way to her home phone.

She started to dial, imagining him telling her that it was already too late. But her finger stopped halfway through with the most horrifying thought.

I was just about to call you, she heard the detective saying, *we found your daughter's body in—*

"STOP IT!" Alison yelled at herself.

She shook away the image of Sarah on a slab and finished dialing the number. But then she slammed the handset back into its cradle before it even started ringing, running toward the door the second she heard a car pulling into the drive.

She was barely throttling her panic attack as she looked out the window and saw Eleanor's BMW — black as the woman's heart — parking beside Alison's Cayenne.

She clenched and unclenched her fists repeatedly while watching Eleanor get out of the passenger side. Then — knowing what she would see and feeling momentarily grateful that she wasn't holding glass — as Sarah climbed out of the driver's side, each of them held a handful of shopping bags.

Alison opened the door before either of them stepped onto the porch, but she was careful not to start yelling like every molecule of her wanted (maybe even needed) to. She kept her tone even, but directed her question to Sarah rather than Eleanor.

"Where have you been?"

But of course her mother-in-law jumped in front of the answer. And in the sharpest possible contrast to last night, Eleanor now sounded sweet as could possibly be. "I took her shopping for clothes."

Like that's what she needs right now? "She has plenty of clothes."

"She needed something appropriate for her father's funeral." Her voice still like sugar. "I asked her and she said she didn't have what she needed."

Sarah looked away from Alison, avoiding eye contact with her mother.

There were too many places to take this argument, and Eleanor wasn't capable of honestly fielding a single one of them. So with her panic having mostly dissolved, and pure fury still writhing inside her, Alison calmly turned back to her daughter.

"I've been calling you all afternoon."

Sarah shrugged. "I thought you knew?"

Still calm, but only barely: "How would I know?"

"Nana said she told you."

"Well, she absolutely did not."

"I sent you a text." Eleanor had a smirk in her eyes; Alison would have been willing to bet every cent in her unfrozen bank accounts that the old bat already knew what Alison was about to tell her.

"The police confiscated my phone." She turned to Sarah. "Go to your room. Your grandmother and I need to talk."

"I didn't do anything wrong."

"Do I sound like I'm accusing you of anything?"

Alison's stare must have been fierce, because for once her daughter didn't back down.

Sarah started walking away.

"Sweetheart!" Eleanor called, holding two shopping bags high like a trophy.

"Oh yeah. Thanks."

Then Sarah smiled and came to get them while Eleanor eyed Alison with a shit-eating grin.

She remembered last night:

"Thanks, Mom."

"For what?"

"For not making me leave with that cunt."

What a difference a day made.

She waited until Sarah was out of earshot, then turned her controlled rage on Eleanor.

"You're not her mother and you can't be pulling shit like this. It wasn't acceptable before yesterday, and it's not acceptable now, regardless of what's happened. I was worried sick about her."

"You should really go and splash some water on your face. You look terrible."

"Sorry I'm not ready for my photoshoot. My husband was murdered yesterday, and my mother-in-law is being a bitch like usual."

"I'm being a bitch?" Eleanor pointed to herself. "What is it that makes me bitchy in particular? Is it the fact that I took my granddaughter shopping, or—"

"How about because you were standing here in my living room less than twenty-four hours ago threatening to take both my daughter and my house away?"

"You are clearly in no condition to care for a child right now, dear—"

"Don't you dare *dear* me."

"—and I see it as a grandmother's duty to do what she can in this time of crisis."

"Is that why you threatened me last night? To do what you can in a time of crisis?"

"We were all a little upset last night. I think we all said some things we didn't mean. Do you not remember threatening to call the police on me?"

"I remember last night just fine." Eleanor had a way of rearranging conversations so that she stayed on top of them, and Alison couldn't afford to let that start happening now. "Why don't we focus on today. You took my daughter without my knowledge or permission."

"I took *my* granddaughter shopping so that she would have appropriate attire for *my* son's funeral, and I sent you a text out of courtesy to keep you in the loop." Then she shrugged and gave Alison a pathetic little shake of her head. "This is exactly the kind of thing that Tom was always worried about with you."

"What's that supposed to mean?"

"You know you've never been especially adept at the social stuff, dear. Even back in high school you were so … is *awkward* the proper word?"

"I'm not doing this with you. Not now, and not ever again."

"What is it we're doing, exactly?" And again with that crap-caked smile.

Alison held her tongue.

Eleanor said, "I do hope you'll be able to hold it together for the funeral."

Again she said nothing.

"It would be a shame if you were unable to make it."

Alison tasted blood as it trickled from the interior of her bottom lip into her mouth.

"There is a certain … *dignity* … one must have in

attending a funeral, regardless of where we might have come from."

"Tom was my husband." Eleanor had finally baited a response right out of her. "I have every right to attend his funeral, and there's nothing you can do to stop me."

She laughed. "Oh, dear. You don't really believe that, do you? I pay for your family membership at Rolling Knolls, so I do believe it's my right to decide which members of the family that membership pertains to."

"You need to leave my house. Right now."

"And here we are again." But having proven her point, Eleanor was already on her way to the door. "Please consider what I'm saying. It was bad enough the way you were always embarrassing Tommy in front of his friends, ever since high school, really. If you couldn't manage to make my son proud while he was still alive, the least you can do is hold it together for an afternoon while we honor his memory."

"Thank you for taking Sarah shopping," Alison said, to keep from punching Eleanor in her stomach and laughing while all the wind left her body. "I'll see you later."

Then she shuffled Eleanor toward the door before she knew what was happening.

The hag hadn't even left the driveway before Alison knew exactly what she needed, and the only place she could get it.

So she scribbled a note for Sarah and went there.

Chapter Eleven

ALISON HAD COME to Provisions on a mission.

She didn't care that it was the most shi-shi grocery store around, if anything she wished she could find Ridiculous Raspberry somewhere else. Like a corner liquor store. But nope, Alison had seen the ice cream at exactly one place. The vanilla swirl was absurdly delicious and the raspberry so perfectly sweet and tart that the smell tickled her nostrils just thinking about it. Together the taste was … well, *ridiculous.* Alison had only found the flavor because she was on a constant pursuit of confections to please Tom, but he was picky and only wanted "pure ingredients." He never really cared for Ridiculous Raspberry, though it worked well enough in theory and looked great on the label, but it was a favorite for both Sarah and her mother. Better, a bowl of Ridiculous Raspberry had always been a great way for the girls to bond. It was the only gluten-free ice cream that Alison loved as much as Mexican Vanilla from The Inside Scoop. Or *almost* as much. Mexican Vanilla was ambrosia on her tongue, but she would have to be feeling even worse than she did now, considering a lactose intolerance put Alison on her ass, every time.

She wanted to get away for a few minutes, but it felt like everyone was watching her. She kept looking up and down the aisles, over her shoulder, and around every corner. Alison had yet to see anyone she recognized, but that didn't make her feel any less inspected.

She had come for the ice cream, but hated being out and didn't want to waste the trip. So she grabbed a cart and loaded it with a few ingredients to supplement what was in the fridge to get them (just her and Sarah now) through the week.

Her cart was a cornucopia of comfort. A half-dozen bottles of wine, which she told herself was only to get the ten-percent discount Provisions offered with the purchase of six or more bottles, but really it was because that allowed her one bottle per day for nearly a week. In addition to all those bottles for her, there were three bags of potato chips, several boxes of frozen crap like pizza rolls that Alison couldn't stand but Sarah loved, plus the five pints of Ridiculous Raspberry, which was an admittedly embarrassing amount.

But the junk food wasn't for Alison. It was an apology for Sarah. And the ice cream was for them to enjoy together. Because right now they weren't even speaking after that blowup with Eleanor.

Her words were still like a knife inside Alison, but the aftermath with her daughter felt several degrees worse.

Please consider what I'm saying. It was bad enough the way you were always embarrassing Tom in front of his friends, ever since high school, really. If you couldn't manage to make my son proud while he was still alive, the least you can do is hold it together for an afternoon while we honor his memory.

What kind of a person would say that to their son's

widow? It was unconscionable. And considering that Sarah understood exactly how cruel her grandmother could be, her aligning with the harpy felt especially hurtful. Alison had been hoping for some support, if not downright expecting it. But Eleanor's ugly and rather humiliating parting shot had only opened the door for Sarah to kick her mother down yet another flight of metaphorical stairs, and sent her tumbling into a dingy emotional basement.

The cart also had meat and vegetables, but nothing based around any sort of plan. Alison realized that she'd been shopping in somewhat of a daze, not really paying much attention to anything, mindlessly adding items to her cart that matched her usual haul. Plus all the junk food.

Her ice cream was melting. She really should go.

She could do a better job next time.

With what money? Alison thought once she was in line and unloading her items onto a conveyor belt. She really should have thought this out. If her accounts were frozen, then her credit cards wouldn't work. She was spending what little cash she had on an unorganized haul.

She should put everything back and get out of line. Abandon her cart and escape this place.

She felt suddenly ashamed, hoping the woman ahead didn't turn back to see the mess of a widow. She grabbed a pint of Ridiculous Raspberry and—

Too late. Tiffany pulled up right behind her.

Alison wanted to grab the guacamole from her cart, pop the lid, and throw the creamy mess all over her face.

"Alison-ohmygawd," Tiffany blurted, the four words leaving her mouth as one and a half. "I would ask how you could possibly be grocery shopping at a time like this, but I guess everyone has to eat, right?"

She glanced at the cart as her face scrunched in judgment — Tiffany was so well-oiled at being a bitch that Alison wasn't sure if the expression was involuntary or not.

She grabbed one of the wine bottles with a laugh. "You sure you have enough, *hon*?" Then she returned it to its spot in the carrier and whispered, "I'm sorry. I guess that's not very funny." But her smirk said otherwise.

Alison didn't know how to respond, not to Tiffany's presence, nor to her words. She needed to escape the grocery store, but now she was boxed in with one of the few people in this world who could compete with Eleanor for the Last Person Alison Wanted To See Right Now award. And instead of making an excuse, agreeing that she did indeed need another few bottles of wine, or maybe some more meat, Alison was loading the conveyer like an automaton.

"Are you okay?" Now Tiffany was glaring at her. "You're not saying anything."

"I'm fine." Alison shoved a hundred-pound smile onto her face. "Just really tired."

"I bet." She looked understanding, even sympathetic, but it was all an act. Alison could feel a few different sentiments creeping behind Tiffany's artifice and wanted to rip them right out of her soul.

The cashier was almost finished scanning Alison's groceries, which meant she only had moments left to save herself.

"I'm such a dummy sometimes …" Alison slapped the side of the head. "Can you do me a big favor?"

"What's that?" Tiffany sounded suspicious.

"I forgot to grab a carton of milk. Could you please—"

"You're not actually drinking milk, are you? Like from a cow?" She glanced at the other side of the conveyor belt where a bag boy was putting Alison's ice cream into a bag. "Oh. I guess you probably do."

"Almond milk will be fine. Thank you."

"You sure you don't want macadamia?"

"Even better." Alison's smile was getting harder to hold, and her seconds now an endangered species. Another customer pulled his cart behind Tiffany's. Tall and bald with an absurdly expensive-looking watch. He looked like the kind of man who believed that patience was for poor people.

"The regular size? Or should I try to find something smaller, since it's just the two of you now?"

Alison ignored the bait, desperate to get Tiffany out of there fast so she could ditch Provisions and the tidal wave of humiliation now rolling toward her shore.

"Please, Tiff" — she had never called her *Tiff* before — "we're running out of time."

"Sorry," said the cashier, turning to look at the two women pretending to like each other, "but you're already out of it."

Tiffany shrugged. "Guess you'll have to get your milk the next time. Just remember that there's a reason chimpanzees don't eat dairy."

"$174.38," said the cashier, still looking at them.

"Oh, of course," Alison replied, trying not to visibly panic as she dug through her purse.

Trying even harder not to feel the heat of Tiffany's deprecating stare.

"I'm so sorry," Alison said, abandoning her faux search and turning to the cashier. "It looks like I forgot my wallet at home—"

"Oh my!" Tiffany covered her mouth in mock surprise.

A heavyset woman wearing too much Chanel (in both clothing and perfume) pulled her cart behind Mr. Rolex (or whatever) and gave the line a dirty look.

The bag boy stopped bagging.

The cashier was looking at Alison, waiting to see what she was going to do.

Loudly, Tiffany said, "I can pay for her groceries."

"It's really fine. I can come back with my wallet and—"

"Nonsense! That's what friends are for. And besides, it's only a matter of time before the police freeze your accounts, if they haven't already." Then to the cashier and bag boy, the two people behind her in line, and to anyone else in relative proximity, Tiffany finished her artificially sweetened assault. "My friend here is being harassed by the police thanks to a completely false rumor that is sure to be cleared up soon."

Alison held her tears, allowed Tiffany to pay for her embarrassing collection of groceries — including "one carton of macadamia milk, please" that she was forced to feign even more gratitude for — then carried her bags to the Cayenne.

But there was a man waiting for her when she opened the rear door. He had about the same amount of stubble on his head as he had on his face, a denim jacket that might have been from the 80s over a red and gray checked flannel, and an aroma that made her think of coffee and weed.

"Mrs. Tom," he said.

"Can I help you?" Alison asked the man, pretending she was brave.

"I was going to help *you*." He pointed to her already loaded bags. "But it looks like you're good. So why don't we just go for a ride."

"I'm not going anywhere with you."

"I think you are." An assertive nod, followed by a glimpse of his gun as he lifted the flannel to show her. "We won't be long. Do as I say and you'll be right back to your pretty little life in no time." Then to accentuate his point.

"Let's make this easy on both of us, or maybe I should say *all of us*. I'm sure you don't want to bring that beautiful daughter into this unfortunate situation."

Alison glanced around for help, but no one was paying attention.

She considered yelling, knowing that even her loudest scream wouldn't stop a bullet, and if all those television shows had been telling her the truth, then this man looked like the kind of person who would shoot her in a parking lot and leave her to die.

"So," he looked around, then lifted his shirt again, "what's it gonna be?"

Chapter Twelve

ALISON'S HEART had never beat harder.

Looking at the dead-eyed man staring back at her now, she wondered if this was the day it would finally stop beating altogether. A week ago she believed in her wonderful life, but now Alison understood how quickly it could all disappear. Or be taken away from her.

"Tell me where we're going," she demanded.

He nodded toward the Cayenne and repeated his directive. "Get in the car."

"Not until you—"

"That ain't how this works." He shook his head, then leaned forward and gave her an even more menacing growl. "You've got five seconds to decide, lady."

Alison wondered if the cops stationed outside her house would notice if she didn't return, or even better, if there might be officers watching her now. But probably not. A guy like this probably knew exactly what he was doing and felt safe enough snatching her right out of a Provisions parking lot. She was a dead woman driving the moment she started the Cayenne. He would make her drive him to somewhere remote, a place where he could kill her and no one would ever even read about it.

And there was nothing she could do to change her situation that wasn't suicide.

One last look around the lot — hoping for the first time in her life that she might see Tiffany — but there wasn't a single soul looking her way.

"Fine." Alison adopted a pose of defeat and started toward the driver's door.

But the assailant kept watching her, apparently waiting to make his move until she was inside, shockingly confident considering Alison would be peeling out of the parking lot just seconds after she sat.

Except … of course that's what he was anticipating. And if she did that, then he'd probably end up shooting her through the window and turning her Cayenne into a luxury coffin.

He finally stepped forward as her hand found the latch.

But then she took off, racing back toward the Provisions entrance.

Her attacker had apparently anticipated that too. Alison made it five furious steps before he had one hand around her upper arm and the other covering her mouth.

"Do that again and you'll be the first of Tom's two girls I take care of tonight. You got me?"

She whimpered *yes*, then he let her go so she could walk to the Cayenne herself, looking around the lot same as she was. He seemed clearly relieved, but Alison was appalled that even now no one was watching.

"Where do you want me to go?" She tried to keep her fingers from trembling on the wheel as her assailant climbed into the backseat and aimed the gun squarely at the base of her skull.

"Ninth and Chestnut."

She looked at him in the rearview, feeling her eyes widen in harmony with the sight. She swallowed, said nothing, then turned the engine and started driving toward one of her city's worst neighborhoods.

"I'm assuming you know where that is?" muttered the predator behind her.

She nodded, keeping her eyes out the windshield.

Of course Alison knew the area, though she had never dared to drive there. Even people who didn't live anywhere near Las Orillas still knew the quarter as Chalupa Row — a once insulting moniker, recently reclaimed by residents of the mostly Hispanic neighborhood, after the barrio had turned eternally notorious with the track "Baracho Sunset," recorded by hip-hop legend Boneyard the Baptist.

They didn't trade a single word on their way to Chalupa Row. Alison spent the entire trip thinking about ways she could maybe escape, chased by daymares of her getting shot in the back of her head with every attempt. And worse, imagining what the monster in the backseat might do to her daughter.

She was driving on Tenth, a block from Chestnut. "Where am I going? Where should I park?"

"Make a left here," he said.

So she swung a left onto Chestnut, then followed his finger to an ancient Victorian sagging on the corner. She parked in front of a stop sign, wondering if the Cayenne would be safe, immediately realizing how absurd that particular concern was in light of her full suite of more pressing problems. For the last mile, every storefront and sign had been written in Español, and though Alison was hardly the whitest person she knew, she still felt like a bag of flour behind the wheel of a two-year-old Porsche.

She pulled up in front of the old house — painted in

heavily faded shades of pink and yellow — then killed the engine, even though it felt a bit like stopping her heart.

The man opened his door on the driver's side, his gun still aimed at the back of her head. "You see that little shed over to the side of the house? That's where we're going. You scream when we get out of the car, I'll put a bullet in you. Look around or do anything to get yourself noticed on your way to the door, I'll put a bullet in you. Mutter under your breath before we're both inside with the door closed behind us, I'll put a bullet in you. And just in case you're wondering, yes, this is exactly the kind of neighborhood where a white woman could get shot in broad daylight. Even so, it's in both our interests to avoid any unnecessary attention. We clear?"

"We're clear." Alison nodded and got out of the car.

Surely she was marching to her own execution, but what else could she do but keep her eyes straight and her chin up, controlling her breath as she waited for her executioner to open the gate, then resuming her lead to the shack.

She stopped in front of the door,

He opened it, waved Alison inside, then closed the door behind them. "One Mrs. Tom, order up."

Alison looked around, as much as she dared. The interior made the shack seem slightly larger than it had from the outside. She entered into a cramped room — a pair of couches, one love seat, and several armchairs — that felt both claustrophobic and dangerous, with a half-dozen men chattering in Spanish. There was a closed door behind them.

Her kidnapper made himself comfortable on the nearest armchair. Alison still didn't dare to sit.

A handsome man with dark skin and a pitch-black goatee was eyeing her like meat behind the display case at

Provisions. She turned his way, figuring Goatee for the boss.

"Hola … me llamo Alison."

Goatee laughed and jabbered fast enough to leave her four-word attempt at sharing a tongue twitching in humiliation.

"Where am I? Wh-what do you want from me?" Alison asked, even more embarrassed by her stutter than she had been by her Spanish.

Goatee turned to Kidnapper. "Why don't you get Ms. Tanner a glass of water. She seems parched." Then back to her. "Are you parched?"

"I'm fine." Alison obviously sounded like the opposite.

"Why don't you sit." The man barely made it sound like a question. He gestured toward one of the empty chairs. "How about there."

Alison sat, feeling as though she had no other choice.

Her kidnapper was already back with the water.

"Gracias, Gustavo." Goatee over-enunciated his words with a sly smile as he nodded toward Alison's kidnapper before returning his eyes to her. "Please. Drink."

She sipped until the water was all gone, realizing as she did that this was the same voice she had heard in that menacing message.

She sat frozen in her seat, unnerved by all the Spanish chatter, picking up the occasional word, but never enough to string anything into an actual thought.

Goatee waved his hand around the room and said, "Vamanos."

He over enunciated with a laugh, but this time the room emptied, with Gustavo and the gang leaving through the rear door. Then she and Goatee were alone. He still had his gaze bolted to her, and Alison was still wishing she could sink down into her chair until she disappeared.

"Do you know why you are here, Ms. Tanner?"

Alison was scared to answer. She wanted to smart off, maybe say something like, *Because you like to kidnap people?* So she kept her mouth closed, not trusting herself to open it.

Goatee continued. "I understand that it might be frightening, getting accosted by Gustavo in the parking lot of your overpriced grocery store. It was not my first choice to bring you here to this place, but I must confess that I don't appreciate being stood up."

Alison swallowed.

"Only one of us was at Rainbow Lagoon at five pm today—"

"I didn't know."

"I think you did, Ms. Tanner. I think you heard my message and were scared to do the right thing."

She swallowed again.

"Do you know what it is I do for a living?" Goatee asked.

Besides murder people?

"You're a drug dealer," she dared.

He gave her another laugh. "You say that with a curl of your lip. Is it fair to say that you have a problem with my chosen profession?"

Terrified as she was of answering incorrectly, Alison was even more scared of him calling out her dishonesty, then showing her what they did to liars like her.

"It's illegal."

He shrugged. "That is a problem with the law, not a problem with me. Is there really any difference between a doctor prescribing medicine to a patient because they request it, or because that doctor has been bribed to write as many prescriptions as possible by the pharmaceutical companies, and me selling the same or similar medicine directly to the customers who want it?"

"Yes," Alison said. "There's a big difference."

"Oh?" He smiled, seeming genuinely curious. "Please explain it to me, Ms. Tanner. What is the big difference between our businesses, besides the permission to operate that the pharmaceutical companies have purchased from the politicians."

"You're selling to addicts."

"And they are not?" A hearty laugh. "Do you really think that doctors have the time or inclination to monitor even a fraction of their patients? Do you really believe that they are on top of all the self-medicating that happens at home?"

"They have a legal right."

"Ah …" He nodded. "The politicians."

"Their drugs are made in a lab."

"All drugs are made in a lab, Ms. Tanner."

"There are inspections and—"

"We have inspections, too. The only difference between their operations and mine is that they have paid for permission that is not available to me at any cost. Does this mean that they are right and I am wrong in your eyes?"

"That's not what I said."

"But it is what you believe?"

"The world is a better place — or at least a *safer place* — when people follow the law."

He held her eyes, but said nothing.

She tried again. "There are laws for a reason."

But the words both felt and sounded hollow as they left her mouth.

"What about your husband? Was Tomás a man who followed the law? Was he making the world a better, safer place for all of us?"

"I have no idea *what* Tom was doing."

"That does not answer my question, Ms. Tanner." Another smile.

"What do you want me to say?" Then again: "Why am I here?"

"Your husband owed me a substantial sum of money."

"I'm sorry about that."

"For better or worse. That is what they say." Goatee shrugged. "This right now is the *worse* part. Tomás ditched his supply to avoid getting caught by the cops. Or so he told me. I suppose we'll never know now that he is no longer with us. But the bottom line is that his debt is unpaid."

"How much does … *did* he owe you?" The acid in her stomach was churning, but she couldn't ignore where her host apparently wanted their conversation to go.

"If Tomás were still alive, he would owe me $125,000—"

"$125,000!"

"—but now that obligation belongs entirely to you."

Alison shook her head. "I don't have that kind of money."

"It is a small sum in the scheme of things. A woman like you, with your house and car and family connections … you can, and will, make good on your debt."

"You don't understand. I'm broke. The police have frozen my accounts. My parents are dead, and my mother-in-law hates me. There's no way I can—"

"If you cannot afford the meal, then it is time to wash dishes, yes?" He looked at her, but didn't wait more than a moment to see if she'd answer. "You can work off your debt by taking over the route."

Her insides turned even icier. Not only did Alison feel the heart-wrenching confirmation that Tom (or Tomás) had been dealing drugs, and not only did his debt now belong to her, this drug-dealing lowlife was now requesting that she break the law in a major way herself.

She shook head again. "I'm sorry. I will find a way to pay you. But I don't know the first thing about selling—"

"There is nothing to learn. Your inventory will be easier to move than boxes of Girl Scout cookies."

"I can't," Alison insisted.

"Do you have my money?"

"No, but I—"

"Then you will be taking over your former husband's route."

"But—"

"This is not a negotiation."

"I understand." Alison nodded. "I'm responsible for Tom's debt. But please, I can find some other way to pay you."

"You are correct, Ms. Tanner. There are many ways." Goatee nodded in agreement. "Your daughter is quite good-looking, for example. I'm positive we could make good with her instead."

Alison swallowed, unwilling to let him bear witness to more of her terror. "Just tell me what I have to do."

"The first thing you must do is understand the situation you are in."

"I think you've made it clear."

He smiled to acknowledge her bravery. "I am a man of my word, and I promise that if you go to the police I will kill both you and your daughter. Do you believe me, Ms. Tanner?"

Alison nodded, desperate not to cry.

"Excellent." Goatee continued. "If you are arrested and your inventory is confiscated, that will only add to your debt. I suggest you take better care of your supply than Tomás did."

"But I still don't know what I'm supposed to do … I don't know anything about his route or—"

"I will send someone to help you get going. Here," Goatee pulled a phone from his pocket like a magic trick, "take this and expect your instructions soon."

Alison took the phone. "Who are you?"

"A businessman who would prefer that you not die, who also understands that life does not always give us what we want."

"I mean your name."

"That is not something you will ever get to know." Goatee shook his head and stood from the chair, apparently finished with her. "But you can call me Goliat."

Chapter Thirteen

THURSDAY …

"PLEASE, Mom! I can't believe you're doing this to me!"

But Alison held her ground. "I'm not doing anything to you! I'm trying to maintain some semblance of normalcy right now."

"But my father died!"

"Yes, he did. Turns out, my husband has also passed. But guess what, Sarah? I don't get to clock out from life. I'm still responsible for taking care of all the little things that are expected of me."

Alison didn't just mean all the countless responsibilities that Sarah was already aware of, she was also referring to the mounting duties her daughter could never ever find out about. Like the one today, that had her headed to the Towne Center where she was supposed to pick up her inventory and meet her 'supervisor' at noon. She had seen the text on her new burner a few minutes after waking up, but Sarah was on her before she could even start brewing the coffee.

"I'm sorry that you have to deal with so much right now, Mom. Really, I am. But doesn't my staying home from school give you one less thing on your plate? You don't have to worry about dropping me off or picking me up, or—"

"No, Sarah. It doesn't give me 'one less thing to worry about.' If you're home from school, then you're one more thing I have to manage."

"I'm sixteen years old! You don't have to manage me!"

"Weren't you caught smoking an illegal substance just—"

"It's not illegal anymore, Mom."

"Well, it's illegal for you."

"You still haven't given me a good reason as to why I have to go. All of my teachers will understand."

"This isn't about your teachers. This is about me, and you, and what's best for our family. Besides, weren't you the one wanting to go back early yesterday, refusing to stay suspended? Why the change of heart now?"

"Yesterday, I was still in shock. Now, I don't know … I've had time with it, and I —" Sarah trailed off.

Alison stared at her daughter and realized besides that first night, she hadn't really asked how her daughter was dealing with all of this. Alison felt like a shitty mom, but at the same time, she didn't have the luxury of diving deep into her or Sarah's emotional state while also trying to keep them both alive.

She thought about hugging her, but Sarah looked like she didn't want to be hugged and was seconds from yelling. The best thing Alison could do was to try and keep things steady or they might never get out the door.

"It's in our best interest to pretend that everything is normal right now."

"Oh. Got it." Sarah nodded adolescent annoyance.

"What is that you *have*, Sarah?"

"It's fine. I'm used to it."

Now she was really starting to piss Alison off. "And what is it you're used to?"

"You caring about what everyone else thinks instead of caring about what's best for me."

"I'm sorry you feel that way. But I can assure you, 'what's best for you' is the *only* thing I'm thinking about right now."

Other than my new life as the newest Las Orillas drug dealer, of course.

"Sure, Mom."

"You'll be safe at school."

"I'll also be safe at home. You can't just—" Sarah stopped, looking closer at Alison and apparently seeing something worrying on her mother's face. "What is it, Mom? What aren't you telling me?"

"Nothing you don't already know."

"Then I'm sure you won't mind telling me again. Pretend you're talking about how I never take out the trash like I'm supposed to."

"Your father was murdered."

"So, what aren't you telling me?"

"Maybe he has some unfinished business."

Sarah laughed at her. "*Or* … you could just be even more paranoid than usual."

"Do you think the police officers watching our house right now are paranoid?" Alison asked, knowing she shouldn't have let that slip before the words were out of her mouth.

"What cops?" Sarah looked serious, perhaps even scared.

"Go look out the window. See the Tahoe? That's LOPD."

"What do they want?"

"I don't know exactly. Maybe to protect us, or maybe to see if I'm dealing drugs like my husband was."

"I can't tell if you're being sarcastic. Do the police really think Dad was doing that?"

"Yes. They do." The admission hurt, but she had no choice. "Our bank accounts have all been frozen while the police are looking into it."

"What does that mean? We don't have any money? How long will it take for the police to clear this all up? And why are they accusing him — it's not like they could possibly have any evidence." Sarah swallowed, and the next bit came in a stutter. "D-Do they?"

Alison had no idea how much of the truth she should share. These were uncharted waters, with bloodthirsty sharks swimming all around her.

"The police haven't told me anything."

"They might not have told you much, but I bet you know more than you're telling me."

"Please … can we talk about this later? It's a school day."

"So you keep telling me."

"We can discuss this when you get home." *After I've finished with my first day of drug dealing to service your father's debts.*

"How about now? I deserve to know."

"What is it you want to know, Sarah?" Alison sighed. "Exactly."

"Why do the police think he did it? Do they have any evidence?"

"I don't know what they have."

"You talked to them, right? You must have *some idea.*" Then, Sarah changed tactics, sending an arrow of inquiry into her pounding heart. "Do *you* think he did it?"

Alison walked over to the living room couch and sat.

Sensing the sudden gravity, Sarah followed, taking a seat right beside Alison while awaiting her mother's response.

"I didn't want to, but yes, I believe that your father was dealing drugs."

"No," she whimpered. "He couldn't have been! What did the police say to make you think that?"

"It's not what they said so much as *how* they said it."

"What does *that* mean?"

She sighed again, then tried to explain. "They weren't asking questions to figure out if he was guilty of dealing. In every way that part felt like a foregone conclusion."

"Then what were they asking?"

"They wanted to know how much I knew."

"And that's why they're outside our house right now? You weren't kidding about that?"

"Definitely not. And yes, I'm sure that's why they're out there." Then a truth to cover her little white lie. "The police are investigating to find out what we knew."

"But didn't you already tell them that you didn't know anything?"

"That isn't exactly easy to prove. Right now it's just my word." Then she lied again. "They want to talk some more today, and I really need you in school so there's one less worry on my mind."

Sarah slowly nodded, finally seeming to get it. But then she said, "What about his go-bag?"

"His what?"

"His go-bag. Let's say Dad really was dealing drugs. Then he had to be good at it, right?"

"What makes you say that?"

Sarah shrugged. "Dad was great at everything he tried."

Apparently not his consulting business. "What's your point?"

"He probably had a go-bag stashed somewhere. With a bunch of cash and fake passports and whatever. So, have you looked for his go-bag?"

"This isn't a TV show, Sarah."

"So, no. You haven't looked."

"If your father had something like that in the house, then I'm sure the police found it while they were turning the place upside down."

"So it could be in a locker somewhere. Or a safety deposit box—"

"Theoretically, yes. But I wouldn't even know where to start looking, and right now I need to focus on the things I can control."

"That sounds about right," Sarah scoffed.

"Can you please finish getting ready for school?"

"Sure. Just tell me the plan first. What are we going to do? For money and—"

"I'm trying to figure all of that out."

"So I'm just supposed to pretend like everything is normal?"

"To the best of your abilities, yes." Alison took Sarah's hands into hers. Then she softened her voice and restated her argument. "I'm really sorry about all of this. I can't even begin to imagine what you're going through right now. But we're in this together, and I need your help. *Please* … just a few more days. Go to school and pretend that things are normal. Give me a chance to figure all of this out. Give me a chance to help make things normal again. I need you with me on this, Sarah. We're in this together."

Sarah looked back at her, appearing to have a hundred and one arguments all loaded in the chamber and ready to fire. A pregnant moment yawned on for far too long.

Until she finally nodded and said, "Okay, Mom."

Then Sarah stood from the sofa, left the living room, and returned a few minutes later all ready for school.

"Thank you," Alison said.

Sarah nodded, then left the house.

Alison followed her to the car, juggling too many thoughts on the way. Her daughter was in danger until she finally figured this out. She couldn't allow pride to endanger her further.

Meaning, Alison would have to let Eleanor take her if she couldn't figure out something fast.

She climbed into the Cayenne and started the car.

Today was a big day. Alison would be following in Tom's footsteps to start her new life of crime.

But she needed to make a stop first.

One that might hopefully buy her a bit of time.

Chapter Fourteen

"You've gotta be kidding me," Alison muttered to herself.

She looked up at the sign, shaking her head. She knew the pawn shop was called The Last Resort because she'd seen the place on her phone. She also knew it was a dump, thanks to all the reviews. But reading between the lines, Alison could also tell that the man who owned the place was a kind soul, and that insight felt like enough of a compass to follow.

But, in person, the place reeked of a despair she could have never imagined.

Someone had stolen eight out of thirteen letters from the sign, leaving the five that spelled *Later* above the filthy remainders left behind by the rest of the pilfered alphabet. The building itself was nondescript, short and wide with no discernible features and only a small bank of miserly windows. A trio of garbage bins were all stuffed to the brim, with high piles of bulging bags sitting on either side. A few feet away, halfway between the building's corner and the entrance, two filthy men lay head to head. She smelled urine and feces and worse.

Then Alison swallowed her fears and entered The Last Resort.

With her funds frozen, and Eleanor being her only outlet for money, Alison had no other choice. She had no idea about the total value of her haul, but it would surely be enough to get by for at least a little while. It wouldn't even hurt that much to sell the collection. She had never been much of a jewelry person. But even when they were kids, Tom had always loved gifting her with shiny baubles. He'd started with simple bracelets and necklaces. His indulgences grew over time, until he was buying her precious gemstones and embarrassing karats more often than not.

Alison had tens of thousands of dollars here, at least. At this point she wouldn't be surprised to find out that Tom had been laundering money by way of her jewelry. Paying in cash with high sums of unreported income. This haul might be all she needed to pay her mortgage for the foreseeable future, and take care of Sarah without her grandmother's interference.

What if there was enough to pay off Goliat as well?

Other than the memories of Tom, there wasn't anything she wasn't willing to let go of. And right now, Alison wasn't too fond of remembering even the best of her former husband. She would keep her wedding ring, and the diamond locket her parents had given her the day she graduated from college. Everything else could go.

"Can I help you?" asked the kindly old man at the counter.

"Jorge?" Alison asked.

"Do we know each other?" The old man smiled.

She shook her head. "I read about your shop online."

"Did you read the one that said, *the thousand-year-old man who runs the place smells like a human fart?*"

Alison nodded. "I did read that one." Then she shook her head. "But you don't smell like a fart, human or otherwise."

"I do when I fart," Jorge admitted, leaning forward as he pointed at her closed box of jewelry. "Nice-looking little trunk. Like a casket for a fancy raccoon. You interested in unloading the box or some treasures inside it?"

Alison lifted the lid and gestured for Jorge to look for himself.

He slid the box closer toward him and rifled through the contents. His face kept changing, each expression equally unreadable. When it seemed like he was all done, Jorge went through the contents again, this time removing each piece one at a time, then returning the full lot to the box only after he had arranged the entire lineup into separate rows.

But Alison sensed no excitement from the old man, surprising considering how much seeing the closed raccoon casket had brightened his eyes.

Jorge finally sighed and looked up at her.

"What is it?" Alison asked.

"That's costume jewelry."

"What does that mean?"

"What is it you were hoping for when you came in here?" Jorge asked, instead of answering a question she knew the answer to.

"I need a lot of money fast."

"You wouldn't be here if you didn't. How much do you need?"

"As much as I can get."

"*As much as I can get* isn't a number."

$125K to start. "Twenty grand?"

"Is that a question?" Jorge smiled and pushed the haul back across the counter. "That box is worth more than all the jewelry in it."

"How much is the box worth?"

"I'd have to look it up. Maybe $500?"

Alison was about to throw up. "But you looked so excited … at first."

"It's a beautiful box. Plus, your wedding ring is the real deal. Same for that locket you're wearing. Of course I was excited."

"So a thousand dollars for everything?"

He offered Alison a kind yet sad-sounding laugh. "I'm sorry. Like I said, I'll have to look up the box, but every-thing else …" Another kind smile. "We'll see what we can do."

Jorge disappeared most of the way. Alison watched a scrap of his head swaying back and forth as he sat down on a stool (judging by his relative height) just out of sight. A few minutes later he slid off of the stool and walked back over to his side of the counter.

"The box isn't worth quite as much as I thought … and all the jewelry is still just … well, it is what it is. But I'd be happy to give you $500."

"For the box?"

"For everything." His smile was kind enough to let Alison know what he was doing.

But she had to ask anyway. "Is that really the highest you can go?"

His smile cracked as it widened, the truth that $500 was already a favor even more apparent on Jorge's face, despite his obviously trying to hide it. "I'm afraid it is."

Alison looked back at him in shock, unable to answer. Five hundred dollars wouldn't cover her mortgage, or a single one of her credit cards. It wasn't even enough to survive for a week.

"How much for this?" She yanked off her wedding ring and handed it over to Jorge as fury for Tom percolated up to the surface of her mind.

He gave her another sad little smile and returned to his stool. Three minutes later he was standing in front of her again. "It's a nice ring … but not as nice as it looks," Jorge said, handing Alison the ring.

"Can you be more specific?"

"I can give you five thousand—"

"It's worth at least five times that!"

Jorge shook his head. "Twice that if we're being generous. Realistically, around $7500. I've been at this long enough to know honest trouble when I see it in front of me, and I'm sorry for whatever you're going through. You're welcome to ask around if you'd like, but I can't imagine you'll find another offer nearly this generous."

She twirled the ring in her hand, thinking.

He pointed at her locket. "Your necklace might be worth around a thousand."

Now she really didn't know what to do. It would kill her to lose the locket, much more than the wedding ring, because to hell with Tom right now. But a thousand dollars would at least buy her some time, and selling the locket would allow her to keep the ring, which would help in her battle with Eleanor. Her son's ring suddenly missing from Alison's finger could be the thing to push her over the edge and into actually taking Sarah away from her.

She unfastened her necklace and handed it over to Jorge.

A few minutes later he was back, and counting out $1,600 in cash, telling her that the necklace appraised for slightly more than he thought it would, but Alison wasn't sure if she believed him. Kindness seemed to be the old man's kryptonite, just like one reviewer of The Last Resort had said.

And he didn't smell like fart.

"Thank you." She put the money in her purse and turned to go.

"The blood bank pays more for plasma than blood," Jorge said.

"I'm sorry?" Alison turned back around.

Jorge handed her a piece of paper, some sort of printout.

She took the paper and read it.

"I keep those on hand, just in case," Jorge explained.

It was a neatly printed list of local homeless shelters, food banks, plus the addresses and phone numbers for three different Las Orillas social work offices.

"Thank you," she said again, half humbled and the other half horrified.

Alison dragged herself toward the SUV, feeling leaden as Tom's betrayals kept gaining weight and were getting harder to carry. She was glad to be rid of her jewelry box, now knowing it both harbored and represented a lifetime of lies. Even before his turn to crime, her husband had been playing a dishonest hand.

She felt disgusting, starting the Porsche, pulling away from The Last Resort in an absurdly overpriced SUV. A stupid purchase, considering she probably owed more than the thing was worth.

She wasn't raised rich, but until a few minutes ago when Jorge handed her his pre-printed flyer, Alison had never worried about being homeless. Her rage threatened to unseat her. She might need to pull over just to start breathing again.

How could he have not considered the consequences of all his lies when it came to her and Sarah?

Had his wife and daughter really meant nothing to him?

Until her trip to the pawn shop, Alison had really believed that there would be some way out of this mess. But now she realized how deep her trouble actually was.

And that's where she would stay, until the police released her accounts. Though, according to the law, that might be never, seeing as her husband was not only a criminal, but an enemy in the country's war on drugs.

She turned the corner, headed for the Towne Center, tallying her next best moves. She could squat in the house until the bank foreclosed on her, and that would buy them a few months … but what about after that? Tom took out an equity loan on the house just last year, so it wasn't like she could tap potential funds there.

Let alone make a payment.

Dammit! Maybe even *shit.* Or *FUCK!*

Even though she had wanted to work, and at times even begged that she be permitted, thanks to Tom's insistence that she let him provide for them both, Alison hadn't worked a regular job in years.

What was she even qualified to do? Flip burgers at a Sloppy's? Probably not even that.

Maybe she was going about this all wrong.

Maybe it was time for her to visit Detective Ian Banks.

Maybe she should just give him Goliat's burner, and tell him the truth.

Except then the detective would have exactly what he had been looking for — proof that she had played a part in Tom's criminal activity, even if it wasn't really true.

Why did she wait so long, if she had nothing to hide? That would be the detective's first question. Alison could rarely argue her way out of anything. Ian would talk circles around her before eventually deciding she was complicit with Tom and tossing her in jail.

And even if he did believe her, could the police protect her from Goliat and who knew how many men he had working for him? TV had taught her that there guys probably even above Goliat — an endless number of dealers and their muscle eager to make an example of Tom's family. Images she'd seen from Mexican newspapers and media flashed in her mind, beheaded journalists, politicians, entire families murdered, examples made of them.

Shit like this wasn't confined to just other countries. Tom's corpse was proof. And how could she trust the police to have the manpower, let alone desire or ability, to protect her and Sarah?

But at the same time, how could she trust Goliat? He'd already killed Tom. What was to say he wouldn't kill her after she paid his debt? She was a potential witness — didn't killers kill anyone who could rat them out?

Alison needed to clear her mind before she did what she still couldn't believe she was doing. So she turned on the radio and managed to pretend that her entire world wasn't falling apart for the next fifteen minutes, her attention fully back on the drive as she passed Sarah's school.

She exhaled, reminding herself that she was doing the right thing.

Four lights later she turned into the Towne Center, ready to ruin the rest of her life to save Sarah's.

Chapter Fifteen

ALISON WAS PARKED in the underground lot with the nose of her Porsche pointed squarely at Walmart's open mouth, where a greeter stood at the entrance, waving people inside. The woman looked a century old from where Alison was still sitting in her driver's seat. She must look like a withered apple up close.

She was supposed to meet a man named Miguel outside The Noodle Exchange in three minutes. It would take that, if not four or five, to get there. She shouldn't be wasting time, but still she couldn't force herself out of the car.

The police were probably following her.

Of course they were. She was being naive to believe anything otherwise.

If they were parked outside her house, then of course they would put a tail on her when she left.

But that was fine. She didn't have to worry about a tail if she took whatever this Miguel gave her directly to Detective Ian Banks.

Alison wasn't here to officially take over Tom's illicit

route, or learn the ropes on how one might go about pulling off such a highly illegal activity. And she certainly wasn't at the Towne Center to pick up her first supply of illegal drugs.

Alison looked in her rearview, saw the same big fat nothing she had seen with every single glance, then finally got out of the SUV and started toward Ross, thinking that she might be dressing for less herself the next time she had to go shopping for her or Sarah.

Not that her daughter would ever be caught dead wearing—

She stopped cold. And swallowed hard.

Then she quickly reset herself before her daughter turned around, marching toward a table in front of The Noodle Exchange, where Sarah was apparently ditching school with one of the cool kids — he had a full head of dark hair and a smile made for trouble.

"Sarah!" Alison called out a few feet from their table.

Sarah turned around, and so did her apparent ditch mate, both of them smiling, holding chopsticks, perfectly poised over their bowls of lo mein.

"What are you doing here?" Alison snapped, losing her cool a little too fast. She still had no idea what she was even looking at.

Sarah looked down at her bowl, then dramatically over to her chopsticks before fixing a wilting gaze on her mother. "Eating lunch."

"And who are you eating lunch with?"

"My friend, Miguel." Sarah nodded toward the kid eating his noodles at her table. "Miguel, that's my mom. Good luck."

Her heart turned icy. *Miguel. My 'supervisor.'*

Goliat had effectively slipped another noose around her

neck, and she hadn't felt the rope until it was already kissing her skin.

He stood and offered his hand. "It's nice to meet you, Mrs. Tanner."

"Alison," she muttered, dumbfounded but shaking it off as she turned to Sarah. "Why are you out of school?"

"I'm not out of school. It's lunch, and I have an off-campus pass."

"I asked you not to leave the school."

"Um, no you didn't." Sarah shook her head.

"It was implied," Alison argued, poorly.

"That's not how it works, Mom." Sarah laughed at her. "So, what? Are you following me now?"

"No. I was getting lunch." Alison nodded at The Noodle Exchange.

"Uh-huh." Sarah smirked. "Called a ceasefire on your war with gluten, did you?"

"Why don't you go inside and order me something." She nodded at the restaurant again.

"Why don't you go and order it yourself?"

"Because I'd like to have a little chat with Miguel."

"He didn't do anything," Sarah said.

"I didn't say that he did."

Miguel gave the situation a shrug and her daughter a smile. "I don't mind talking to your mom."

"What are you going to talk about?" Sarah asked Alison. "Why can't I be here? I haven't done anything wrong."

"Then stop acting guilty and go get me some noodles. Extra gluten."

Sarah held out her hand, waiting for Alison to fill it with money like usual.

"I'll pay you back," Alison said without apology, staring Sarah down and daring her to argue until she finally turned around and marched inside The Noodle Exchange, trying to slam a door that refused to comply.

"What the hell are you doing with my daughter?" Alison growled, claiming Sarah's seat. "No one said anything about her being involved in this."

"She's not involved in this, Mrs. Tanner. I'm a senior at Sarah's school. We know each other, not well, but well enough. I invited her to lunch and she said yes. Imagine the cops are watching us right now. Don't you think it's a lot less suspicious, you and me talking with your daughter instead of alone?"

"Are you the Miguel that got my daughter in trouble?"

"I was one of the kids smoking with Sarah, if that's what you mean." He nodded without apology.

"So you've been spying on my daughter?"

"Not spying at all. My boss asks me to keep an eye on her, I don't ask why, I just do."

"And how long ago did he ask you to start stalking her?"

"Again, not stalking her. But not long ago. A few weeks. She's a good girl. You did a great job."

"I don't need you to compliment my parenting." Alison glared at him, hating how he was trying to threaten her without being menacing. "Why are you trying to intimidate me? I'm doing everything I was asked to do."

Miguel shook his head. "No one is trying to intimidate you. Me and—"

"We'll meet somewhere else later. You need to go. Sarah's not involved in this, and you need to stay away from her."

"I can't do that, Mrs. Tanner. Unless you want the police to think you're some kind of cougar, this is the best play we've got."

Alison laughed, acutely uncomfortable. She glanced

inside The Noodle Exchange and saw that Sarah was already in front of the line, ordering her mother something with gluten.

"Look …" Miguel's voice sounded kind, and had since her arrival at the table. "I swear on my Grandma Rosa, I have no intentions of hurting your daughter. That's not who I am, and it's not the kind of thing I do. I'm in high school, remember? This is the least suspicious way to communicate — passing messages between us using Sarah so we don't have to meet as often."

"So, she is involved."

"Only as much as you want her to be."

"What's that supposed to mean?" Alison asked.

"You slip a note in her backpack, I'll make sure to get it. You make it easier on all of us by filling her in, then I fully support the honesty. Either way, Sarah helps us both stay under the radar.

"She can't know anything about this."

"Secrets it is, then." He nodded.

"I don't trust you."

"And I don't trust you." He still sounded kind, even if his words had hardened.

"I'm not the criminal."

He acknowledged her with a nod. "And thus you'll have zero hesitation turning a person like me into the police to save yourself."

"*Thus*?" she repeated. "And a 'person like you' — does that mean a criminal?"

"From your perspective, sure."

"Aren't you breaking the law?" Alison asked.

"Aren't *you*?" He gave her a knowing smile as Sarah came outside carrying a bowl of noodles.

"So, now you're in my seat?" Sarah tried to hand Alison the food.

She reached into her purse, grabbed the fob, then handed it to Sarah. "I'm parked on the first floor facing Walmart. Take your food and my food. You can wait for me in the car."

"Why am I in trouble?"

"You're not in trouble."

"Then why are you acting like I'm in trouble?"

"I promise, you're not in trouble. Say goodbye to Miguel, and I'll meet you in the car—"

"What are you guys talking about?" Sarah asked.

"I will catch you up later," Alison said.

Sarah glared at her mother, but then finally shook her head in fury and grabbed her half-eaten bowl of noodles before stomping away.

"Maybe you could try to understand what she's going through," Miguel insulted her.

"Maybe you could try to not be a teenage drug dealer corrupting my daughter. And since she's now waiting in the car for me, maybe we could get going with my own descent into hell."

Miguel looked like he might reply with a soliloquy, but then he stood with what seemed to be a full body shrug and started walking toward the far side of the underground parking lot, opposite from where Sarah should be waiting for her mother.

But what if she wasn't?

Alison swallowed the cold creep and continued to follow Miguel. Into the parking garage and over to his vehicle. She eyed it in surprise.

"You drive a Saturn?"

"What?" Miguel gave her a smile. "You don't like cars that are made entirely of plastic?"

"Do they even make these anymore?"

"Nope." He shook his head. "Believe me, that's a good

thing."

"So why do you drive it?"

"Because it's what I drive." He opened the trunk, pulled out a JanSport backpack, then shoved it into her hand and started blurting words faster than she could sort them. "There's a price sheet in the bag. I'll be back in a few days to collect the cut for Goliat. That's usually sixty percent, but seeing as you're working debt, that's going to be eighty percent to the house and twenty back to you …"

That's when he lost her.

Miguel finally stopped talking when Alison started to hyperventilate.

"You gonna be okay?"

Alison nodded, finally recovering enough breath to not answer his question. "What am I selling?"

"What aren't you selling?" He laughed along with his shrug. "You got Xanax, Valium, Ritalin, Oxy, Percocet, Adderall, Dexedrine, Ambien, Tramadol, fentanyl, coke, MDMA, X, LSD and of course, weed for little bitches who want to smoke, but don't want any record of ever having gone to a dispensary."

She kept on nodding along, but barely paying attention to Miguel, more focused on how she could get the backpack to Detective Banks without Goliat knowing what she did. Or Sarah. Maybe she had enough to bargain her way out of trouble. She could tell Ian about the old Victorian on Ninth and Chestnut. She could—

"Are you hearing me?" Miguel asked. "You don't look like you're listening."

"Of course I'm listening. How am I supposed to contact the junkies my husband was selling to?"

Miguel gave Alison an admonishing look. "They're clients, not junkies."

"Can't they be both?"

"If Goliat hears you disrespecting the clients, he won't be happy."

"Is he ever happy?" Alison asked.

"All the time." Miguel closed the trunk.

"That doesn't answer my question — I still don't have any idea who my husband was selling to."

"Your husband probably kept a list somewhere," Miguel said.

"I don't think so." She shook her head. "He would have memorized it."

"Of course he would have. But he still might have kept a copy somewhere, either before he memorized it, or as a 'just in case.' That's what I do." Miguel shrugged. "I think that's what we all do."

She shook her head again. "Tom probably would have thrown the list away, because he wouldn't have wanted me to find it."

"Doesn't seem like you were looking too hard."

"The cops ripped the place apart. And I went through everything after they did for any evidence of what they were telling me he was doing. But I didn't find anything. No envelope taped to the backside of a drawer, nothing tucked into the back of a picture frame. No secret compartments inside his desk. Nothing in the family safe. *Nothing* ... unless the police have—"

"He would have hid it someplace smarter than that."

"Like where?"

"I used to peel up the insole of an old shoe partway, then hide thin stuff under there. Like a piece of paper."

"Where do you hide things now?"

He shook his head. "You don't need to know that. Any other questions?"

"What happens if I want out?"

"We all want out. But life happens, or you wouldn't be here, right?"

"How did life happen to you?"

"Don't worry about me. I'm doing just fine."

Sure looks like it, dealing drugs out of the back of your Saturn.

She shouldered the bag.

Miguel said, "Don't get caught."

"I wasn't planning on it."

"The police so much as catch a whiff of what you're doing, you'll lose Sarah forever."

"Thanks for voicing my worst fears out loud. I super appreciate it."

He gave her a nod. "I'll be in touch."

Alison nodded back, then started across the lot toward Walmart.

The truth was a rock in her throat. Miguel was right: If the cops figured out that she had taken over Tom's route, she would lose her daughter forever.

So for now, it looked like Alison Tanner would be dealing drugs in secret, same as her former husband. Unless she went to the police, in which case she could end up just as dead.

She threw the bag into the back, then went to the driver's side door and climbed inside. Sarah was staring at her phone, scrolling through her LiveLyfe feed.

"What's up with giving the third degree to my friend?" Sarah asked before Alison closed her door, still not looking at her mom.

"How long have you known him?" She turned the engine and began to back out of her space.

"I don't know? A couple of weeks? What — is it my turn for an inquisition now?"

Alison didn't answer.

"So you're just going to ignore me now?" Sarah said

after a long and yawning moment where Alison didn't answer.

"I'm not ignoring you."

"Well, you're definitely not talking to me. Can you please just tell me why you were having a conversation with Miguel?"

"When we get home." Alison gripped the steering wheel tightly enough to sprain her fingers.

"Why not now?"

"Because I'm driving."

"You can't drive and talk?"

"Not when I'm thinking."

"Are you thinking about your conversation with Miguel? Because if so, maybe you could just say whatever you're thinking out loud."

Alison didn't answer her.

Or say anything else until they were home.

Five minutes later, the argument exploded.

Chapter Sixteen

"I have every right to know!" Sarah screamed at her mother.

"And I'll tell you if you'll just calm down!"

"I AM CALM! YOU'RE THE ONE WHO'S NOT CALM!"

Alison stared until her daughter backed down.

"I'm sorry for yelling," Sarah finally said. "I just want to know why you were talking to Miguel, and every time I ask you change the subject, or avoid the question entirely."

"I was worried about you, okay?"

"What are you worried about? That you weren't embarrassing me enough? Now that Dad's gone you'll have to take care of all the humiliation for both of my parents, even though that's what you were already doing?"

"That's not fair. Or nice." Alison could barely focus on the conversation with most of her attention still on the JanSport in the back of her Cayenne. She should have parked in the garage instead of the driveway. What if the police went digging through her—

"You know what's not fair?" Sarah cut into her

thoughts. "Having your mother follow you to the Towne Center, then suffering Death by Embarrassment."

"Isn't that a little dramatic?"

"This whole thing feels *a lot* dramatic. Why did you feel the need to make me fetch your food, before sending me off to the car like I'm a ten-year-old?"

"I wouldn't have let you wait in the car alone when you were ten."

"Exactly," Sarah said. "So, again: *What's your problem with Miguel?*"

"People like him live a dangerous life, okay?"

"BECAUSE HE'S MEXICAN?"

"No!" Alison finally lost it. "Because he's a drug dealer!"

"You are so racist."

"I'm not being racist, Sarah. Is he or is he not the same Miguel you were—"

"He shares his weed with a couple of kids from school. It's not a big deal." She laughed, shaking her head like Alison was the village idiot.

"And you saying that just proves my point."

"I'm sure it does." She kept shaking her head. "Didn't *Dad* turn out to be a drug dealer? And, gasp, he wasn't even Mexican!"

"Yes, Sarah. He did. Which is exactly why you need to keep up the appearance of NOT HANGING OUT WITH OTHER DRUG DEALERS. The last thing we need right now is for the cops to think that you and I are selling too."

Hypocrisy kept laying eggs inside Alison, making her want to wither.

"And why would they think that?" Sarah asked, staring back at her.

"How would I know?" Alison threw her hands in the air. "I'm still surprised that they're looking into us at all."

"But you think Dad was guilty?"

Alison nodded. "Probably."

"Why were you talking to Miguel?"

"He looked like a witness I saw when I was down at the station," she lied. "So I wanted to see if he knew anything."

"Did he?"

"No." She shook her head, desperately wanting for Sarah to stop asking her questions.

"All that time, while I was inside ordering noodles you had no intention of eating, then again when you had me waiting in the car. What did you guys talk about?"

"Nothing, really. I asked him a few questions, but he didn't seem to know anything."

"So you sent me away for nothing."

"I guess …"

"He's *my* friend. So don't you think Miguel would tell me if he knew something about what happened to Dad?"

Not on your life. "Not necessarily."

"Maybe you shouldn't have sent me away."

"Maybe you're right." But no, Sarah wasn't even in the orbit of right.

"Maybe you should stop treating me like a stupid little kid." Then she turned in a huff and marched out of the living room.

Moments later Alison heard her slamming door.

Finally. She went outside with a big black garbage bag and started emptying everything from inside the Cayenne into it. She kept the car clean, so there wasn't much. But the cops across the street didn't know that. She emptied the glovebox into the bag, plus all the empty grocery totes she usually took into Provisions, plus one of Sarah's books that she'd left in the back seat, and some soccer cleats that had been in the trunk for more than a year, because Alison had to choose her battles, and the one about where Sarah's cleats actually lived had turned into a cold war.

Miguel's backpack was on top, but the big black bag looked bulky enough to hopefully mask her activities as she carried her poorly disguised illegal haul inside the house and into her bedroom.

She locked her door, opened the backpack, and dumped everything onto her bed.

Staring down at the mess of baggies, she began to feel overwhelmed, not knowing exactly what she was looking at, or what the hell to do next. Simple organization usually helped when too many thoughts started swamping her, so she unlocked her door, peeked into the hallway, and dashed to her craft room for a multi-compartment organizer.

She emptied the contents into a tidy pile and took the empty box back into her bedroom.

Alison laughed to herself, because what else could she do? She had bought this thirty-two-piece organizer to keep her beading supplies all in one place. But now she found a much better use for her purchase — it wasn't just great for beads and cords and other crafting supplies, Alison had found the ideal organizer for sorting all of her drugs before selling them!

She checked the door again, cursing her own paranoia before returning to the bed and beginning to label the various compartments on the box, trying to focus on that simple task while excising paranoid thoughts of Eleanor from infiltrating her head.

But no matter how hard Alison worked to keep her mother-in-law out of her mind, the demon seed kept making herself at home. Like she owned the place. Or was in the process of repossessing it.

She looked down at her work, once the various compartments were labeled and the appropriate pills were all matched. But Alison still didn't really understand what she was looking at, or how she could get started on the illegal work that might save their lives.

Again Alison wondered how she was supposed to take over Tom's route without knowing any of his clients. She heard Miguel in her head: *I used to peel up the insole of an old shoe partway, then hide thin stuff under there. Like a piece of paper.*

She went to Tom's closet and inspected his collection of shoes. Her anger grew every time a new pair found her hands. He had caviar tastes, ranging from relatively inexpensive Samuel Hubbards at around $300 a pair to his Salvatore Ferragamos, which were surely more than a grand. Unlike Alison's jewelry, his shoes were all surely the real deal. Too bad the demand for used footwear was so much weaker than the aftermarket for precious metals and gemstones.

Sitting amid all that luxury footwear, Alison saw a pair she didn't recognize. A Grand Troy oxford from Cole Haan, probably no more than a hundred bucks. And since she had never seen that particular pair, Tom must have bought them himself.

So she took out the shoes and peeled up the insole on the left one. Finding nothing, she peeled up the insole on the right one next, and sure enough discovered a folded piece of paper full of tiny writing she didn't understand. Some kind of code, with stuff like *roo 319 X white, pdl OP 20,* and *2rot green flower* written in miniature letter and numbers.

She sat on the bed, perking her ears, suddenly twice as nervous that Sarah would suddenly start pounding on her closed door, demanding to know why it was locked.

She stared down at the list, trying to untangle the truth

of what she was even looking at, and wondering how she might ever figure it out. The code didn't appear to be anything obvious, like phone numbers or addresses. Nicknames didn't strike her as right either. She had never heard Tom refer to anyone by the name *Roo,* or *Puddle* or *Two-Rot.*

But then something occurred to her, and Alison reached over to the freshly stocked caboodle of drugs and plucked one of the pills from its compartment. Sure enough, the tablet had numbers and letters imprinted onto its face. She dropped the pill back into the box, picked up another, then felt the thrill of a lead. The fourth pill she looked at had a happy face on it instead of writing, but she refused to let that confuse or deter her.

Alison was on her burner phone a few minutes later, googling what turned out to be a straightforward answer. The pharmaceutical industry used standard coding to identify their various pills, and looking at them now it no longer seemed like a secret language that she could never decipher. She clicked a link and was taken to a site that gave her a way to look up each of the pills by imprint.

The site also reported that ecstasy often had a flower or some other symbol stamped onto the tablet — a happy face in her case. Green had to be weed. And if so, then white could be the little baggies of cocaine.

Knowing all of that felt like enough to break the code, or so Alison thought as she gave it a try.

The first word in the cypher probably referred to the customer in some way … but how?

She couldn't figure it out.

Alison stared at the slip, turned it around and studied the other side in case Tom had used invisible ink and his secret messages might suddenly appear, then dropped the paper onto the bed and began plucking pills out of the box to investigate them again one at a time.

But none of that really helped, and her anxiety was threatening to spiral out of control. She kept imagining that knock on her door. She kept hearing Sarah demanding to know what she was doing. And she kept feeling increasingly certain that even if her daughter wasn't curious, the cops outside her house would be.

More than anything else right now, she needed to bury the evidence of her wrongdoing.

Just like Tom had been doing all along.

Unfortunately, Alison had no idea where to hide the stash. It wasn't like she could just shove all of those drugs into his shoes. But she did need a place that 'belonged to Tom,' so if that if the police did march back in with their warrants, Alison could still swear that she didn't know it was there.

Alison slipped the storage container into the backpack, slung it over her shoulder, opened the door and peeked into the hallway, then scurried into the garage feeling like the entire world might be watching.

Surely the police had left cameras in the house to keep an eye on her.

And if not, then maybe Goliat had.

Alison ignored her paranoia and walked directly over to Tom's tool cabinet — the best hiding place in the garage, even if it was a bit obvious. The cobalt cabinet was tall, with a bottom drawer that should be deep enough to hide the bag if she layered a few other items on top of it.

Moving a few things around to make room for the bag, her hand found a phone, cleverly concealed in the back and fixed to the top. She smiled as her hand closed around it.

She left the drugs in the garage and took the phone back into her bedroom. Then she powered it on, and compared the contacts to those on her list. Despite the illegality and all she had to do, Alison wanted to squeal when she saw that they matched.

The excitement was short-lived.

Because now, Alison knew that she would have to make her first call.

She looked at the list, then at the phone.

She repeated the cycle several times, stirring her courage as she did.

Then finally, she worked up enough nerve to dial the number for Tom's client *Roo*.

One ring and Alison's heart stopped when the other end answered.

"Hello?" Tiffany sounded uncertain.

But Alison knew enough to kill the call.

The phone buzzed in her hand a second later. Then again as Alison stared down at it, wondering if she should answer, and knowing that she had no choice.

"Hello?" Alison answered, disguising her voice with what sounded like a mouthful of gravel.

"Who is this?" Tiffany asked. "How did you get this number?"

"This is Karma." It was the first thing she thought of. "I'm taking over the route."

"Oh, fantastic." Tiffany sounded relieved, despite her total lack of enthusiasm. "I'm almost out of coke and wasn't sure if I could get more."

"I have more," Alison said, still in disbelief at what she was doing.

"Do you have any molly? And can you come by today … the usual place?"

"Yes, and yes." But holy shit, was she really going to do this? "But you'll have to tell me where the 'usual place' is. I only have your number."

"Oh. Sure. I'll text you the address. Along with what I need. See you whenever."

Then Tiffany was gone.

And Alison had to acknowledge that, yes, she was really doing this.

She didn't have a choice. Not when she could still hear Goliat in her head, calmly suggesting that Sarah work off her father's debt as a prostitute.

So for now, Alison would have to do this.

Just long enough to make the $125K and get Goliat off her back.

Tom's secret phone buzzed in her hand again, this time with a text.

Alison looked down at the screen, shaking her head as she read Tiffany's message.

"Of course," she muttered to herself.

Now she just needed a way to sell Tiffany her drugs in public without getting caught.

Chapter Seventeen

ALISON PEDALED FASTER, cycling through a sudden and rather surprising burst of exhilaration.

The emotion was short-lived because she needed it to die down a bit or she'd look like a cat on meth. She couldn't even enjoy the ride — bike rides usually relaxed her — because she was entering the lion's den with a bag full of drugs. It didn't help that this illicit transaction would be conducted with her biggest frenemy. Every time Alison dared to believe that the nightmare couldn't get worse, it did.

So she had to kill the burst of pride that her thighs weren't on fire, despite the raw power behind her furious pedaling. All those hours in the gym — *all those hours for Tom* — were finally paying off.

But none of that mattered now.

It only mattered that she was about to break the law.

In public.

With Tiffany.

She wanted to think *At least it can't get any worse,* but that was daring fate to crash through the facade of her picket fence life yet again. So instead she thought, *I can do this*, and pedaled even harder.

She pulled up to Rolling Knolls, looking around the park and wanting to laugh out loud, both because it would feel relieving to exhale with a gust of mirth, artificial though it might be, and at the absurdity of her realization that the country club might not even have a place to lock up her bike.

Members of the Rolling Knolls Cycling Club were the only people who ever rode in on a bike, so their rides were all harbored in an exclusive area meant only for them.

Tom had bought them all bikes on a lark one day — business must have been good that week — but the last time she could remember them all riding together, Sarah had been around seven or so. That was three bikes ago for her. Alison still had her powder blue cruiser, and was far from aging out of it. This felt so much better than all that pedaling to nowhere she had done in the gym and on her Peloton.

Alison pulled up to the front entrance and realized that of course there wouldn't be anywhere for her to lock the bike.

She leaned her bike against the wall and went inside, her heart rate somehow accelerating even more as she crossed through the country club foyer on to the next leg on her tour of hell.

Can u get in2 RK like Tom? Tiffany had texted.

Alison ignored her fury and texted back, *Of course.*

"How are you, Mrs. Tanner?" Lionel, one of the club's doormen, greeted her.

"Great!" she said with her best faux smile as she waved and passed him.

A few more long strides and she would be halfway there. Maybe then she could finally stop freaking out. That baggie full of coke and a half-dozen pills made it like trying to hear a song behind the sound coming from an over-turned amp that had been cranked all the way up.

The drugs were hidden in a tin of bath salts, so it wasn't like she could trip and fall and watch her life end in slow motion as everything spilled out of her purse. But paranoia kept eating her insides like maggots chewing through garbage.

Paranoia was what put Alison on her bike in the first place. On her way to the front door she got the worst feeling, just a few breaths from an absolute certainty, and somehow knew that if she left in her car the cops might pull her over and ask a few questions.

So she ditched her burner and slipped out of the house with only her purse and the powder blue bike, leaving through the back with her heart pounding like a *STOMP* live show.

That paranoia never left her. Even after she was sure the cops weren't following, Alison started wondering if they could have planted a tracker in her purse while she was being questioned. For five blocks she cycled through a catalog of TV shows, trying to remember any time when something like that had happened. She came up with two, but both of those shows were barely realistic.

But maybe the police had a second car. Alison had seen that exact scenario play out more times than she could count. The bad guy would have his eyes on the one vehicle he already knew about, while a second one cut a right behind him and slipped onto his tail.

Still, Alison had been aware of all the cars around her, and none seemed to stay for too long. It was kind of hard to be subtle trailing a bicycle.

It might have been Pavlovian considering how often an afternoon in the spa had done her wonders, or unbridled relief that she was finally on her way to the luxurious locker room, but Alison felt a promise of relaxation as she opened the door and stepped inside.

She nodded at Teagan, the receptionist manning the front, then exhaled as she entered the locker room, scanning the area for Tiffany.

"Oh my God … you have to be kidding me!" Tiffany laughed and covered her mouth, looking to her left and right, clearly disappointed that she didn't have an audience with whom she could share her delight. She was sitting in front of her locker, treating the bench like a throne. "Tell me this isn't just a coincidence. You're not here for why I think you might be here, are you?" Another laugh, with a dramatic wave of her perfectly manicured hand. "Say it ain't so!"

"Why is it you think I'm here?"

Tiffany stopped laughing, but only to study her. She narrowed her eyes at Alison, took a long moment to chew on her thoughts, then finished her recital with a smirk. "So he really did tell you." She shrugged. "I figured he was keeping you in the dark."

I figured he was keeping you in the dark.

Tiffany's words echoed in her head. There was something uncomfortably knowing in them.

"Can you please keep your voice down?"

Tiffany laughed and waved her hand again. "No one cares."

"*I* care."

"Like I said." Another laugh. "So, what do you have for me?"

"Nothing if you can't communicate in a—"

"Doing something cool for once clearly hasn't made you any cooler." Tiffany held out her hand, looking dramatically around to prove that no one was there.

"This is the part where you present me with my purchase."

Alison sighed and started digging for the bath salts, wanting to get out of the locker room and away from Tiffany more than she wanted to win this little whatever-it-was. She rummaged to the bottom, closed her hand around the prize, and pulled it out of her purse.

"Outstanding work," Tiffany said with the verbal equivalent of rolling her eyes, looking at Alison's bath salts. "It's like you've been doing this for years."

Alison handed her the Ziploc bag from inside the bath salts, only realizing at that moment — and more than a second too late — that now she would have to wait for Tiffany to hand her the money.

Alison had given her the power again.

Something about Tiffany had always made the animal inside Alison want to claw at her face. But that feeling had never been stronger than now. The way Tiffany was still sitting down, looking up at Alison standing over her, yet still acting taller, like she knew many things that Alison didn't.

Tiffany glanced in the Ziploc, then stood with a smirk.

She turned around, opened her locker and stuffed the bag inside, then rummaged around, probably just to keep her back to Alison longer.

Once Tiffany finally turned around, Alison held out her hand.

Tiffany sat back down and looked up at Alison. "What? Are you in a hurry?"

"I have places to go."

"Oh, come on, Alison. You have a few minutes to sit."

"I have a full day."

"Tom always sat." Tiffany flashed a smile that felt more like a wink.

And Alison finally asked the question burning her mind. "Were you and Tom having an affair?"

Tiffany insulted her with yet another laugh, followed by yet another wave of her hand. "An *affair*? Please. Don't be so bourgeois."

"That's not an answer."

"Isn't it, though?" Tiffany looked back at Alison as she stood, shaking her head and letting Alison know how disappointed she was that they couldn't chat longer. She opened her locker again, rummaged inside, then emerged with payment and an insult. A pair of hundred-dollar bills, one fifty, and an Abraham Lincoln on the top. A $5 tip for Alison's troubles.

As if she had just delivered a goddamned pizza.

"You gave me too much." Alison held out the five, then shook the bill at Tiffany in refusal.

"Please. I'm sure every bit helps right now."

Alison closed her fist around the money and left the locker room without another word.

Most embarrassing, Tiffany's little tip was ten percent of her take-home. Alison would only get $50 of the $250, the rest would go to Goliat.

She would have to sell a mountain of drugs to make even her most basic ends meet.

Alison left the country club, climbed onto her bike, and road back home amid a symphony of neighborhood noises, passing traffic, and her own tempest of thoughts.

All that thinking even seemed to be going somewhere, until it suddenly hit a wall at the sight of what was clearly a rental car parked across the street from her house.

The Tahoe was gone, and so was the Crown Victoria.

She suddenly missed the officers down to her marrow.

Because the young man sitting in the rented Mazda

didn't look like he belonged in this neighborhood at all. Now Goliat was keeping an eye on her too.

Well, at least he would see Alison doing her job.

The worst was over. If she could sell to Tiffany, then Alison could sell to anyone.

So she slipped back inside her house through the back, returned her bike to the garage, checked on Sarah to make sure she could still hear her daughter breathing through the door, then locked herself inside her bedroom with the burner and Tom's list.

Alison hit pay dirt on her very first call.

Chapter Eighteen

For once, Alison refused to let paranoia get the best of her.

She couldn't afford the heart attack that might hit her if she refused to heed the warnings. If the cops weren't in front of her place, then she wasn't going to worry about driving. The Mazda would be easy to spot, and Alison also supposed that she didn't really care if Goliat saw her dealing.

Alison thought she recognized the second client on Tom's list, both by the ever-so-slight drawl in his voice and by the address once he texted, but she was a hundred percent sure it was Jake after pulling up in front of the handsome eco-friendly house, built using only repurposed materials.

She had heard about Tom's "buddy over on Charlemagne" for years, and was introduced to him a couple of times at the club, always quickly with an efficient exit right afterward. Alison only knew what Tom had told her, which was admittedly little, despite her having dug for more nearly every time his name came up.

Jake and Tom had served in the military together. Jake made millions investing his inheritance after getting out. He could have been a hotshot stockbroker, according to Tom, but decided early on that he didn't want to be on that particular hamster wheel. So instead he spent his life as an angel investor and a groovy biohacker — Tom tended to share more about this part of Jake's personality, without ever really saying much that Alison really understood, or found an onramp to caring about.

He answered before she knocked, smiling at her as he opened the door in a way that somehow seemed to acknowledge that a good-looking woman was standing on his porch, without in any way making her feel the slightest bit uncomfortable.

"Well, come in …" He opened his door all the way.

The interior looked as striking as she had imagined. Architecturally impressive, and with a magazine-ready decor, yet still somehow warm.

Why would a man like this feel the need to buy illegal MDMA?

"You wanna sit?" He gestured toward the couch. Unlike Tiffany's invitation, his felt genuinely friendly.

She nodded and took a seat on the far side of a gunmetal-gray couch.

Jake sat on the other side, and pulled a dark wooden box on the glass coffee table toward him. He lifted the lid, gestured down at what appeared to be several rows of hand-rolled cigarettes — *joints?* — in various colored paper.

He nodded down at the box. "Care to join me? I've got varietals."

"I don't smoke." She shook her head, not knowing what he meant by *varietals,* nor wanting to ask.

"Not even weed?" This newfound knowledge seemed to seriously surprise him.

"I don't smoke anything." She shook her head again.

"That's a shame." He shrugged. "I figured everyone smoked weed by now. Especially ..."

"Especially what?" Alison asked after he failed to finish his thought.

"Nothing." He laughed, but made it sound like a compliment. "You sure?"

Jake glanced at the box again and grabbed one of his joints — in mint green paper — from the top before closing the lid and snatching a lighter sitting right beside it.

Then he lit the tip and took a long drag.

"You don't smoke outside?" Alison asked.

"Only when I want to be outside. Otherwise, I like the smell."

"I don't have any ... marijuana with me. I didn't know that's what you wanted."

"Does it look like I need any weed?" Another glance at the box, this time with a chuckle. "Each color is a different strain. Red is Scarface, brown is Old-Fashioned, yellow is Chemdawg, pink is Girl Scout Cookies, the white is Irish Cream, dark green is Purple Haze, and this one right here ..." He took another drag. "That's Green Unicorn. You sure you don't want to try? Green Unicorn is good for a first-timer, or an all-timer like me. I rotate my strains, but Unicorn never leaves the lineup."

He grinned and pushed the box back toward her.

"Maybe next time." Alison smiled, shaking her head and wishing she didn't feel so supremely awkward. She laughed, like this was all a big joke. "So, just the MDMA for you, then?"

Jake answered her seriously. "MDMA is the only thing

in your inventory besides weed that I'm willing to put in my body."

"You say that like it's a power food."

"No." He shook his head and took another drag. "I say it like someone who went through some serious shit in the military, and have recently stumbled into a little success while experimenting with MDMA for therapeutic treatment of trauma."

Alison laughed without meaning to. "So you're using an illegal drug to treat your PTSD?"

Jake shrugged. *No big deal.*

Then he offered her an impossibly charming smile. "It works a lot better than all the legal ones."

"Because it makes you forget all your troubles?" Alison asked.

"No." His brittle little laugh sounded gentle and sad. "Because it makes you remember."

She wasn't sure what that meant, and didn't want to ask. So instead she pulled out a Ziploc bag from inside her purse and passed it across the table like freshly dealt cards.

He took the bag and shoved it into his pocket with barely a glance.

"It's awful, what happened to Tom." His voice was kind and his manner inviting. "I'm awful sorry you're having to go through all of that. Is there anything I can do?"

"Not unless you want to buy a *lot* of drugs." Alison laughed, but it sounded as uncomfortable as it felt, and Jake failed to nibble her bait. She changed the subject, so that maybe she could leave this house with something more than a few dollars cleared from an obligation that shouldn't even belong to her. "How stupid do you think I am?"

"I'm sorry." He blew out a plume of smoke, clearly

taken aback. "I don't think you're stupid at all. What makes you say that?"

"I don't mean you, specifically." She shook head. "But I can't believe that I never suspected what Tom was up to. I feel like everyone at the club must have known … except me."

"Nah, not everyone …" Jake gave her a casual shake of his head. "Just the cool people."

"I always thought Tom was a good, moral person. Finding all of this out after he died …"

Alison was having a hard enough time finishing her thoughts without Jake looking at her like that.

"So Tom selling drugs makes him a bad, immoral person?"

"That's not what I'm saying—"

"How about me?" Jake asked, his drawl slightly stronger, his tone still non-threatening. "Does buying MDMA to help my PTSD make me bad or immoral?"

"I'm sorry." She stopped there, unsure of what else to say.

Jake took another long drag before he continued. "The pharmaceutical companies, most of them are 'bad' at best. And even if the drug war isn't immoral, judging by the results, it might as well be."

"You think the war on drugs is a bad idea?"

"Long jail sentences even for people who pose no violent threat to society, and for countless others who are utterly innocent, not doing anything different for their mind and body than what you do with a glass of wine, or what most folks with a bad injury and a prescription for painkillers do to ease their suffering?"

"That sounds like a gross over-simplification," Alison argued.

"No more so than the other side. I'm not talking conspiracy theory, these facts are readily available."

"What facts?" In her experience, people loved to throw that word around, even when they weren't anywhere near any quantifiable details.

"Like the United States puts more people behind bars than any other country."

"We're a big country," Alison said.

"We have four percent of the world's population and twenty percent of its prisoners. And again, for what? We're legislating behavior, spending a fortune, and still failing to fix the problem. Plenty of adults can manage drug or alcohol use while still raising families and going to work. Time marches on but our policies can't keep up. Sure, we have the slow roll toward cannabis legalization, but by now we've also had presidents who once used drugs in their youths still hypocritically supporting the war."

"Or they're doing what they see is the right thing, now that they've grown up," Alison replied.

Everyone made mistakes. It's what you did in the aftermath that mattered. Why were they even having this argument?

Jake continued. "The prohibition of alcohol gave rise to organized crime, and the same thing is happening now. The drug war drives trade into the hands of criminals, leading to violence that is, and always will be, much more dangerous than the drugs themselves."

It was definitely time to get out of here. Jake was clearly a deep thinker, and he had such a soothing manner that made for easy listening even if she disagreed with every other word. Yes, Alison was breaking the law, but that didn't mean she would turn hypocrite and denounce her beliefs to justify her illegal activity. It surprised her that someone as obviously smart and well-educated as Jake wouldn't understand the nature of evil.

"Drugs destroy people's lives," Alison said, instead of *I really should be going now.*

"You're right. So does driving. How do you feel about outlawing that?"

"There's a big difference between driving and meth."

"Again, you are absolutely right." Jake crushed his mostly finished joint into an ashtray. "But there is also a big difference between coke or meth and a bit of weed, or nibbling on some sight-bestowing mushrooms, which I kept telling Tom he should really start considering over all them pills."

"Illegal drugs cause crime."

"You, Alison Tanner, are on an absolute roll. Yes, there is too much drug-related violence in the ghettos, same as there's too much gang-related violence along the country's southern border. But guess what? If we make it all legal, then we eliminate the black market. Most customers would rather purchase their intoxicants from ordinary stores, and businesses like that settle their disputes with lawyers instead of bullets. You ever hear of a beer or tobacco gang? Portugal decriminalized every drug under the sun. And contrary to every Henny Penny out there, the sky still hasn't fallen. No surge in drug abuse — in fact, the number of young users and serious addicts in Portugal both dropped."

Jake paused, leaning back against the cushions as if to quiet himself.

It was the perfect exit, if she could just let him have the win. But for some reason Alison didn't understand she simply couldn't let the issue go.

"We wouldn't have a drug war without any reason."

He laughed. "We have a drug war because Richard

Nixon got his panties wadded in front of Congress, insisting that if we didn't destroy the drug menace it would surely obliterate us. But that was all the way back in '71, and even all these decades later there aren't enough people in power willing to question those original, antiquated, outdated and disproven assumptions."

Alison didn't know what to say or how to respond. And it seemed like Jake could go on for a year without stopping.

He took a deep breath with a shake of his head. "I'm sorry. Really. Sometimes I tend to go on."

"You've obviously thought about this a lot." She gave him a smile.

"That, I have." He smiled back as he stood. "Give me a second, I'll be right back."

Jake disappeared from the living room. Alison had assumed he was going to get her money. And he was, but he also returned with an iced coffee to go, freshly prepared for her in what was surely an eco-friendly gourmet kitchen.

"My favorite recipe." He handed her both the iced coffee and an envelope presumably filled with her payment. "You'll love it, I promise."

It might have been his smile, or the warmth of his voice, or it could have simply been that Tom's old friend was the first person who had been truly kind to her since the catastrophe, but for whatever reason, she was surprised to feel a genuine connection. More importantly, Jake had managed to make her feel safe.

"Tom wasn't a bad guy," he told her at the door.

Alison turned back to look at him. "Did he always use drugs?"

"I never saw him do anything other than a little weed once in a while, and that's an herb if you ask me. But I knew Tom for longer than I've known most people, and he was a good guy, Alison. He went through a lot, and never really dealt with how angry he was at his father, but a good guy for sure."

"Did he ever talk about us? His family, I mean?"

"He talked a lot about Sarah. He always wanted to make sure she had a great life. That was really important to him."

"What about me?" Alison asked. "What did he say about me?"

"Mostly good stuff, I promise." Jake gave her a knowing smile, followed by a change of subject. "I owed Tom a debt I can never repay, so I'll do whatever I can to help you. Just ask."

How about giving me a hundred and twenty-five grand? Do you think you could do that? Though, of course she knew that wasn't possible. Even an angel couldn't invest in the devil without leaving a paper trail.

"Thank you … why do you — why did you owe him?"

"That's between me and the angels now." Another smile and a tip of his head, gently nudging Alison toward the door.

She thanked him again, then left his handsome house with a smile, picturing him lighting back up before she even turned the engine.

She pulled into the street with a singular thought, her eyes on the lookout for cops.

Alison was less than a mile from home when one of them stopped her.

Chapter Nineteen

ALISON SAW the blue-and-red lights flashing and wondered how long the cops had been behind her.

It couldn't have been more than a few seconds, considering how much she'd been looking in every direction for either the police or one of Goliat's men.

But there was no doubt about what she was seeing now.

So she threw on her blinker, waited another few seconds while checking her mirrors, then crossed over into the right lane before pulling over to the side, noting with a sliver of misplaced pride that her hands had been at ten and two on the wheel before she noticed the officer behind her.

The radio was already off, but Alison reached over and pulled her license and registration out of the glovebox after she killed the engine.

She set the folder in her lap, wondering what was taking so long.

Alison glanced into the rearview and noticed that she hadn't been pulled over by a cruiser. The cop was driving a black sedan, though she didn't know the make and didn't want to get caught looking too long or closely enough that she could be accused of caring either way.

Only after he was finally out of his car and on the way to hers did she realize exactly who it had to be. Then his face appeared on the other side of her window and Alison knew for sure.

Detective Banks gestured for her to lower the window, which she was already doing while cursing herself for not having it all the way down before he got there.

"Evening, Ms. Tanner." He gave her a nod and another long second to think. "Mind if I ask what you're doing?"

"You mean, besides driving?"

"Where are you driving to?"

"Nowhere in particular. I just have a lot going on in my head right now, as I'm sure you can imagine. The house is feeling claustrophobic. I figured a drive might help me clear my head."

"How is your daughter doing?"

"I'm sorry?" Alison said, instead of *How dare you.*

"Your daughter … is the house claustrophobic for her as well?"

"What are you actually asking me, Detective Banks?"

He shrugged. "I'm just wondering if you needed to go out for a drive to try and clear your head, or if maybe you were picking up some of the slack in your family business."

"Believe me, no one wants to pay for *my* consulting," Alison replied as if her answer were serious.

"Think they'd be willing to pay top dollar for controlled substances?"

He looked at her without blinking, waiting to see what Alison might do next. She stared back at him, playing the housewife who knew too little.

Apparently that had been her role in life, until Tom died and turned her into the reluctant lead character in a crime show. She was afraid of saying the wrong thing or making the wrong move, and reasonably confident that saying little to nothing was the right way to go. She didn't have so much as a contact buzz from sitting next to Jake, but the scent of his Unicorn might still be on her.

Detective Banks finally broke their stalemate with a request that sounded more like an order. "Mind if I take a look inside the vehicle?"

Alison didn't have anything incriminating on her, or in the car. It wasn't like anyone could ever prove where the cash had come from. But she didn't trust the situation, and cops were always planting evidence, both on TV and in the actual news.

"I would," she said.

"Really?" He raised his eyebrows in either real or mock surprise. "I imagine that someone with nothing to hide wouldn't mind a little look-see at all."

Legally, Alison didn't have to answer. So she didn't.

The detective continued. "Let me guess, you've been boning up on your rights and figure you don't have to cooperate …"

Alison wanted to tell him that he was half right, she didn't have to cooperate. Instead she stayed silent.

"We found evidence that you knew about Tom's dealing. I can promise you, Ms. Tanner, it's in your best interest to let me search the vehicle right now."

Maybe she should just let him search, and maybe that would kill his suspicions and help this to all go away. But the detective's expression persuaded her otherwise. Something behind his eyes told her that he'd already found Alison guilty, and even a clean SUV couldn't convince him of her innocence.

"If you have proof, then can't you just go ahead and arrest me right now?"

"I'm trying to help you."

"You'll forgive me for not seeing it that way."

"Last chance." He gave her a grave look to underscore his offer.

But Alison kept looking straight ahead, responding only with the corner of her left eye.

He sighed, then told her to hold on, that he would be right back.

It felt like forever before he returned. She expected more bluffing, more of an attempt to get Alison cracking before he was forced to let her go. But instead he issued her a ticket for speeding.

"You've gotta be kidding me …" Alison said, scrawling her signature onto the bottom. "We both know I wasn't speeding."

"You're welcome to contest it in court." Banks wasn't smiling, but she could clearly see the gesture itching to surface from under his solemn expression.

He handed Alison her copy of the ticket, told her that he'd be checking in with her again soon, then turned around and walked back to his car.

She drove the rest of her way home, wondering if this would all be over by the court date. If not, Alison probably wouldn't even be able to pay for a speeding ticket, let alone hold onto her house, and the daughter she was trying her best to raise behind its walls.

But more than anything, Alison was glad she hadn't believed the detective's lies. It would have been a mistake to confide in him, or to throw herself on the mercy of the court. Banks was looking to close his case, and for that he needed someone to blame. Or punish.

She couldn't let that person be her.

And she couldn't let anything happen to Sarah.

For right now Alison needed to keep going, and avoid as much conflict as she possibly could.

You're almost home, she told herself.

But, of course, that's where the next conflict was waiting.

Chapter Twenty

ALISON AND SARAH had been knee-deep in battle ever since she got back home, but now their little mother-daughter duel was turning into an all-out war.

Sarah was stomping through the living room, then the kitchen on her way to the garage — the last place in the house that Alison wanted her to be right now, or for the foreseeable future.

"Just stop. Please …" She hated her begging voice, but Sarah refused to listen to any of the others as Alison trailed behind her. "I'm telling you, we should just call a plumber."

"We're not calling a plumber." Sarah opened the door and crossed the threshold into the garage, then restated her point with slightly different words just in case her mother had missed it the first time. "*Dad* wouldn't call a plumber."

Well, DAD got us into this mess! Alison wanted to scream but didn't, holding her anger the same as her calm, drawing a deep breath before answering in her most placid voice.

"Dad isn't here."

Sarah reeled around on her. "DON'T YOU THINK I KNOW THAT?"

Then she marched over to Tom's work area and started digging around, not yet opening drawers of that cobalt blue tool box, but surely only moments from doing so.

Her scream had been deafening, yet Alison saw that as a positive development. Sarah was seconds from sobbing. Then the *tantrumy* teenager would temporarily vanish again, only to reappear and rip at Alison's emotions at some other inopportune time in the future.

But at least for now, once her tears started to fall, Sarah might need her mommy again.

She yanked open one of the tool box drawers, vaguely in the middle, four drawers up from the jackpot. Alison let her riffle around inside for a few seconds, then watched her do the same thing to the drawers above and below it, not really actually looking in any one of the three.

"You're not going to find it in there," Alison said, at what felt like the perfect moment to draw Sarah's attention away from the toolbox.

"How do you know?" She turned to her mother, spittle flying from her bottom lip.

"Because your father never put anything away, including the wrench he used to fix your bathroom sink. He would have just left it on a counter somewhere. But I still think we should call the plumber."

"Dad showed me how to fix it! He said that was something I should know how to do!"

"Your father was always great at that." Alison smiled, even though it hurt her stomach to say anything nice about the man who had murdered the best parts of her life in the coldest of blood. "And he was right, that *is* something you should know how to do. But we can't afford any disasters right now — I would much rather call a plumber to fix your leaky bathroom sink now, then after—"

"So you don't think I can fix it."

"That's not what I'm saying, Sarah. But—"

"I already told you: Dad showed me! It's a loose pipe under the sink. I just need to find the wrench so I can tighten it."

Then she turned back around and yanked the bottom drawer open.

Alison slammed it back shut. Immediately, as if by instinct. "You need to stop and listen to me." She stopped just shy of *right now, young lady*, waiting for Sarah to meet her eyes before going further. "I understand why you want to fix your own sink, but I need you to understand why this isn't the right time."

She waited a beat, obviously trying to stifle her tears. The first one fell anyway. "But my sink is broken *right now*." Her plea was pitiful and she knew it, and the sound of her own misery made her cry harder.

Alison pulled Sarah against her, grateful that she allowed it, and that the embrace was keeping her away from the tool chest.

Soon enough her weeping settled into nothing.

After a long stillness about the length of a song, Sarah started crying again. Softly at first, barely a whimper, but then her mewling swelled to a crescendo with the mood of a gray and gathering storm.

She pulled away and pushed her mother, seemingly for no reason.

"THIS IS ALL YOUR FAULT!" Sarah looked like she wanted to give her another shove, but instead she spun around and ran back out of the garage.

Alison didn't know if it really was all her fault, because she wasn't sure what Sarah was referring to. Maybe it was and maybe it wasn't. Despite all the awful things Tom had done to their family, she sure as hell wasn't innocent. At the very least, Alison had turned a blind eye to a lot of wrongdoing, because she wanted to believe in her husband, and that her entire life wasn't a lie.

If she had even *tried* to look, then surely she would have seen enough of the truth to start digging deeper. Maybe Tom would be in prison right now, or maybe they would be divorced, but he would probably still be alive.

And Sarah would hate her anyway.

Alison sighed, turning her gaze to the bottom drawer, sticking out of the toolbox like a mocking tongue. Even with everything already ruined, the situation could still get even worse. She had illegal drugs in the house. A discovered stash could finish them off. But where could she hide them?

She'd figured that Tom's toolbox was about the safest place away from Sarah as possible, having forgotten all about her daughter's leaky sink. It always sucked when they argued, but it felt exponentially worse when Alison knew she was wrong.

Maybe she should have helped her find the wrench instead of refusing to hear her. Fear had swallowed her logic. Now Sarah was pissed at her again, and Alison still didn't know what to do.

There had to be somewhere in the house where she would never look, no matter what.

She raided Alison's closet all the time, and even though Tom's side would have been safe before his accident (murder), their daughter had started sleeping in his T-shirts.

She wasn't about to rob her of another way to cope. She wished she could afford to put Sarah into therapy. They had been suffering from an ever-worsening case of *Teenagitis* before Tom's death, and Sarah's emotions were now understandably out of control. She needed to talk about all of this with someone who didn't already know her. A therapist was the best way for her to deal with what had happened, but that solution cost a couple hundred dollars per hour. Alison couldn't afford the first hour, let alone the however many Sarah might actually need.

She couldn't even afford pay for a plumber.

It was humiliating, having a wealthy mother-in-law who wouldn't flip a nickel her way. Alison's cut of the drugs she was selling sure as hell wouldn't help. She would probably need new "clients," in addition to the ones on her list, just to keep them eating in their house with the lights on.

She looked around the garage, searching for a hiding place while trying to ignore all the memories. Barring them from the gates of her mind like refugees fleeing a civil war over her personal history.

Over and over she had to keep asking herself: *Has my life been a lie?*

The question was an arrow and her brain had a full quiver.

She shoved all of the gloom and defeat to the floor of herself, focusing instead on hiding the drugs to keep them safe. She was torn between keeping them close to her — maybe under her mattress? — and maintaining believable deniability by hiding them with Tom's things, which Sarah would be much more likely to go through.

Alison's heart was already aching enough, but it hurt even harder when her eyes finally found the perfect place. A box of old baby clothes she never had the heart to give away. For the longest time, really up until a few years ago, she had always hoped and even sometimes believed that they would have another child.

But now Alison knew for sure what she had felt and ignored for more than a decade.

Tom had never been interested in having a big family.

Really, Tom had only been interested in satisfying himself.

And now she was left cleaning a mess she didn't even know he'd been making.

She pulled the box of clothes down from its shelf and carried it over to the toolbox. Then she put the backpack into the box and buried it under a pile of memories.

She returned the box to its shelf with a sigh and went back to her bedroom.

Then she got her phone and reintroduced herself to the devil.

Chapter Twenty-One

Friday …

ALISON PULLED INTO HER DRIVEWAY, eyes fixed on the rearview as she killed the engine and sat.

No Tahoe. No sedan. No rental.

And yet not seeing any signs of her usual watchers only unsettled her further.

She got out of the SUV, her nerves on fire thanks to the baggie of coke, jostling around like a pack of gum in her purse. One of her clients was a no-show.

Most of her wanted to leave the coke in her Cayenne, unreasonably sure that Detective Ian Banks would accost her at some point between the driver's side door and her porch. But a big enough part of her knew she was being paranoid, and another part unreasonably wondered if they would search her SUV with drug-sniffing dogs.

She opened her front door, ducked inside while still managing to look like a perfectly normal woman entering her house. Alison planted her back against the door on the other side, a gesture she saw all the time onscreen, but never really believed or had the inclination to do in real life. Until now.

She looked at her watch. Sarah should be home any minute now.

Fifteen minutes to decompress. She wanted to open a bottle, but didn't want Sarah to see it, so she emptied a glass of water down her gullet instead, gulping the whole thing before she refilled it two-thirds to the top and started to slowly sip.

She sat on her sofa, thinking. Parsing her thoughts into two separate piles. The stuff she couldn't get out of her head, but needed to box up and ponder later, and the stuff she had to leave churning up front because those thoughts were too powerful for her to even try and order them around.

Her drop-offs were … interesting. Her second day at it, and the gig wasn't really anything like she expected. The first two calls had been exceptions to the rule, due to their extreme nature. Eleanor was the only person in the world who would have been a worse first client than Tiffany. And Jake was the one of Tom's friends she would have most wanted to have a conversation with. Those polar experiences boosted her confidence enough to text most of Tom's list.

Around half of her lines in the water replied, with a handful trying to make appointments, and others either wishing her well or telling Alison that an order would be coming soon. She always identified herself as Tom's wife immediately, and kept the language vague. Maybe the half who didn't answer weren't willing to risk it, making her wonder how she might recover those missing clients.

She took five and deferred the rest for later. Even that

felt like too many, but without any other means of generating income, she had to get going.

Alison had taken the first five clients who accepted her conditions. She wanted no more than five transactions — again, even that felt almost absurdly risky — with all of them taking place in Provisions. The cops wouldn't follow her into the grocery store, and if they did, then it would be game over before she even moved her first piece onto the board.

She took her appointments ten minutes apart and spent just under an hour shopping, leaving with a full cart made of large, low-cost items. Enough to fill her bags. Rice, beans, oats, and flour. She would have to figure out something else for next time, and institute a rule to deal with the no-shows.

But yes, it would have been a good day, considering. If not for that second thought that lived like an axe in the stump of her mind. Tom's funeral tomorrow, or so said the almost comically insulting e-vite Alison had opened while taking her first sip of coffee that morning.

The funeral turned her stomach, and the thought of Eleanor parading around like she could already picture her doing turned it even harder. She was a snake lying in the grass of Alison's life, spewing venom on behalf of her son.

Surely the serpent would strike at his funeral.

By this time tomorrow it would be in the past, but until then his burial felt like a haunting. Like—

The door opened and Sarah entered the house.

But she wasn't alone.

"Hey, Mom."

"Hey, Mom," Miguel echoed.

"Don't call her that," Sarah said, her voice teasing as she gave him a playful shove. "She'll get all mad at us."

"Will she send us to your room?" Miguel laughed.

Sarah joined him. And Alison wanted to strangle them both. "You didn't tell me you were bringing company over."

"*See*." Sarah turned to Miguel. "I told you."

"And what did you tell him?"

"Nothing." But then she laughed. "So. Can Miguel help me with my homework?"

"Sure. In the living room. After he and I have a little talk."

"Why not in my room? And what do you two need to talk about?"

"You know why not in your room, and if I wanted you to be a part of the conversation, then I would ask you to stay instead of telling you to go and take a few minutes to settle in. So please, go to the bathroom—"

"I don't have to go to the bathroom."

"Get something to eat, then, and put your things away. What are you studying?"

"What do you mean?" Sarah asked.

"You said you had homework."

"Oh." Sarah shrugged. "History. Miguel is great at history."

"It's true." Miguel nodded, but his smirk was pushing all of her buttons.

"I'll see you in a few minutes," Alison said.

"Fine. Whatever." Then Sarah left them alone and went to her room.

Alison pointed to the sofa, then went over herself, grabbing her purse from the coffee table before plopping onto the cushion. She pulled out an envelope and handed it to Miguel as he took a seat next to her, slipping the envelope into his pocket without even looking.

"You short?" he asked.

"I don't know how much I'm supposed to deliver, other

than *almost everything I'm making,* but the eighty percent is there."

"So what did you want to talk about?"

"There's gotta be another way," Alison said.

"You're taking over for Tom." A tiny shake of his head. "You're in it now, and there ain't no way out of it."

"But I'm only in it until my debt is paid. So how can I pay off what I owe faster? Even if the cops stop watching me and I can double what I'm bringing in now, it feels like I'll be doing this for a couple of years."

"A couple of years is better than jail or worse, isn't it?"

"There has to be a better way to make money."

"Making money isn't the problem," Miguel said, shaking his head. "Believe me, you're much better off doing what you're doing, even if it takes you a lot longer to do it."

"What's the problem?"

He shrugged. "The more a job pays, the bigger the risk."

"What kind of risk?" Alison asked.

"Even if there isn't a bigger risk to your life, the kinds of payouts you're looking for come with heavy sentences if you get caught. That's why they're worth so much."

"Like what?"

"Like smuggling."

Alison sighed. There was zero chance she could be a smuggler. The paranoia would eat her alive.

"Have you ever smuggled anything?"

He shook his head. "No way. And I'm never gonna offer. Once you're in, you're in."

"So you're just a dealer, then." Alison meant to insult him.

But Miguel didn't take it that way. "At least I don't charge sales tax."

"What would your parents think if they knew you were dealing?"

"No idea." Another shrug. "My mom OD'd when I was seven, and my dad isn't around."

"Who do you live with?"

"Foster parents. And they couldn't give less of a shit what I do as long as their checks keep coming in, and I stay out of trouble."

"So drug dealing is fine?" Alison asked, stirred by disbelief.

"As long as they don't know."

"And you're okay … with what you do?"

"*With what I do*?" Miguel gave her a careless laugh. "Yes, I'm perfectly fine with supplying a little escape for profit so I can start my life right. And I'm not interested in your judgment. You can enjoy your libations all you want to. But other people can make different choices. I'll be able to pay for college, between what I've saved and my scholarships. There's no other way I could do that. So yes, I'm not just okay with what I do, I'm damn proud of myself for getting it done."

"Scholarships … that's great … Where do you want to go?"

"Maybe MIT. But probably Stanford since I don't really want to leave California."

"MIT and Stanford, really?"

"Don't look so surprised," Miguel said.

"I'm not." She was. "It's just … what do you want to study?"

"I want to be an engineer."

"Why?"

"I'm good at fixing things. Solving problems. We've got a lot to deal with, right? Controlling and preventing pollution, developing new medicines, even urban development

… I'm not sure yet what kind of engineer I want to be, I just know it's where I want to go."

Alison was shaking her head.

Miguel said, "Again: you don't have to look so surprised."

"You're so smart. Why would you want to get mixed up in all of this?"

"Not sure *wanting* had anything to do with it. Like I said, when you're in, you're in. I got in a long time ago, and that's where I've been living ever since."

"But you think Goliat will let you leave when it's time for college?"

Miguel nodded. "We have an understanding."

"How well did you know Tom?"

"Abrupt change of subject … Not very."

"And how well is that?" Alison pressed.

"I met him a couple of times."

"Was one of those times the night he was hit?" She surprised herself with the question.

Miguel too; she could see it all over his face.

"What happened?" Alison asked.

He shook his head. "Nothing."

"It wasn't 'nothing.' My husband was murdered. What happened, Miguel?"

"Keep it down," he cautioned, patting the air with his hands.

She took a breath and repeated her question in a softer voice. "*What happened?*"

"I'm not exactly sure. But it had something to do with Rottweiler."

"A dog?"

"Nah. A person, vicious as a dog."

"Who is that?"

"A seriously dangerous dude. He's into some bad shit."

"Like drugs?"

"Like human trafficking." His face withered along with the words. "Rottweiler's people have killed two of Goliat's men. They mutilated a third before sending him back with the message, *Join me or this happens to you.* Apparently there was a big powwow where Goliat tried to negotiate a peace, and the Big Dog, as they sometimes call him, pulled a Genghis Khan."

"What does that mean?" Alison asked.

"Genghis used to give towns a chance to surrender and peacefully join his kingdom before he attacked; but any who refused, he went out of his way to slaughter and lay waste to everything. His way of encouraging others to join him peacefully. And it worked, more often than not …"

Miguel stopped.

Her heart skipped a beat as she looked up and saw Sarah entering the living room, having just caught the tail end of their conversation. Alison wondered how much she had heard.

"See. I told you he was great at history." Sarah smiled at him.

"It's important," Miguel agreed with a nod. "Because those who don't know their history are doomed to repeat it."

Chapter Twenty-Two

SATURDAY ...

WHEN ALISON WAS on her deathbed pondering the many years behind her, this day would surely be among the very worst of her memories.

The closed casket was on full display, and the preacher had already finished his spiel. He had invited the mourners to come up one at a time to pay their final respects, and Alison had watched the assembly stand in line to say goodbye from the sidelines.

All of that had been expected. Same for Eleanor's performative histrionics. But Alison failed to anticipate the flurry of rage the sight would stir up inside her. Eleanor holding court as if *she* was the widow. Alison didn't doubt that her emotions were real — she did lose her son, after all — but that didn't make it any less maudlin and performative. It was so uncomfortably tacky, the way she was making it all about her.

"Why can't I go up there?" Sarah griped to her mother,

after Alison had held her back for more than a quarter hour.

"Your father would have wanted us to say our goodbyes after everyone else." That sounded true enough.

And Sarah seemed to accept it.

They stayed in place with Sarah holding her hand, softly sobbing against her shoulder while Alison forced a smile onto her face to greet every well-wisher coming her way. That was easier than trying not to glare at Eleanor.

"Can we go now?" Sarah asked, once it seemed that they were the only mourners left. Alison nodded and led the way. But then Sarah stopped her in front of the casket. "Do you mind if I have a moment alone with him?"

"Of course," Alison said, trying not to feel hurt.

Then she fell several steps back and did her best not to listen, catching a few words here and there, anyway.

"… that no matter what … you'll always be with me … soul … bird chirping … singing to me … butterfly … remembering all the things you said …" A long pause followed by a choking sob and a string of gibberish through which Alison understood only a single word. "*Forever.*"

Then Sarah turned toward her with a bottomless exhale and mumbled, "I'll be outside," before leaving her mother alone with the casket.

Only after she was gone and Alison was standing almost flush against the closed metal box did she realize that her fists were clenched tightly enough to hurt. And it was only upon seeing them closed and feeling the crescents biting into her skin did she realize just how angry she was.

Alison had to mutter through clenched teeth while looking down at the coffin to keep her bile from spilling like lava over her bottom lip.

"You lied to me. You cheated on me. And worst of all,

you abandoned me." A deep breath. "I'm so, so, *so* fucking angry at you right now." Another breath. "If something happens to Sarah because of what you did, I promise that I'll be right next to you in Hell, spending my eternity making sure you never forget that this is all your fault."

"Such ugly things to say at your husband's funeral," Eleanor said from behind her, with what sounded a bit to Alison like whimsy in her voice.

She spun around to face her mother-in-law, realizing for the first time that she wasn't even sure if Eleanor still fit that definition. Was "in-law" a social relationship, or a legal one?

Their marriage vows had agreed with the traditional *till death do us part*. But now that was over, and Alison didn't know what was next. Only that Eleanor would want more than her share, same as always.

"You're not even going to give me my time to mourn?"

"That didn't sound at all like mourning to me." Eleanor tried to hand her an envelope.

Alison shook her head, refusing to take whatever it was. "I don't want that."

"You don't even know what it is."

"I know where it came from."

"Stop being a baby," Eleanor scoffed. "The result is inevitable."

"The result of *what?*"

Eleanor shoved the envelope into her hands, then forcibly closed her fingers around it. "This is a custody agreement for Sarah. It's inevitable, dear—"

"You're not taking my daughter!"

"—you haven't got the money to fight me, so you might as well sign the paperwork and make this easier on all of us."

"I will *never* sign any of this." Alison dropped the envelope on the floor. "And I will *never* let you have control over Sarah, so you can ruin her like you ruin everything else."

"You better watch what you say to me."

"Or what? You'll try and take my daughter away from me—"

"*My granddaughter.*"

"—or threaten to take my house? Tell me that I can't fight? Do everything you can to make me feel small?"

Eleanor laughed, as if wanting to prove Alison's point for her. "Tom always said you were foolish."

She shook her head. "That asshole may have said a lot of things, but I don't believe that he ever said that. Because I was only a fool when it came to his lies, and he never would have wanted his mommy to know about all of those."

Eleanor blanched and fell a step back.

Alison wasn't sure if she had ever enjoyed anything more.

So she stepped into the empty space and lowered her voice to a rolling whisper that vibrated with a raw yet insistent anger, threatening to go nuclear and cover the funeral in a blanket of emotional radioactivity if Eleanor wasn't smart enough to listen, or even worse was dumb enough to interrupt.

Alison owned the moment, and she could have spent it screaming all of the things she had ever wanted to say to this terrible human.

But instead she said, "I'm sorry you have to spend the rest of your life knowing that your son was a liar, a cheater and a drug dealer. But if you think I'm going to let you raise my daughter, after the job you did with Tom, then you are out of your motherfucking mind."

Chapter Twenty-Three

Alison's life was really in the shitter.

She couldn't even shed her paranoia while standing in line for ice cream. Plus, apparently she was using words like *shitter* now. Life kept piling on top of her. From bad, to worse, to Eleanor. Her mother-in-law had always acted like the semi-silent adversary while Tom was still alive. But now that Alison's childhood sweetheart was no longer with them, there was nothing quiet about her role as the primary antagonist in Alison's life.

Or at least she would be, if Alison wasn't so busy being bullied by both the bad guys and the good guys alike.

She was self-medicating. With ice cream, and not from the grocery store. Alison was standing in line at The Inside Scoop, waiting to pay for a pint of Mexican Vanilla, fresh from the freezer. To hell with her lactose intolerance, this place had the best ice cream in Las Orillas. Maybe the world. A little Mexican Vanilla melting in her mouth might help to ease her and Sarah's suffering after the funeral.

But she couldn't stop looking over her shoulder. Couldn't stop dreading that something else would go wrong. That someone — good guy or bad guy, right now they felt sort of the same — would suddenly appear to redirect the course of her life yet again. Any second now.

Would her life ever feel normal again?

"That'll be $7.71," said the cashier when it was finally Alison's turn.

She nodded and handed him a ten, her stomach flopping along with the transaction as she remembered her life just a week ago, when ten dollars felt like nothing, and she didn't care about the city's obnoxiously high ten-and-a-quarter-percent sales tax.

The cashier — sixteen or seventeen with a wide smile and shockingly smooth skin for a kid who worked in an ice cream parlor — bagged the pint and handed Alison her change. "And that'll be two dollars and twenty-nine cents back. Thank you for enjoying our ice cream at The Inside Scoop!"

"You're very welcome." Alison smiled back at him, with a fleeting moment of comfort.

She looked around the parlor on her way to the door, paranoia still attempting to lead the way.

She opened the door with one hand, Mexican Vanilla tucked in its bright white bag with The Inside Scoop's vibrant logo tucked under the crook of her opposite arm. She made it three steps from the entrance — just past the small assembly of empty tables out front — before a large imposing man was suddenly standing in her way.

For less than a second she wanted to scream, suddenly certain that the man standing in front of her was there to end her life. He was tall, almost a giant compared to her. Not just with his height, at least six-foot-four if she was guessing, but shoulders that looked like they might give the man trouble squeezing through the average door frame. Imposing, scary even after she settled, but after that first second had passed Alison realized that the man inspired a different strain of fright.

"I understand you have a problem. I have a solution to your troubles."

"And I have pepper spray," she told him, her hand closing around the canister in her purse.

"Relax, Mrs. Tanner. I'm not here to hurt you." He added a warm smile to his understanding nod, as though to make up for his dominant size, sudden appearance, and overbearing stance. "I'm with the DEA."

What Mr. Drug Enforcement Officer apparently believed might improve their situation, quite clearly made everything worse. The pepper spray was out of her purse and the snarl was on Alison's face as she looked around to see if anyone else was watching. She couldn't see anyone, not that *that* meant nobody was watching.

It wasn't like the man was dressed in all black with DEA stenciled across his chest, but she was still unreasonably sure that anyone who saw them talking would know *exactly* who he was.

And if the wrong person spied them, *Sarah* would pay for her mistake.

"I have to go," Alison said, attempting to pass the man.

"Please, Mrs. Tanner. Take a seat," he said, still blocking her exit as he pointed to one of the many empty chairs in the parlor. "I believe that you're innocent and I would very much like to help you."

Alison was smart enough to know she shouldn't believe a word out of this man's law-enforcing mouth, but his voice, and something in his demeanor, were too comforting for her to ignore.

This wasn't just anyone professing her possible innocence, it was the DEA. That mattered. Detective Ian Banks was treating her as guilty until proven innocent, and probably couldn't do anything to help or protect her against Goliat and his people. The DEA, though, had more resources. More firepower to maybe end her nightmare.

So Alison sat.

And the man took his seat across from her. "Name's Ellis Munk." He handed her a card. "I can see that you're nervous, but let me assure you that right now you're perfectly safe."

"What about ten minutes from now?"

"That's all up to you, Mrs. Tanner."

"How so?"

"Like I said, I think you're innocent. Banks" — Ellis made a face — "well, Banks doesn't know dick, and neither do any of the schlubs working under him."

He paused, looking at Alison and apparently waiting for her to respond. When she said nothing, Ellis continued. "Don't bother confirming or denying, but I think I can understand some of what you're involved in. And believe me, I'm not after you."

"Who *are* you after?"

"Goliat." Then he stopped again. Looked at her again. Waited for her to respond again.

This time something surely showed on her face, despite her trying to stop it.

"I'm listening," she said.

Ellis seemed to sink ever-so-slightly lower in his seat, as if seeking new ways to put Alison at ease. "Any involvement on your part in your husband's activities will be forgiven if you agree to help me."

"He's not my husband." A dumb thing to say, but she needed to say something.

"Your former husband, then."

"I was never involved in his business."

"I'm not saying you were."

"I thought he ran a consulting company until the day he died." Then she corrected herself. "The day he was murdered."

"I'm sure that's all true." Ellis gave her an understanding nod. "But let's not talk about what happened before Tom was taken away from you. I'm not interested in any of that. I only care about right now and what's going to happen next. I'm invested in *you*, Mrs. Tanner."

Alison looked to her left and right again. Lightly at first, then wildly around. She wanted to hear more of whatever this DEA man had to say, but Goliat had given her strict orders to stay away from the cops if she wanted Sarah to keep breathing.

And it wasn't like she could pretend that the drug dealer hadn't had her watched.

"Knock it off," Ellis said.

"I'm sorry?"

"Stop looking around like that. No one knows who I am, so right now you could be talking to anyone. You're only drawing attention to our conversation. I can protect you, and eventually get you out of this mess. But you have to—"

"How can you do that?"

"My task force is taking this case away from LOPD. That means it's up to me now whether or not you stay out of jail."

She swallowed hard, feeling like a cartoon character as the lump slid down her throat. Frightened as she was, for the first time Alison was also willing to believe. "You'll let us walk right now if I tell you everything?"

It was a terrifying thing to say out loud. Again Alison wondered if it was possible that she had been bugged somehow.

He shook his head. "Sorry, Mrs. Tanner, but it's not that simple. I need someone inside Goliat's organization."

"For how long?"

He shrugged. "Long as it takes."

"What does that mean? A few weeks, a few months … a year?" That last word came out sounding like a curse.

"You want a promise, then I'm sure it'll be closer to the last one."

She shook her head. "I need to get out of this, not deeper inside. One week of it and I'm going out of my mind. I can't exactly—"

"What is it you need to get out of, Mrs. Tanner? I could definitely help to arrange your escape." He shrugged again, but this time there seemed something cold in his gesture. "But I'm sure you wouldn't like where an early flight out of this will send you."

"Are you threatening me?"

"Not at all. It's a simple fact: if we don't have what we need to bring in the big dog, then we round up as many of the puppies as we can."

"What would I have to do?" She forced herself to hold his gaze without looking around, wondering if his lifeline might really be able to save her.

He gave her a tiny smile. "Have you learned anything so far?"

"Like what?"

"Like anything." His tiny smile widened with invitation.

Alison opened her mouth, but then she realized the size of her potential mistake, and the danger she might be redirecting away from her and right toward Sarah, then closed it instead.

"We can start with something small. Like I said: *anything*."

She cleared her throat but nothing came out.

"It's simple, Mrs. Tanner." The slightest edge had entered his voice. "You give me a sign of good faith right now and I promise to make sure that when this is all over, you and your daughter go free." A pair of beats to let that sink in, then Ellis finished his thought. "A new life with no jail time. You want a new identity in Witness Protection?" He offered her a knowing shrug. "I can get you that, too."

"Have you heard of a guy named Rottweiler?" Alison asked.

"Keep talking …" Ellis gave her a nod.

"He was involved in Tom's death."

"And how do you know this?"

"From one of the guys I met at Goliat's place." No reason she needed to fink on Miguel. At least not yet.

"And he just told you this?"

Alison shook her head. "Two guys were talking. I overheard them."

"They were talking in English?" Ellis asked.

Only a few questions into their conversation and she was already seeing the inherent danger in telling even the simplest lies. "Mostly, yeah."

"How do you know they didn't want you to hear what they were saying?"

"I guess I don't." She shrugged; it seemed like the safest answer.

"So, what about Rottweiler?"

"He's into some bad shit."

"The guy who either killed your husband, or had something to do with his murder is into some 'bad shit.' *That's* what you have for me?"

"No. The actual intel was that Rottweiler had something to do with Tom's murder." Was *intel* the right word? "It sounds like human trafficking might account for some of that bad shit he's into."

"In what way does it 'sound like' that?"

"From what the two guys were saying," Alison clarified. Sort of.

"Mostly in English."

"Right." She nodded, wondering if he was buying any of this. "Apparently Rottweiler's people killed two of Goliat's men. There was some big meeting where Rottweiler pulled a Genghis Khan."

Alison stopped. Waited for Ellis to ask for clarification.

But he only nodded back at her instead.

"Does that help?" Alison asked.

"It might. Might not. Sounds awfully convenient, you knowing all of that. Unless there's something else you're not telling me?" Ellis raised his eyebrows at her.

"No, sir." Alison held his gaze, wondering why she was defending Miguel.

Was it because of Sarah, or something else?

He nodded slowly, surely disbelieving her.

"What do you want me to do?"

"Whatever they ask you to do, for now. Keep your eyes and ears open. Anything you learn might be valuable. I'll be in touch." Ellis stood.

"How will I get a hold of you?" Alison asked.

"Like I said, *I'll be in touch.* Keep an eye out for the blind coyote."

Then he turned around and started walking away.

"What does that mean?" Alison called after him.

But Ellis never turned back around, leaving his informant with her surely melted Mexican Vanilla and the heavy doubt that instead of fixing things, she had just made the biggest mistake of her life.

Chapter Twenty-Four

TUESDAY ...

THREE DAYS.

It had been three days since Ellis sat Alison down in front of The Inside Scoop. Three days and he still hadn't reached out to her. Three days, including two with Sarah at school all day, and Alison going out of her goddamned mind, worrying about her safety while texting her way through Tom's list of potential clients and facing ever-diminishing returns.

She had lucked out the other day getting all of her transactions in a one-hour window at Provisions. As Alison soon discovered, people desperate for a fix will do just about anything. But it had been a buyer's market ever since. She had plenty of inventory, but most of her customers — or potential customers — wanted to meet at the same place they had always met Tom.

But he must have gone to the country club on some sort of schedule. Alison was nervous going in and out of

Rolling Knolls as often as she was. Surely the police would be on to her. There was nothing cool about her itinerary: *sell drugs as often as possible, no matter where you have to go.*

And yet despite all that desperation, Alison still didn't have what she needed to survive. How long would she have to wait before a pint of Mexican Vanilla no longer felt like a luxury? How long before she could be sure that all this was behind her and Sarah was safe?

After going through the entire list of non-responses yet again, Alison did the last thing she wanted to do and texted Tiffany, aware of her schedule enough to know she would almost for sure be on her way to Pilates at the ladies' spa right about now.

I'm heading to the club. I'm stopping by the store on my way. Need anything?

No answer from Tiffany.

Even after Alison tried again.

She looked at the time, saw that she still had five minutes until Pilates, and hit the contact to call Tiffany's phone.

"No thanks," she answered.

"You're not out of groceries?" Alison asked.

"I actually am. Or at least I'm out of avocados, and what's the point of living without nature's butter, am I right?" Tiffany didn't really want to know. "I think you're actually asking about my cocaine supply. But that's doing just fine."

"Do you think you'll be needing more any time soon?" She felt humiliated begging, and like a bronze-plated idiot still worrying that her call was somehow being intercepted. Even if the burner wasn't being monitored, Tiffany's line could be.

"Definitely. I really like coke. But I have a new supplier."

"A new supplier?"

"His molly is *primo*."

"But—"

"I mean, Tom's was Chanel but this dude's is Prada."

"—we already have a relationship."

"Only because of Tom. We both know you and I wouldn't ever have anything to say to one another if not for him. So guess what?" The bitch actually giggled. "Now we don't have to. I figured I'd buy from you to honor Tom's memory or whatever. But that was then and this is now."

"What happened in between then and now?" Alison asked, hating Tiffany with a new and undiluted purity.

"When you first texted I was like, *Boo-hoo! Poor little Alison just lost her hubby and the cops might even lock her up for what Tommy was doing!* But now, the new guy is giving me a discount."

"I'll give you a discount," Alison said, hating her even more.

"That's okay. You're making me late for Pilates."

Then Tiffany was gone and Alison was squeezing the phone hard enough to break either it or her hand. She glared at the screen for several long and angry seconds before dropping the phone next to her on the couch.

"Fucking bitch."

Again she returned to her list. But scrolling down while scanning every contact from top to bottom was sending her deeper and deeper into despair. Tiffany's excuse wasn't unique, and was feeling less like an excuse. Fewer customers were answering, but those who still had manners enough to respond said the same thing as her frenemy. They also had a new source, and therefore wouldn't be needing anything in the future. Of course they would let her know if anything changed.

As similar replies started to pile atop each other, Alison felt ever more frantic. Now, after talking to Tiffany and looking through the list again, she finally saw what might be happening here.

This wasn't just about former clients being scared of getting caught, or not wanting to deal with Alison after her husband had gone down. Her client list was being targeted.

Did that mean that Rottweiler's people had been assigned to take over Tom's route?

And if so, how could she ever pay off her debt to Goliat, or learn enough to buy her way out of trouble with the DEA?

She leaned back against the cushions, longing for wine.

Then she leaned forward and stood, walking to the kitchen, already deciding to uncork one of her few remaining bottles. A little drinking might help her to figure out what the hell she should do next.

Ellis said that he would contact her and left no means for the other way around, making any plans having to do with talking to him dead on arrival.

She obviously couldn't tell Goliat about her meeting with the DEA agent, but Alison was also terrified to tell him about her dwindling client list. She could clearly imagine him telling her that setbacks were her problem, not his. If she made it his problem, then they had a problem.

She filled her glass and returned to the living room. Scooped her phone up from the coffee table on her way to sitting, already scrolling through her contacts to Miguel. She hit his name and listened to the ringing.

"Mrs. Tanner," he answered.

"Please stop calling me that. Alison. Or if you want to give me a cool nickname, I guess now's the time." She laughed to herself, feeling feisty.

"Is everything okay?"

"What can I say, life is a generous pour." Alison laughed again.

"You don't sound okay."

"I have like, no customers, Miguel."

He sighed.

"What does that mean?" Alison asked.

"I've heard the same thing from a few other guys. I've been fine, but a couple of us have been hit. Rottweiler's moving in. No surprise there. Though it is happening fast."

"What should I do?"

"It's a turf war."

"Well, I've never been in a turf war, Miguel. So forgive me if I'm not exactly sure what a turf war entails. Do I need to start bringing my AK to work?"

"Do you have an AK?"

"NO I DON'T HAVE AN AK!" Alison was suddenly on her feet, and splashing wine onto the carpet. *Goddammit.*

Or actually: *MOTHERFUCKER!*

Miguel laughed. "It's cool, Alison. Make yourself a smoothie."

"Why would I do that?"

"Because chill pills are played out."

Alison surprised herself with a laugh. "Seriously. What should I do?"

"Offer your clients a discount."

"That comes out of my end, right?"

"Of course it does," Miguel said.

She could picture him shrugging.

"Or you could try and find some new clients," he suggested.

Alison laughed again, an accidental self-conscious twitter. "Should I go to the mall for that? Or would it be better if I stood on Seaside Drive in a sandwich board with my best offer and a number?"

"Is that a prostitution joke?" Miguel asked.

"No!" Now she felt embarrassed. "I was still talking about drugs!"

Because that was so much better.

"Oh. That sounded like a prostitution joke."

"This isn't helping, Miguel. What can I do?"

"Those were serious suggestions. You're running a business. If you ran a pharmacy and another pharmacy moved in across the street overnight, and your once-loyal customers started going there, you would either need to figure out way to get those old customers back, or find new ones to make up the difference. No guns in that turf war either."

"That's easier said than—"

Something that sounded like a metal dumpster rolling over in an alleyway exploded in her ear. Alison yelped in unison with Miguel doing something similar on the other side of the line.

"Are you—"

But then the call went dead.

She looked down at her phone, heart pounding.

Again she gripped it too hard, and again wondered which would be the first to go between her hand and the handset.

She drew a deep breath, the kind she used to draw in yoga, back when her life wasn't a nightmare, hoping that the worst hadn't happened and Miguel was still alive.

She returned her glass to the kitchen, instead of drinking the wine like she wanted to.

Then she prepared a little gift box for Tiffany, got in the Cayenne, and drove to Rolling Knolls.

A baggie of coke and a half-dozen pills. Her usual

order, so far as Alison knew. No charge, if Tiffany agreed to a standing order. Half-price if she only wanted Alison's generous gift for today. Yes, she would be taking a big hit whichever way Tiffany decided, but the tax was worth it. If she could land Tiffany, she could land anyone.

Because what Alison really needed was free rein of the country club, without Tiffany making life difficult. It might even be worth supplying her on the house, if she could help Alison generate enough customers to make up the difference.

Potentially working with her in any capacity was a nightmare, but it was still better than the alternative and whatever might happen with Sarah's safety, or jail for Alison.

So *this* was where her life had spiraled down to.

She wondered if it was time to rethink parking on the far side of the lot as she swung her Cayenne into an empty space. She liked the exercise of constantly walking from her SUV to the country club entrance, but it was surely suspicious.

"Afternoon, Mrs. Tanner." Lionel gave her a nod as he opened the door. Was there something sarcastic in the way he'd said that, or was Alison only imagining things? She liked it so much more when he wasn't here.

"Afternoon, Lionel."

And then she was inside.

But Alison still had ten minutes until Pilates was over, so she grabbed a coffee and pretended to look at some unflattering blouses in the clubhouse shop while acting like people weren't looking and talking about her.

How many times has she been here this week?

And right after her husband died.

Tiffany saw her standing a few feet from the entrance as she came out of class. "What are you doing here?"

"I brought you a present." Alison handed her the box.

Or she would have, but Tiffany refused to take it. "Is that what I think it is?"

"No charge." Alison offered it to her again.

Tiffany still refused, now falling a step back and laughing in her face. "I don't want anything you have. Now that you don't have what I want."

"What's that supposed to mean?" Alison asked. *Is that a reference to her fucking Tom?*

"It's supposed to mean that if you don't get out of my face right now I'm calling security and telling them that you tried to sell me drugs."

"I can show them your texts."

"From your burner to mine?" Tiffany grinned. "Good luck with that."

Alison stared back at her dumbfounded, box in her hand, unsure of what to say or do next. She wanted to think that Tiffany was bluffing, but Tiffany was only slightly better than Eleanor. If she promised to fink on Alison and deny her involvement, Alison had to believe that she would deliver on that vow. If Tiffany got her banned from the club, then Alison wouldn't even be able to connect with the few clients she still had.

"So. Is that all?" Tiffany glared at Alison, daring her to … do anything.

"I was just trying to be nice," Alison said, because apparently she couldn't think of anything weaker.

Then she turned and left, feeling Tiffany staring daggers at the back of her head.

"I thought so," Alison heard her say ahead of yet another laugh.

She gritted her teeth and kept walking.

"Afternoon, Lionel."

"Afternoon, Mrs. Tanner," said the doorman behind her.

She walked across the lot nursing aches in her heart, mind, and body.

Why wasn't the DEA agent calling her?

Not that it would help if he did. Because what did she possibly have to bargain with?

Maybe she could send him to that old Victorian on Ninth and Chestnut?

Except, of course he would already know about that place. And even if he didn't, what if the information wasn't useful? Maybe Ellis would act on her tip and find nothing. Then Goliat would retaliate against Alison for her betrayal, if she was lucky. Sarah would be the target if she wasn't. Or both if fate hit her with something even worse than the worst.

Realizing that she'd been walking in a daze, Alison focused on the Cayenne in front of her.

And saw a stranger she had never seen before.

She wanted to think that he wasn't there for her. But then he ruined everything.

"Afternoon, Mrs. Tanner."

And for some reason she couldn't help but feel certain she was staring into the eyes of the man who had murdered her husband.

Chapter Twenty-Five

"AFTERNOON, MRS. TANNER," the man repeated.

"Who are you and what are you doing in front of my car?" She tried to control the shaking in her voice, and hands.

He looked dramatically behind him and back at Alison with a comically stupefied expression. "I thought that was an SUV?" Then he scratched his head while shaking it. "I guess they taught us all wrong in chop shop school, right?"

"I don't know what you're talking about."

"Sure you do." The man smiled. His teeth were so much whiter than Alison would have expected — an observation that only proved his point. "You see a guy like me with big pants and a tattoo on my neck, and I must be up to no good … right?"

"You're preventing me from getting into my car. Are you up to some good I don't know about?"

"Fair. Fair." He nodded while laughing, holding her eyes as he grinned. "Just admit you were being a little racist."

"I'm not racist."

"Classist, then." Still grinning.

A hundred percent of Alison's possible answers sounded wrong in her head, so instead she stayed silent.

"How about we settle on stereotype? Murder to manslaughter, I see how it is. You gotta feel good about yourself."

"Why are you here?" Alison asked.

"You mean in a country club parking lot looking like I do?"

"No. I mean stopping me from getting into my car."

"I got a text from a concerned citizen that you were—"

"When did she text you? I was *just* in there!"

"Maybe she expected you."

"So it *was* Tiffany."

"That's just one of the many friends we have in common," he said.

"What's your name?" Alison asked. "It's good manners to tell someone your name when you're accosting them."

"I'm Sancho."

"Is that your real name?"

"I'm just giving you one that fits with your preconceptions and that's easy to remember."

"Do you have some problem with me? I'm half-Mexican, you know." She wasn't.

"Me?" He pointed to his chest and shook his head. "I don't have a problem with you at all. But Rottweiler, well, that's why I'm here." Then he leaned forward and whispered to let Alison in on the rest of his little secret. "We don't want him to *ever* have a problem with you. Once the big dog decides to put his choppers on you, even a bone the size of a T-Bird won't be enough to make him let go."

"I don't have any problem with Mr. Rottweiler."

"Might want to consider never putting *Mr.* in front of *Rottweiler* again to keep it that way."

"My point is, I'm not trying to offend him."

Sancho shrugged. "Maybe you weren't *trying*, but selling in another man's territory is deeply offensive nonetheless. Would you put your dick into another man's wife?"

"I don't have a dick, so no, I wouldn't."

"Your husband had a dick."

"My husband *was* a dick. What's your point?"

Another shrug. "That maybe you should learn a lesson from what happened to him."

"What do you know about what happened to my husband?" The lump in her throat was too thick to swallow but she shoved it down anyway. The way he was looking at her, the coldness in his dark eyes, she felt even more certain that she was standing just inches from Tom's killer.

"I read in the paper that he died in a freak shootout … wasn't he missing his eyeballs or something?"

"Are you the person who murdered my husband?" Alison was almost proud of herself, standing up to a genuine gangster with her bottom lip only barely quivering.

"Now why would a nice guy like me ever want to take another man's life?"

"You killed him," Alison said, her lip curled in accusation.

"I've never even killed a chicken."

"Then you were there when he died!" The second she said it, Alison saw something flash in the man's eyes. "Just admit that you were there!"

"I don't know what you're talking about." But a sideways smile said that he did.

"Tell me what happened." She could feel her jaw twitching.

"Like I said, no se what the fuck you're talking about."

"You don't know or you won't say?"

"I won't even say whether I know." Sancho held his smile while changing the subject. "So, can I assume we understand each other?"

"What? That you can steal all of my customers and there's nothing I can do about it? Sure, I guess I understand fine."

"Good girl." He glanced around the parking lot while situating his body, looking like he was preparing to leave. "You got a problem with any of this, you'll need to take it up with Rottweiler."

"Wait!" Alison called out to his back as he started walking away.

He turned back, eyebrows raised.

"How do I talk to Rottweiler … if I want to take it up with him?"

Sancho laughed and shook his head. "You don't want to do that."

"You just said—"

"I know what I said, *Karen*. But believe me, this ain't like demanding a manager."

"My name's not Karen." Then she got it, and stood up for herself anyway. "But I want to speak with him. There are more than enough customers for us all to share. Rolling Knolls should be mine. Or someplace else. I don't even know where my territory is. This is all new to me. I wouldn't even be in this if you all didn't kill Tom."

"Your territory is wherever Rottweiler gives you permission to sell."

"And where is that?"

"You'll know when you're violating his terms, because he'll send me down here to tell you."

"How do I talk to Rottweiler?" Alison tried again.

"How about I do you the one-time courtesy of pretending like I didn't hear you say that?"

"What if I insist? Or maybe I end this right now by screaming at the top of my lungs? The security guards will come running right over here, you know. See that guy over there standing in front of the entrance? His name is Lionel and he carries a gun."

Lionel had probably never even held a gun, or seen one in real life.

"You could do that." Sancho nodded with a careless shrug. "But you're smart, so you won't. A really clever girl," he tapped the side of his head, "will know that the best course of action when it comes to dealing with a man like Rottweiler is to make sure he doesn't have a problem with you."

He walked away, but turned back around once more halfway to his motorcycle. "And you definitely wouldn't want him to develop any interest in your extremely hot but underage daughter."

Sancho swung one leg over the motorcycle, and after a fast and furious rev of his engine, he was roaring past her and out of the Rolling Knolls parking lot.

Alison looked over at Lionel. Sure enough, the waste of a doorman was pretending not to notice anything happening.

After losing a valuable couple of seconds wondering what the hell was wrong with her, she was in the driver's seat, cranking her own engine and offering Lionel a sloppy wave as she left the club.

She swung a hard left onto the outgoing road, toward the road and away from the amenities, unwilling to let that asshole out of her sight.

Maybe he was on his way to see Rottweiler. After dealing with her, Sancho was *probably* on his way to see Rottweiler. And if she could figure out where the big dog was staying, then maybe she could trade that information to the DEA agent for a ticket out of this mess.

Unfortunately, following someone on a motorcycle was yet another thing that seemed so much easier on TV. After a series of turns, some sharp and others loose, with two in a row that seemed entirely unnecessary, Alison finally lost sight of Sancho.

She kept driving, looking left and right across every intersection, retracing her route with an ever-swelling sense of defeat.

Then insult to injury — just seconds after she finally surrendered her search and switched to the left lane so she could make a U-turn for home, she saw Sancho already headed that way, screaming by on his motorcycle and flipping her the bird while she waited to turn.

Panic ate at her insides.

Alison tore into the intersection, spun the Cayenne around when she really should have waited, and floored the gas in pursuit of Sancho.

Maybe she was being paranoid and maybe she wasn't. But if the latter was true, then he might be on his way to her house to kidnap Sarah, and punish Alison for tailing him.

She didn't see Sancho anywhere.

So Alison drove even faster.

Chapter Twenty-Six

ALISON SWUNG HARD into her own driveway, opening the door before her engine was off.

She didn't see any cops in front of the house, and hadn't for a couple of days now. She also didn't see the guy that Goliat had (presumably) been staking her out in the rental car. But most important for her peace of mind, Alison saw zero sign of Sancho, and hadn't heard the roar of his motorcycle since it passed her headed in the opposite direction.

She felt desperate to see Sarah. But then she opened the front door, glanced into the living room, and saw her daughter and Miguel sitting side-by-side on the couch, with Alison's nightmare displayed on the coffee table in front of them.

It would have been better if they were having sex. Maybe.

Alison didn't have the words to explain the situation, or herself. The JanSport had been entirely emptied, with the fabric shell of her portable pharmacy lying like the shed skin of a serpent on the floor, inventory spread across the coffee table.

In what felt like slow motion, Sarah turned from staring at all those separated baggies of drugs to meeting her mother's gaze as she closed the door behind her.

Miguel mouthed the words *I'm sorry*.

But Sarah looked like fury itself. "Tell me the truth. What is this?"

"Not what it looks like?" Alison tried to smile, but no attempt had ever felt more awkward on her face. She imagined Eleanor knocking on the front door. Or worse, barging in without asking like she used to do all the time when her lying asshole of a son was still alive and sowing the seeds that would germinate to ruin her life.

"Then what is it?" Sarah was clenching her jaw, just like her mother.

"It's … complicated." Alison would have to do better than that, but she was still in shock and buying time.

"Is *this* why Dad is dead?"

"What do you mean?" Alison asked. Because, yes, drugs were the reason her father was dead, but for some reason that didn't seem to be the question Sarah was asking.

"Did he try to stop you from dealing? And that's how he—"

"No! Of course not!" Alison threw her hands in the air, taken aback, looking over at Miguel as she started to pace the living room. But he wasn't helping — maybe because he didn't know what she would want Sarah to know. Besides *nothing*.

"So these aren't *your* drugs?" Sarah pointed to the haul.

"No." Alison shook her head. "Not exactly. Your father was the one dealing."

"Then why is all this shit under your mattress? You had

to know it was there. Why not get rid of the evidence after … what happened?" Sarah choked on that last part, but she still (barely) managed to keep things together.

"What were you doing looking under my mattress?" Alison snapped.

Pure instinct. There was zero chance she could be ascending to any moral high ground here. And she shouldn't even try. She should be setting the best possible example for her daughter.

"I deserve answers," Sarah said.

"Of course you do," Alison agreed with a nod, realizing that these next few minutes might be the hardest of her life. Even worse than the funeral, or any single exchange with Eleanor. Sucking up to Tiffany and her little country club clique despite all their endless efforts to humiliate her was nothing compared to this.

Even worse than finding out her marriage was little more than a charade with her as co-star, playing the part of *unwitting fool.*

But, no. It was this moment right now. Confessing to her daughter that, yes, she was indeed a drug dealer. She took seat on the couch, with Sarah sitting between her and Miguel. Then, with a sigh, she admitted the truth.

"Yes. I have been selling drugs. But not because I want to. Your father owed a hundred and twenty-five thousand dollars to some very terrible people."

"The person he was selling for?" Sarah asked

"Yes. Exactly. And that person insisted that one of us pay him back."

"One of us?" Sarah touched her chest. "How would I … oh."

"So it's not like I had any choice in the matter." Alison shook her head. "Miguel has been helping me to figure out how—"

"MIGUEL!" Sarah vaulted to her feet.

"Just listen—"

"NONE OF THIS MAKES ANY SENSE!" She cut her mother off, drew several breaths in the following moments of pure silence, then finished her thought in a still fiery but much softer voice. "But you hate drugs, Mom. You won't even smoke a cigarette."

"I—"

"You wouldn't take Vicodin when you had that surgery on your wrist!"

"I still don't—"

"And Dad was dealing first?" Sarah collapsed back in an armchair on the other side of the room, then leaned forward to stare daggers at Alison and her apparent partner in crime. "I thought adults were supposed to be responsible for doing the right thing. Isn't that what you've been telling me, like every day of my whole entire life?"

"That hasn't changed, Sarah. We still—"

"Do you remember how hard you yelled at me for smoking a joint at school? AND YOU'RE DEALING DRUGS!"

"I wasn't—"

"You volunteered to run the anti-drug assembly when I was in fifth grade!" Her voice kept rising in both volume and pitch, a lightning-filled twister rolling onto the farm. "YOU PRETEND TO BE SO PERFECT, BUT YOU'RE ACTUALLY THE WORST MOTHER IN HISTORY!"

Sarah turned to Miguel. "And *you*." She drew several heaving breaths. "I thought you were hanging around with me because you liked me! Do you know how humiliating it feels to like someone and think they might like you back and realize they weren't ever really interested you? And worse …" Her voice cracked and she choked twice before resetting to get the last of it out. "And worse, that person was really only using you to get near your mother?"

She finally exhaled and caught her breath. Alison and Miguel looked back at her, neither of them seeming to wonder what they should say so much as uncertain whether it felt safe enough to do so.

"I'm sorry," Alison finally said.

"I do like you, Sarah. I've always liked you."

Her face changed, now playing hopscotch with an array of emotions. Rage and anguish, embarrassment and despair. Then, after a flare of what appeared to be fury followed by the raw acknowledgment of a concrete reality, her expression seemed to settle on *resolve*.

Sarah said, "We have to run. Somewhere this Goliat guy can't find us."

Miguel was already shaking his head. "You can't just run."

She turned her body so she was fully facing Alison, with her back to Miguel. "Somewhere out of state. How much could—"

"He'll find you wherever you go," Miguel interrupted. "You don't have enough money to disappear for real."

Sarah reeled back around on him. "DOES IT SOUND LIKE I'M TALKING TO YOU?"

Alison held her calm in the face of Sarah's thunder to address Miguel. "Surely *someone* has gotten out at some point. You can't possibly expect us to believe that every person who crosses his path gets a life sentence of indentured servitude. You're going to college — so what's our way out?"

"Doing everything I promised Goliat I would do. He sees himself as a businessman. He honors all of his contracts, and has zero tolerance for people who don't do the same. Narcs get killed and deserters get hunted down.

But Goliat never breaks his promise. You want to be free of this mess, then pay off your debt and *then* you can walk away."

"You should ask Grandma for help," Sarah said.

"That isn't an option." Alison shook her head.

"Then I'll ask her—"

"You will do no such thing!" Alison spun around, using the two inches she still had on Sarah to bore down into her eyes. "Your grandmother won't help us. Worse, she'll use what you tell her to take you away from me. Act like you wouldn't mind that outcome all you want to, but we both know the truth."

"Well, we have to do *something*," Sarah said, crossing her arms.

"Do you think this is new information?" Alison glared at her. "Do you think I haven't been trying?" She sighed, knowing the next words were dangerous, but willing to let them go anyway. "Have you ever thought about working with the DEA?"

Miguel shook his head. "There are easier ways to kill myself."

"What if—"

"I suggest you don't even say that next part out loud. Whatever it is. You talk to the DEA and Goliat will find out. Then you'll wish he killed you quick."

"I'm just saying."

"No way." Miguel shook his head, cutting her off again. "I don't want to hear it. And if you're thinking of going to the DEA after we're done here, then it was nice knowing the both of you. As far as my understanding of the way things work, you don't know enough to save your life. I'm not dying because you want to cut a deal."

So, a big *NO* on telling Miguel about her friendly neighborhood DEA agent, Ellis.

"Fine," Alison pretended to agree. "No DEA."

"Then what's the plan?" Sarah asked.

"For now? Same as it has been. Go to school and act normal—"

"Are you kidding me?"

"Does it sound like I'm kidding?" But then Alison barreled forward without any intention of giving Sarah so much as a second to respond. "You need to be in school because—"

"No way, Mom." Sarah vehemently shook her head. "I'm in as much trouble as you are. And you don't get to pull the adult card after what you've done. I mean, look at this!" She jabbed an accusing finger at the coffee table full of her mother's illegal inventory.

"You're right. I don't have the authority to pull the adult card." Alison paused, wanting Sarah to feel the weight of her acknowledgment before moving on. "But that's not why I'm suggesting that you stick to your usual schedule. The detective already suspects me. So it will be even harder than it already is for me to do all the things I need to do if he's *also* suspicious of you."

Sarah shrugged. "Or maybe suspecting me would create a distraction for you, thereby making it *easier* for you to—"

"Absolutely not." Alison shook her head. "Promise me that you'll do as I ask here."

"I don't have to—"

"Promise me, Sarah."

The way she said those three words made it hard for her daughter to refuse. Alison glared at her, waiting for an answer. But Sarah kept staring back, her bottom lip twitching, neither of them willing to break the stalemate.

"I know you don't want to hear this," Miguel said to Sarah, his face and body both full of reluctance. "But I agree with your mom. Things should look as close to normal as possible."

"Of course you do." She crossed her arms. A statue of betrayal.

"Promise me," Alison said.

Sarah opened her mouth to answer.

But then their landline started to ring.

Chapter Twenty-Seven

THE LANDLINE *NEVER* RANG.

So this was guaranteed bad news. Someone official: a clerk from some government office informing her that Sarah was about to be taken away; a lawyer on behalf of one Eleanor Cuntmaven Tanner; the police, on their way to arrest her. Though she couldn't ever remember a TV show in which the police provided suspects the courtesy of a phone call.

"Hello?" Alison answered, fear crawling down her spine like an icy rivulet.

"Hello there," chirped a friendly female voice. "This is Greta."

"Hi, Greta," Alison said, her heart beating triple-time for no apparent reason. This was obviously a marketing call.

"I just wanted to remind you that your book club is meeting at Hill of Beans just fifteen minutes from now."

"My book club?"

"That's right. It's the Hill of Beans on Warner. Don't forget to bring your copy of the *The Blind Coyote*. The author will be there and has promised to sign them. Do you already have the book?"

"I do." Alison found herself nodding, looking over to see Sarah and Miguel both eyeing her with question marks in their expressions.

"Great, then we'll see you there."

The call went dead and Alison hung up the phone.

"Who was that?" Sarah asked.

"Someone I never met."

"That's not an answer," Sarah said.

"It's an answer, just not one that added any clarity to anything," Miguel corrected.

"I've gotta go." Alison grabbed her purse and started toward the door.

Sarah: "Where are you going?"

Miguel: "Where is she going?"

"I'm going for coffee. I'll be back!" Alison opened the door.

"What!" Sarah exclaimed. "When?"

"Soon as I can. Maybe an hour." Then she shut the front door, imagining Sarah and Miguel trading baffled glances as they wondered what the hell had just happened.

Alison barely knew herself. But the words "Blind Coyote" weren't a coincidence. She had been waiting — maybe *dying* — for the DEA agent to get in touch with her. Now someone had on his behalf, and Sarah couldn't get to Warner and Deacon fast enough.

Maybe she was on the way to a possible escape right now. Alison kept telling herself that's exactly what this was, as she made the ten-minute drive in silence, then one final time as she pulled into the shopping center, parking in between TJ Maxx and the Sweet Tooth Smoothies next door.

She hurried out of the SUV with six minutes to spare,

then slowed her gait as she passed the smoothie shop, and the Feelin' Saucy pizzeria, before setting her hand on the Hill of Beans door handle and reminding herself not to yank it.

Alison was slapped by a blast of coffee-scented cold breeze as she entered. She saw Ellis the second after that, just leaving his place in front of the line, wearing a cheap suit and holding two cups of coffee, one per hand as he walked toward her with a smile.

"A cafe mocha." He handed her the one in his right hand. "Your favorite, right?"

Because that wasn't creepy at all.

"How did you know that cafe mochas are my favorite?" Alison asked, narrowing her eyes at the DEA agent who clearly couldn't be trusted. "Have you been following me?"

When was the last time she'd even *had* a cafe mocha?

Ellis laughed. "I asked the barista what the most popular drink here was. She said cafe mochas. Boom. Lucky guess."

"How do I know you didn't put something in my drink?"

He looked thoughtful, but Alison knew Ellis was still only mocking her. "Well, I am part of the enforcement agency that works to *prevent* things like that from happening, but I do understand your lack of trust. So here ..." He offered the drink in his left hand and held the other open and waiting.

"What did you order?"

"A café mocha. I hear it's their most popular drink." He smiled wide.

"I'm fine with what I have, thanks." But then she went ahead and switched them.

"Mind if we sit?" He pointed to a table.

Alison nodded and followed Ellis to the rear, sitting

across from him at a lone table as far from the bustle up front as they could possibly get.

"You have anything you want to tell me?" The agent got started right away.

"You're saying that like I should be telling you something specific."

"Do you have anything specific to share?"

"I don't understand. Are you … is there something …"

"Is there an end to that sentence, Mrs. Tanner?" Then when she didn't immediately answer, he said, "You're acting awfully uncomfortable."

"You're *making* me uncomfortable." She shifted in her seat.

"How exactly am I making you uncomfortable?" Ellis asked, his face neutral.

Unreadable.

"You're acting like I'm guilty of something."

"Are you?"

"I'm not guilty of anything you don't already know about — you called me here. What do you want?"

"To get an—"

"And with only fifteen minutes notice? That's rude." Alison reset herself, realizing the irony. "Sorry for interrupting."

"It's fine." He nodded, then answered her question. "I wanted an update from you."

"I need help."

"That's not an update," Ellis said.

"Sure it is. Since the last time I saw you, I really need some goddamned help!" Alison snapped, then reset herself yet again, glancing around the coffee shop to make sure that no one was watching them. "I'm sorry."

"You said that." Another nod. "What kind of help do you need?"

"I want to be put in the witness protection program."

"Okay then, now we're getting somewhere!" A big grin as Ellis leaned forward in his seat, but the artifice in his glee was apparent, and she realized a beat too late that the agent was making fun of her. "Good to know you've nabbed the bad guy already." He rubbed his hands together and leaned even closer. "Now, tell me what we've got and how you closed this case in record time."

"If I had something to give you, then I wouldn't need help," Alison said, keeping her voice level so Ellis couldn't tell how much he'd offended her.

"You were in a dangerous situation, and you continue to be in a dangerous situation. That fact was established when last we met. So what has changed?"

"I was threatened by a guy who works for Rottweiler. Outside the Rolling Knolls country club. He moved in on my customers, which leaves me in a bad place with Goliat. I'm happy to help you however I can, Agent Ellis, but it's going to be a lot harder to do this job if I'm dead."

"What kind of testimony can you offer us?" Ellis asked.

"I can testify that I had a conversation with one of Rottweiler's men."

"And …?"

"And the guy who threatened me was also there when Tom was murdered."

"He told you that?" Ellis asked.

"He didn't have to." Alison knew how she sounded.

"You've gotta be kidding me." Ellis laughed and shook his head in what appeared to be mockery. "No way we're putting you in WITSEC for that."

She sipped at her coffee, feeling dejected.

"Don't feel bad. This is actually good news."

"How is it *good* news?"

Ellis nodded. "You bring that same *Holy fuck my world is*

falling apart energy to Goliat, and ask him to protect you the way you were just wanting me to, I can guarantee he'll want to leverage that fear and pull you deeper into his rapidly expanding enterprise."

"How so?"

"He'll offer you more protection. But you'll have to get closer to his operation in order to access that protection. Meaning, he'll offer you a job that involves more responsibility and higher pay. That will help you to feel more insulated, while also giving you a means to clear your debt sooner."

"Like what kind of job?" She didn't want to know.

"Like being a drug mule."

"That sounds great!" This couldn't really be happening. Alison had seen this episode plenty of times. "So, what? You make me wear a wire and then the bad guys find it and torture me?"

"You watch too much TV. More like I'll put a GPS tracker on you and stay aware of your location."

"You mean there won't be any way for you to hear what's actually happening?" She tried to keep her voice from sounding frantic.

"So … you *do* want a wire?" Ellis looked at Alison, knowing she didn't.

She felt like freaking all the way out, but that wouldn't do her any good. She could read the DEA agent just fine. TV might have lied to her about wearing a wire, but so far it hadn't seemed to be lying about his personality type. The agent came off as ambitious, maybe in the middle of a brewing midlife crisis, longing for the big bust that might finally validate his career, possibly turn him into an agency superstar.

But like her lawyer, Ellis was cynical. The agent had seen so many guilty people, he figured everybody was always lying about something, including Alison. He probably had zero qualms about putting the people useful to him in harm's way, and for the simplest of reasons: if a person was connected to one of his cases, then they had likely done something to deserve whatever was happening to them. Even if they had only been the beneficiary of an elevated lifestyle like the good wife Alison.

She tried anyway. "Please. Just put Sarah in protection somewhere. If you get her far away and safe, then I'll do whatever you want. I won't be freaking out, so I can concentrate. I'll infiltrate the bad guys and get whatever you need."

"Infiltrate the bad guys, huh?" Ellis chuckled to himself. "The best I can do is get the LOPD to put a protection detail on you."

"No thanks."

"You don't want protection?"

"They already live outside my house sometimes. Once, Goliat had one of his guys watching the cops while they were watching me. So I'm thinking that I'm just as well without them, and that maybe those same officers would be better off staying on the lookout for jaywalkers or something."

"I'm working with local law enforcement and have access to some of their resources. I'll do my best to keep you and Sarah safe, and I'll make sure to take things slowly enough that you're never in any unnecessary risk."

"That hardly sounds like a guarantee …"

"At which point in this conversation did it sound like I was making one?"

"Who is Rottweiler?" Alison shot back with a question of her own.

He just kept looking back at her without answering.

She expected the stalemate to last longer, but then Ellis suddenly grunted, "The bad guy."

"I mean *who is he?*" Then, when he still didn't answer, "Do you know if he killed Tom?"

Ellis shook his head. "Not gonna happen, Tanner."

"So we're dropping the *Mrs.*?"

"I can't share case info with a civilian."

"But you're asking me to—"

"*Especially* an informant who could slip up and reveal what she knows to the very criminals I've been working so hard to catch."

"I know how to keep a secret."

"Does that mean your husband *did* trust you enough to tell you about his business, and you're keeping that secret now, in which case I can't trust you because I know that you've been lying to me? Or does it mean he *didn't* trust you?" Ellis shrugged. "Because if your own husband can't trust you, I'm not sure how you can expect me to."

Ellis looked at her: *Heads I win, tails you lose.*

Might as well try one more time. "I won't slip up."

But he shook his head again. "Rules are rules."

The rules weren't fair, but this wasn't an argument she could even come close to winning.

"Here," Ellis handed her a business card.

She looked down, scanning the text. "Agile Solutions … what is this?"

"A coded business card. Call the number and use that address, then they'll transfer you to me."

"What do I do now?"

"Remember the job with more responsibility and better pay?"

Alison nodded.

"That's what you do."

"And how do I do that?"

"With your best poker face, I suggest." Ellis picked up his cafe mocha and appeared to drain the cup, finishing his drink with a satisfied nod. "And sooner rather than later. Call if you need anything."

Then the agent was gone and Alison was back to being alone.

Chapter Twenty-Eight

"WHERE'S SARAH?" Alison asked when she got home to find Miguel sitting on her couch, scrolling his phone's screen.

"Her friend Brooke came and they took off. She's pissed … at both of us. Said she was going to spend a few nights there. And not to worry about her. Said she just needed time to process."

"And she just left you here?"

"I wanted to make sure you were okay."

Alison was annoyed that her daughter had just gone like that, and left the enemy in her house alone, but it was also just as well. She had a favor to ask Miguel and it was better to make the request without Sarah there.

After she asked, Miguel shook his head.

"No. I've told you a bunch of times Mrs. — *Alison*. Goliat calls you, it doesn't work the other way around. Not if you want things to go your way."

"It's not like I'm asking him for anything. I want to help."

"You don't want to help," he said, still shaking his head. "You want to *offer* him help."

"I don't see the difference." She did. Sort of.

"You and I both know you don't want to help Goliat at all. So you go asking or offering, or whatever, that's going to make him wonder why. Hell, *I'm* wondering why. You take off and come back with this sudden inspiration? Who did you go meet?"

"A potential client. I didn't feel like explaining at the time." She barreled on, before he could question her further. "I keep telling you why, Miguel. And it's not hard to understand! I want to be done with this mess. Out of debt and on with the rest of my life. Can you please just make the call?"

"This isn't going to go how you're imagining." He sighed while dialing.

Goliat must have answered immediately, because Miguel was already spilling several syllables a second, all in Spanish. The words were coming too fast for her to even try and decipher. She heard her name and a few *yeses* and *nos*, plus something about her hair (maybe). But the tone was obvious: Goliat was irritated by the interruption, and agitated at Miguel for his substandard judgment. Just as he had predicted.

Her heart was pounding. Maybe this had been a big mistake. Miguel was now silent, still nodding to himself after a lingering stretch of listening on his end, punctuated by a muffled voice sounding far away but no less dangerous to Alison's ears on the other side of the line.

He finally hung up and met her eyes. "Come on. We need to go right now."

"Is that good or bad?"

"We'll see." But Miguel looked like he knew, straightening his shoulders on the way to the door, his motion reminding her of a warrior donning armor before a battle.

She drove mostly in silence, so the cabin was thick with discomfort until they finally parked in front of the pink and yellow Victorian.

"Good luck," Miguel muttered under his breath, already opening his door and stepping onto what was once a thin strip of lawn but was now a patch of yellow grass surrounded by hard-packed dirt.

Alison followed him through the gate to the small shack in back.

A sudden memory hit her with blunt force trauma. A different man making her lead the way.

You see that little shed over to the side of the house? That's where we're headed. You scream when we get out of the car, I'll put a bullet in you. Look around or do anything to get yourself noticed on your way to the door, I'll put a bullet in you. Mutter under your breath before we're both inside with the door closed behind us, I'll put a bullet in you. And just in case you're wondering, yes, this is exactly the kind of neighborhood where a white woman could get shot in broad daylight.

Miguel opened the shed door and held it open for her.

She looked around, same as last time, feeling a strong wave of déjà vu seeing the couches, love seat, and armchairs. Still claustrophobic and dangerous, still with a half-dozen men chattering in Spanish.

"It's Mrs. Tom," said the man who had put the gun to the back of her head the last time she was here. *Gustavo,* Alison thought.

But the handsome man with the pitch-black goatee acknowledged her with a nod, then gave a general look to everyone in the room, its meaning clear: *Scram,* or *Largarse* as the case may be; Alison was pretty sure she remembered that one from her junior year.

She sat on the couch.

Miguel moved to leave with the others, but Goliat gave him a glance and directed him to the seat beside her. Once they were both situated, the big boss unleashed both eyes and his baritone on Alison.

"Miguel tells me that you have an urgent matter to discuss."

"I wouldn't say it's urgent …" *DAMMIT,* her heart was beating fast.

"Not urgent …" He nodded. "But today. Now. At your convenience. How do you suggest we define our time together?"

"A meeting of the minds," Alison dared.

"I am not interested in your mind." His shrug was somehow more dismissive than his words.

"I want to do more."

"More what?" Goliat looked at her.

She swallowed, wondering if the wrong answer might prompt her death. "I want to get out of Las Orillas and start a new life … for me and my daughter. I know that's impossible while I still owe you, so I'm asking to go 'all in' as they say." A little laugh, because who actually said that? "So if there's anything I can do that might pay more than the way I'm doing things now, I'm willing to—"

Goliat raised a hand to stop her. "You would like a promotion."

It didn't sound like a question, but her timid little *Yes* resembled an answer.

"Do you think you have earned a promotion?" Alison could feel Miguel trying not to look at either of them.

"No. But I'm willing to do any—"

"You are willing to do anything that earns you a promotion, yes?"

Alison nodded.

"Anything that makes you more money. Gets you out faster. Draws you deeper into my organization. Yes?"

She wasn't just sensing a trap, Alison might be knee-deep in one already. "I only want to help."

"That is very generous." Goliat gave her a saccharine smile. "And I do appreciate the offer. I am curious if you would be extending the same generosity if not for a particular gentleman."

"A particular gentleman?" Alison repeated.

"I apologize for the vagaries." That sounded like something Goliat might say before pulling the trigger. "Let me be more specific. I mean the detective you have met with a couple of times now."

"Him?" She laughed like his accusation was nothing and felt one of her feet slip off the tightrope. "Detective Ian Banks? He doesn't believe that I didn't know about Tom's activities before his murder. It's not like I want to deal with him."

"Do you want to deal with the DEA agent?"

Alison wanted to blurt *What are you talking about?*, but Goliat would surely hear the lie in her voice even easier than he'd see it on her face. There was no way to hide from the truth, not if he'd had her followed.

"You know who I'm talking about ..." Goliat offered Alison the warmest of smiles. "Broad-shouldered Black man ... you met him at a coffee shop. A Hill of Beans to be specific."

"That's what I've been trying to tell you! Now do you see why I'm so desperate?" Alison held his eyes, feeling like sudden death was one wayward phrase away. And still she kept going. "They're closing in on me. That's why I need your help."

"I thought you wanted to help me?" Goliat held his smile.

"I *do* want to help you. It's a win-win. You make sure that my daughter and I are protected, I'll do whatever you want me to. Regardless of the risk."

"Regardless of the risk," Goliat repeated, that last word like a hiss.

"Banks and the DEA agent — Ellis is his name — are working together. They want to put me in jail because they think I was Tom's second-in-command. But I can't let that happen." Alison shook her head, allowing that first tear to fall. "If they put me away, then I'll never see my daughter again. My mother-in-law will take her into custody and that'll be it. She's a …"

Alison had a hundred ways to finish that sentence, but her silence was more powerful than any of them. She let it sit like oil in a skillet, sizzling in wait for the meat.

Goliat didn't respond. At least not with his words or even a gesture. He stayed frozen, his penetrating eyes doing all the work. Probing Alison, pressing into her and making her want to back down. But she managed to hold her poise, and her tears.

Still, she probably couldn't do this alone. And right now she was the perfect picture of *All by herself.*

"If it matters, she's a pain in the ass when it comes to the cops," Miguel said, jumping in to lend her a hand. "Totally paranoid. Not only does she do everything she can to avoid them when they're actually there, she's always thinking the pigs are around, even when they're not."

Goliat stared at Miguel without saying a word.

"And they do seem to be harassing her," Miguel added with a shrug.

The big boss finally nodded. "Shame on those officers. Buying her coffee."

"I don't know about any DEA agents or coffee."

Miguel shook his head. "I only know what I've seen. Hope it helps."

Another slow and thoughtful nod from Goliat. "Why are you telling me this, Miguel?"

"Because you like to know everything," he replied without hesitation.

"And do I know everything now?" Goliat asked.

"You couldn't possibly." Miguel looked as bold as he sounded. "But that's things as far as I've seen them for myself. You know I'm not dumb enough to risk my life over some *ama de casa* I barely know. You also know I've seen enough to understand the danger of not playing straight."

But Miguel *wasn't* playing it straight. He was putting his life on the line right now, sticking up for her. If she failed to get enough of whatever Ellis needed to put Goliat in jail, Miguel would probably end up dead. How would she ever be able to live with herself then?

Goliat broke his gaze with Miguel and turned to Alison. "You want a job? I have a job for you."

She nodded, terrified of what might be coming.

"Higher risk, higher reward. This is what you are requesting, yes?"

She kept nodding.

"You do something for me tomorrow, I will erase ten thousand dollars of your debt. How does that sound?"

"It sounds wonderful," Alison said, still waiting to hear the catch. "What do I have to do?"

"You will get a text with an address. Then you will go to that address."

"What will I do … at that address?"

"You will bring your passport. And you will wear something nice."

"But—"

"Like you are going to a party," he finished with a menacing smile.

"But what will I be doing?"

"Right now?" Goliat looked at her. "Right now you will stop asking questions."

So Alison smiled and replied with, "Okay."

But in her head she was calling Ellis, and mentally rehearsing what she was going to say.

"Anything else?" Goliat's eyes made it clear that there was only one answer.

"No." Alison held his eyes, terrified as that made her. "Thank you."

She stood. Then so did Miguel.

"One more thing," said the big boss, giving her chills.

"Yes?"

"Next time, I will be calling you. Today has been your only exception. Do you understand?"

"Yes, sir." She nodded.

"Rodrigo," Goliat corrected her. "After all, you're part of the family now."

"Rodrigo," Alison repeated, feeling like she was half-dead already.

Chapter Twenty-Nine

"AGILE SOLUTIONS," answered a female voice. "How may I direct your call?"

Alison looked down at the card and read the address out loud. "2097 Atherton Ave."

"One moment please …"

She had only been alone in the Cayenne for a few minutes. Alison had driven Miguel back to her house and waited for him to get out of her SUV and into his Saturn and actually leave, before pulling back out of the driveway and driving away from the house.

She didn't have a destination in mind. Alison only knew she needed to keep moving in order to keep thinking.

The Muzak was Michael Bolton. So, insult to injury. Shouldn't the DEA have something cooler to listen to? Even "Bad Boys" was better than this.

The line crackled and Ellis finally brought his gruff voice onto the line. "Mrs. Tanner."

"How did you know it would be me?"

"Your code," he answered impatiently. "Can I assume you have something for me? If so, outstanding job, that was fast. If not, then you and I need to have a conversation about how you're supposed to use this line."

"You said, 'call if you need anything.' Are you telling me you didn't really mean that?"

"What do you need, Tanner?"

"Protection, for a start."

"Maybe we should start recording our conversations. That way you can review the many things you seem unable to remember."

"I don't have any difficulty remembering what we've talked about. This is me following through. You wanted me to get deeper into things, so that's what I did."

"Oh yeah?" Ellis sounded interested. "How so?"

"I told Goliat that I needed protection and that I wanted higher-paying work to help me get out of my situation faster."

"I'm pretty sure I was there when I gave you the strategy. I'd assumed you were occupying my time calling this number right now because you were going to tell me things I didn't already know."

Okay, it was official: Ellis the DEA agent was an asshole.

"I was getting to it," Alison said.

"Get to it faster."

"He wants me to go somewhere."

"Okay … where does he want you to go, Tanner? Are you intentionally drawing this out?"

"I think he wants me to cross the border into Mexico."

"You think or you know?"

"He told me to dress nice, and to bring my passport," she told him.

"Any idea where you might be going?"

"None."

"Don't worry, we'll be on it," Ellis said.

"How will you be on it?"

"Goliat will want you to take your own vehicle. We'll put a GPS locator on it and have eyes on you the entire time."

"You'll know where I am, but how close will you be?"

"Close enough."

That wasn't an answer. "What about Sarah?"

"What about her?" Ellis asked.

"What can we do to make sure she's protected?"

"You mean beyond the officers that have already been assigned? Constantly shadowing her, just like we talked about. Do you think it's inexpensive to have a couple of cops dedicated to keeping you safe at all times?"

"I appreciate that, but—"

"Do you?" Ellis made it sound like Alison didn't even *understand* the word.

"Of course I do. But I didn't ask for any of this."

"How much does your house cost? How about the pretty silver SUV you drive? The one that's basically a Volkswagen you paid tens of thousands of extra dollars for so it says *Porsche* instead."

"I didn't know about any of this."

"How hard did you look, Tanner?"

"I need to know that my daughter is safe, or none of this can ever go anywhere. Cops on the house won't be enough to keep Goliat from killing her if he knows what I'm up to with you."

Alison paused for the drama, then dropped the bomb. "And he already knows that you're trying to recruit me. One of his men saw us talking at the Hill of Beans."

But Ellis refused to treat that like the revelation it was. His words sounded like a shrug. "That changes nothing."

"It absolutely does!" Alison exclaimed, instantly furious. "He'll hurt or kill me if the tiniest thing goes wrong. Do you think I want to end up tortured or dead?"

"Of course you don't. No one does. But that is the risk you're taking here. It doesn't change anything on *my end.*"

"So while I'm on the way to what might be my death, you're not willing to promise that my daughter will protected."

"That's not a promise I can make. I can assure you that there will be two full-time officers keeping an eye on her at all times while we have things in play, and I can urge you to appreciate the gift and stop being self-centered."

"It's not self-centered to want—"

"It's self-centered to think the world revolves around you. You're in danger, yes. But that's what you signed up for. A man like Goliat won't risk getting caught or bringing his empire down to exact punishment on your daughter. Will he kill you if he sees you as a threat?" Ellis gave the question a long second to settle before answering it himself. "Absolutely. Will he harm your daughter while the cops are watching?" She imagined him shaking his head. "I can't imagine he would be that stupid."

"What's the signal for pulling me out?"

"There isn't one."

"Then how will you know when it's time?"

"We won't be pulling you out under any circumstances," Ellis replied without apology.

"YOU'RE JUST GOING TO LET ME DIE?" Alison finally pulled the SUV over to finish her call, roughly a mile from home.

"That's the risk agents have to take."

"I'm not an agent, I'm a—"

"Suspected criminal? This is your way out, Alison. But you need to stop thinking that life works like it does on TV — you can't learn anything real by watching those shows.

We're not blowing an operation just because you're scared."

"What if I—?"

"Uh-uh. You do anything to blow your cover trying to force us to extract you from a situation you got yourself into, then whatever Goliat does or doesn't do to you will be entirely your fault. Are we clear?"

"That I'm totally on my own? That I'm barely getting any guidance from you, even though I've never ever done anything like this? And that if shit hits the fan, I'll just need to brace myself for torture or worse? Yes. *Thank you.* It's all so perfectly clear."

"Excellent," Ellis said, infuriating her further.

Alison finally realized exactly what she had done, making a deal with yet another devil, and this one didn't care in the least whether or not she left the situation alive.

And Ellis was wrong about TV, she had learned plenty. Those shows Tom used to love were still good for some stuff, like letting her know who Ellis really was. The agent probably lost more informants than average, but had one of the best records in the department as a result. And thanks to that record, his superiors likely overlooked his ignoring or bending of the rules.

Alison would bet that good old Ellis wasn't above planting evidence on someone he knew to be guilty, or blackmailing them to do something that might blow their cover, if it got him what he needed to make his next bust.

Ellis Munk was the kind of agent that either infuriated his colleagues or made them jealous, but he probably had few friends because no one really even liked him. Like Alison, most people probably found the man abrasive. And in the field, he was probably trigger-happy like Yosemite Sam.

She should never have agreed to any of this. She

should have run as fast and as far as possible, back when she first got the burner phone.

"How do I know when the tracker has been placed?"

"If the vehicle is in your driveway tonight, then you can rest assured it will have a tracker on it by the time you're pulling out of your driveway tomorrow morning."

"Great." Then, because it felt wrong not to say it: "Thank you."

"Good luck," Ellis said.

Then he hung up the phone.

Her engine was still running. Alison put the Cayenne in drive.

But she didn't go home.

Chapter Thirty

"Slow down," Jake told Alison again, this time patting the air with one hand while he opened his door all the way with the other. "Start over."

She entered the house, walking right by Jake and collapsing down onto the couch in approximately the same spot she had occupied during her last visit to Tom's old Army buddy and client.

"Sorry about that … I …" She had a ton more to say, but none of it wanted to come out. She was sucking air through her teeth instead.

"Breathe …" Jake said, his voice calm enough to guide Alison into following the suggestion. "No reason to hurry. We got time."

He disappeared from the living room, only to return with two glasses of water a few minutes and several hundred fresh breaths later.

"Here you go." He handed her one glass while sipping from the other, lowering himself to the sofa a few feet away from her before leaning forward to set his water on a coaster, next to that same box of pre-rolls still sitting on the coffee table from the last time.

He scooted it closer to him, lifting the lid on its way. Then he took two of the green wrapped joints out of the box, but Alison was already shaking her head.

He narrowed his eyes, disappointed. "You came here for help, am I right?"

Alison nodded.

"So that means you must trust me, am I right?"

She nodded again.

"So then *trust me.*" Jake gave her his biggest grin so far as he offered her the joint.

She held out her hand, finding his smile impossible to refuse, or maybe it was the hitch in her breath she couldn't get rid of, surely triggered by … all of this.

Jake handed Alison the joint, then refreshed her memory. "Green Unicorn. Good for first-timers, or for all-timers like me."

"So I've heard." She took the joint, nervous but wanting to relax, and believing in Jake long enough to see what might happen.

He gestured for her to hold the joint so he could light it. She did, feeling awkward as he flicked the lighter, then as the flame kissed the tip, and still as she heard the barely audible crackle of paper curling toward her to reveal a glowing ember.

She inhaled and immediately started to cough.

"Slow down," Jake said, his voice circling the edges of a drawl.

She finished coughing and tried again. And again and again and again.

They smoked in silence. Until she felt compelled to break it.

"You sure you don't mind the smell?"

"It's one of my favorite smells in the world."

Alison inhaled, not just the smoke in her lungs, but the pungent air hanging like a fog in his handsome living room. She had no idea if the smell was funky or wonderful. It somehow bordered both, though she also felt sure that suspicion and unfamiliarity kept some of the truth of this scent away from her.

Another couple of puffs and she had to stop. She coughed several times in a row and then set her still-burning joint into an ashtray as Jake slid one toward her. Her head was suddenly stuffed full of cotton, and she laughed out loud with the realization that it was also swaying back and forth.

"There it is." Jake grinned at Alison while giving her an appreciative nod.

And yes, there it was … nothing like she had expected. And not all that different from having a glass of chardonnay — at least so far.

She closed her eyes to soak more of it in.

There was a warmth to what she was feeling. A fuzziness perhaps? She couldn't quite explain it, at least not yet, but for some reason the word *wooly* felt kinda sorta right. And in a way that made Alison want to laugh.

She wasn't out of her mind … at least not exactly … or in the way she had been led to believe by the media. Alison remembered people talking about cannabis like the drug could induce a psychotic break. But she didn't feel crazy, nor was she hallucinating.

And yet, the world did seem acutely better in its own little way.

Everything looked sharper. Colors were more intense, and every angle around her seemed closer and rounder. Definitely more reality to deal with, despite its artifice. And yes, Alison also realized that everything she was thinking didn't make as much sense as it should, but she was also aware of how everything she was thinking also made a lot *more* sense than it ever had before.

She felt detached, yet relaxed.

Sure, the fear was still there, but now more like a far-off reality. In the way even the specter of eventual death cannot truly haunt a person in their prime. She felt aware of her terrors; in no way did they cease to exist. But she couldn't exactly embrace the familiar fear that had haunted her recently, so Alison managed to stew in its stillness.

This was *much* nicer than chardonnay.

She took another long hit and leaned back into the couch.

And that's where she stayed for several luxurious seconds. Until something slow and creeping was suddenly in front of her mind, sending her lurching toward the coffee table to drop her still-smoking joint in the ashtray.

"You okay there?" Jake asked, a comfortable mirth still alive in his eyes.

Paranoia was suffocating. Even heavier than the usual variety.

"I'm fine." But she wasn't. "Can cannabis lead to a full psychotic break? How do we know the cops won't barge in — I mean, the window is *right there*!" She pointed to the window in accusation.

But Jake just laughed and took another long drag. He held it in, blew a billowing plume out of both his nose and mouth, then shook his head. "I seriously can't believe this is your first time smoking weed. You do know the herb has been legal for a while now."

"I had a bad experience," Alison said.

"Oh yeah?"

"In high school. I was caught with drugs at a party,

even though they weren't even mine. I took the heat and my parents wanted to kill me. But something good did come from that little misadventure."

Alison laughed, reaching out for the joint and wondering if she really wanted more, of if she was only playing a role. "The drugs actually belonged to Tom. My covering for him nabbed his attention. So he asked me out, and we've been at least sort of together ever since."

"Really?"

"Why does that surprise you?"

"Not sure." Jake shrugged along with his lack of an answer.

"I mean, we were on and off a lot until after college. Tom proposed after he graduated. He didn't get picked up to play professional football like he'd always imagined, so he went into the Army wanting to feel like he was doing something important. His mother *hated* that he proposed. She always thought he could do 'so much better than me.'"

"You say that like it's a quote."

"She literally told me that, all the time. Eleanor is a real piece of work. She's always hated me."

"Why does she hate you?"

"For being a middle-class loser who embarrassed her family and ruined their once outstanding reputation."

"You mean because of the drugs? She never knew they were—"

"*Never.*" Alison shook her head. "No reason to tell her. She would have just found some other way to make it all my fault, anyway. Seriously, the woman wore all black to our wedding. She cried through the whole thing. Sobbed to all her friends. Acted like she was attending a funeral."

"Seriously uncool." Jake took another drag.

"Seriously." Alison nodded, feeling the weed and enjoying it more. Suddenly wanting to chat about everything. "I gave him everything, you know. The only thing I ever wanted was for Tom to be happy. I figured that as long as he thought I was good enough, then it didn't matter what his mother said, or how she might treat me. But I had no idea how much he was cheating on me."

"How do you know he was cheating on you?"

"Are you kidding me?" Alison didn't really want to get started on this, but here she was, already on the way. After one more hit, of course.

"In the seventeen years we were married, the main thing we fought about was how much time he spent at the office, and how he barely had enough for us. Me and Sarah, I mean. But that was all a lie. Tom didn't need to be gone all that time. *He wanted to be.* That hurts. And it hurts how much I played my part. He never tried to change, no matter how many times we fought. Tom always resolved our conflicts with gifts. For me, for Sarah, for both of us. He always promised that we would have more time together in the future. Once he had built the business enough for him to finally step away. He always said that was his dream, too. I'm such an idiot for believing all of that, and for seeing all that hard work as an expression of his love for us, instead of the escape from his family that it was. The escape his ego demanded of him."

Alison drew a deep breath, aware of how upset she sounded, finishing her tirade with an anemic-sounding, "I'm sorry."

"Don't be." Jake shook his head, then gave her an encouraging smile. When she still hadn't spoken after a lingering minute or so, he followed up with a question. "Is that what you meant by 'cheating' — Tom lying about his work? Or do you think he was actually sleeping with someone else?"

She shrugged. "I think he was sleeping with Satan

herself."

"Oh?"

"Tiffany," Alison explained, even though Jake probably didn't know her.

Or did he?

"Sounds like a bitch," Jake said with a smile. "But I'm still not clear. Do you know if Tom was cheating on you for sure, or …?"

She answered with a shrug.

"If they really give it the proper thought, most women can tell if their husbands are cheating. So, if you don't mind my asking, what was the sex like?"

"For the last couple of years … not great," Alison admitted. "Tom usually had what sounded like reasonable excuses to avoid sex. I didn't know he wasn't really working and therefore shouldn't be so tired in the way he always said. I was exhausted myself, trying to be the world's best wife and mom, working to keep up appearances at Rolling Knolls, even though I could never stand the place."

"It's the worst." Jake blew a plume of smoke from his nose.

"I thought of him as passionate in bed, when we did, I guess …" Alison kept going, surprised how easy she was finding it to talk with Tom's old friend about something so intimate. "But I think there was a lot of anger I'm only seeing now … now that I have more context."

"Anger about what?" Jake's tone suggested he knew.

Alison sighed, picked up her Green Unicorn, and took a drag, realizing how much she genuinely wanted to do exactly that as she pulled the smoke into her lungs.

"I think he was angry at me, and at the world." Another little puff. "Angry at the world because it had yet to deliver the magical life that Tom always thought he deserved. He wasn't just the star quarterback in high school — everyone agreed he had the kind of wattage that could last long past his senior year. He was dreaming of a pro career with cars and mansions and yachts and … well, none of that ever happened for him. So after a while he started blaming me for 'dragging him down.' Just like his mother always said I would."

"Did she really say that?"

"*Constantly.*"

"That's fucked up." Jake's slight drawl inspired her to laugh. "So you're saying Tom had a few mommy issues."

"FOR SURE." And wow, did it feel great to finally talk. Or maybe *to be heard* was more like it. "*And* daddy issues. I seriously thought that Tom should have gone to therapy for his parents, but he always refused, *every time* I mentioned it."

"What kind of daddy issues?"

And again, Alison couldn't tell whether Jake knew the answer to his own question or not.

"Tom's father was an alcoholic. He died of liver disease the year after we married. But their relationship was hard to watch before that."

"In what way?"

"In every way." Alison gave Jake a bitter little laugh. "Tom was always trying to get his father's attention, and it didn't really matter how he got it. Eleanor was indulgent with him; she let him do pretty much whatever he wanted, so long as the touchdowns kept coming. But his dad only seemed to have two modes: distant and critical. So Tom was always alternating between wanting free rein and defying authority in order to give his father the finger for never paying attention to him."

Alison laughed, louder and more bitter than the last time. "It's sad and hilarious, looking back and seeing it all so clearly now. Negative attention always gave him such a thrill. Tom saw it as love, but he also wanted the kind of support and caretaking that his mother always provided. And after we got married, I wasn't just the person who gave that to him, I was also the one who supported every little bit of his negative bullshit!"

He was nodding and smoking and watching. But more than anything, Jake was *listening to her*. That attention felt like early morning sun bearing down on a frozen tundra, and Alison couldn't stop absorbing the warmth.

He put out his mostly finished joint in the ashtray and said, "What was his mother like?"

"Do you know her?"

He shook his head. "I've heard a few stories is all."

"Eleanor is one of those syrupy-sweet passive-aggressive women who never has anything bad to say, while constantly giving backhanded compliments and implying the worst. But that was never really the problem. I know plenty of terrible people."

"So what *was* the problem?"

"That Tom never saw it, or never even once took my side."

"Come on, not even once?" Jake used both his smile and drawl to challenge her.

"I wish I could say I was exaggerating, but seriously, Tom saw his mother as perfect. And he was much more attached to her than a grown man should be. He was always gaslighting me, saying that his mom didn't mean the things I was 'reading into her words.' Treating me like I was an idiot. She was constantly undermining me by spoiling our daughter, under the guise of 'providing the basics,' of course. Making me feel like a terrible mom with a childhood that was so deficient, I couldn't possibly know how to properly raise my own daughter."

"Do you have a good relationship with … is it Sarah?"

Alison sighed again. "We used to."

"You mean before all of this?"

"I mean *before* before all of this. We were already fighting a lot. Mostly about her independence and what a 'supremely uncool' mother I am. That's an actual quote. I get it … Sarah wants to be her own person, and before all of this I was so allegiant to being the 'perfect mom' that I was obviously starting to smother her. I understand that …"

"But?"

Alison wished that the ember on her Green Unicorn hadn't died, just not enough to ask Jake for a light. "But even getting it, I still miss the days when we'd watch movies and eat popcorn on the couch together. Do each other's hair and makeup. Dress up in costumes and pretend to be superheroes. Sarah always wanted to be Supergirl, which worked out for me since I'm more of a Wonder Woman gal myself. Not that we were still playing *Justice League* a month ago or anything. Sarah stopped wanting to do the joint costume thing for Halloween in fourth grade, and it never came back. Not just for Halloween, but for all time. She seemed to think it was dumb overnight. A lot of things were like that." Alison shrugged. "I always tried to pretend like I wasn't hurt, even when I totally was."

Jake shook his head. "Maybe that Green Unicorn should be called Truth Serum."

Alison laughed.

"I still can't believe this is your first time smoking."

"You heard my story about what happened in high school. Drugs have always terrified me."

"Not a drug." He shook his head again, this time pointing at the box full of weed. "That right there is a plant. And I heard that story about the two of you in high school, but I heard it a lot differently."

Jake's statement wasn't a surprise. But still, it sobered her.

"I'm sure Tom told all of his stories differently, depending on who he was talking to." Alison swallowed hard, then delivered the question she didn't want to ask but was dying to know the answer to. "Did you know that Tom was cheating on me?"

"No." Jake shook his head. "But probably because he knew I wouldn't have approved."

His eyes were kind and his voice gentle.

"Thank you." Then she fell silent, not knowing what else to say.

"So what did you want to talk about?" Jake asked after their quiet had lingered a little too long.

"Haven't we talked about enough?"

"You were really upset when you first came over … and I don't think it was about all of this. You were saying something about not being able to do it anymore and hyperventilating and stuff." Jake waved his hand in a gesture that was probably meant to indicate her issues with Tom, his parents, and Sarah.

No, Alison had not come over to bitch about her family.

So she told him the whole story: Ian Banks, Ellis Munk, Goliat, Rottweiler, and goddamned Tiffany calling the bad (or badder?) guys to accost her in the country club parking lot. Alison ended the narrative by detailing her last encounter with the big boss and the mounting fear that kept threatening to drown her in unrelenting waves of anxiety before she could finish what she started.

"You must think I'm a terrible person," Alison said when she finished.

"Not at all," he drawled. "But you are in a pickle. So what do you want to do?"

"You mean besides getting in a car with Sarah and just driving somewhere far far away?"

"Why don't you do that?"

"Because I'm terrified that even if Goliat doesn't track me down, the DEA will. Then I'll spend the rest of my life in jail while Eleanor's raising my daughter. It looks like I need to go through with this sting and hope I survive."

"And that this Ellis guy keeps his word."

"Right." Alison grabbed the Green Unicorn, still in the ashtray awaiting her hand. "Can I get a light?"

Jake smiled and went to light the tip of her joint.

She sucked it in, got the ember glowing, pulled in the smoke, then blew it out and kept talking. "I can't even afford a lawyer to fight Eleanor for custody."

"How much do you have?"

"Maybe a thousand dollars." It was only slightly less embarrassing to say out loud than Alison had imagined. "But that'll get eaten by living expenses in a few weeks, even if I decide to stop paying the mortgage."

"I might know someone who can help us out."

"*Us?*" Alison repeated.

"We'll find a way out of this," he assured her.

"I'm broke."

"We'll find a way out of this," Jake repeated. "Let me see what I can do."

"Thank you. I don't know how I can—"

"Don't worry about it. Like I told you, I'm indebted to Tom, whether he's still here or not. And I'm happy to pay up."

"But you still won't tell me why you owe him, will you?"

"Absolutely not." He grinned. "Let's just say he wasn't always a selfish dog."

Chapter Thirty-One

WEDNESDAY …

IF THE CAR *is in your driveway tonight, then you can rest assured it will have a tracker on it by the time you're pulling out of your driveway tomorrow morning.*

Alison remembered the agent's words as she backed out of her driveway. Everything was making her nervous, and no amount of sleep, caffeine, or preparation had changed that. She had her passport in the center console and was dressed "nice," she supposed. But there was a big difference between cocktail party nice and summer brunch nice, or even interviewing for a job nice.

She tried on three different outfits, finding it increasingly absurd that she should give a shit what she was wearing to run drugs, or engage in whatever illegal activity (to save Sarah's life!) she was about to partake in. She finally settled on a simple turquoise blouse and a black pencil skirt, but had been second-guessing the choice ever since she closed the front door behind her.

Alison stopped at a red light and eyed her GPS again. She had another two miles — seven more minutes until she arrived at the address that had been waiting on her burner when she woke up that morning. Despite her costume changes, she was still running twenty minutes early.

But her GPS couldn't account for the three minutes she spent waiting for more than a mile of freight train to stop passing in front of her — knee bouncing the entire time — or for the head-on collision between one of those boxy little Nissans (she had no idea what they were called) and a PT Cruiser. Seeing the latter vehicle usually made her smile since it always accompanied the memory of Tom referring to PT Cruisers as "Borat's dream car," but this time she had to turn away at the sight of all that safety glass like sprinkles around a long smear of blood.

And *that* was why Alison always left early. Despite all the hiccups and holdups, she still made it to her destination with four minutes to spare. A crap spot in the middle of mostly industrial area, but hardly anything she needed a passport for; a strip mall full of broken concrete and a Sloppy's that surely hadn't seen a line in years.

She parked in between the closed pizzeria and a tiny shack that made keys, exactly as she had been ordered to. Alison swallowed, realizing she was in an isolated parking lot. No cameras, so whatever was about to happen would be off the record like the rest of her recent life. A place like this made sense considering their illegal activity, but it also made her feel like she might be about to disappear.

She told herself to stop thinking about all of that, and was wondering what would happen next when the question died in her mind, thanks to the shiny new Mini Cooper pulling up to kiss her SUV on the nose.

Alison wasn't sure who or what she expected to meet

out here on the corner of Nowhere and Forgotten, but it definitely wasn't the tiny woman getting out of the Mini Cooper and walking over.

Alison rolled down her window, observing the contact Goliat had apparently sent her to meet.

She looked like a life-sized doll. Five feet tall or so, with straight raven hair cut sharp at the shoulders. Hoop earrings that Alison probably could have slipped her fist through. A denim jacket that made the 80s proud. Her makeup circled the wagons of whorish and clownish before staking a claim in "general mockery of the art." Over-drawn lips, pencil-thin eyebrows, magenta mascara, and — Alison forced herself not to stare — *glitter*. It was hard to tell the woman's age from behind foundation that looked more like neon bedrock, but she was somewhere between twenty-five and 101.

Surely this couldn't be Goliat's girlfriend. He seemed so sophisticated, while this woman seemed … like something else. She was holding a medium-sized gift bag, pink as a bottle of Pepto-Bismol.

"You who I'm here for, yeah?"

Alison blinked, already needing a moment to catch up. The woman had somehow managed to make her six words sound like only three.

"Yes. I'm Alison." Maybe she should be using a fake name. Probably not, seeing as she was family now. "Did Rodrigo send you?"

"Shit. Rodrigo be making spaghetti when I tell him to. I'm doing him a favor right now."

"Okay."

"This is for you." The woman thrust the gift bag toward Alison while holding out her opposite hand. "You got something for me?"

"Um … no?" Did she? Was she supposed to? "I don't …"

"I'm not saying you're obligated or nothing. I'm just saying it's a long way from Reseda."

"Oh. You mean … am I supposed to—"

"Don't tell Rodrigo."

"About what?" Alison asked.

"About anything. He don't need to know shit."

"Okay," Alison said again. This was all so confusing. She looked inside the bag and saw a gift-wrapped box the size of a large paperback book. "There's a present inside …"

Alison's observation seemed to anger the woman. "Think I don't know what I put in the bag? I'm the one who dumped out all my barrettes to make room!"

"I'm sorry." Alison smiled at her. "I guess what I'm asking is, *am I supposed to open it?*"

"No you're not supposed to open it! What kind of fool-ass question is that?"

"Then who is it for … if you don't mind my asking?"

The woman held out her hand.

"I'm sorry, I—"

"Your phone," she clarified, sounding irritated. "Shit."

Alison handed her burner to the woman. "I'm sorry. I—"

"You said that. Now would you mind shutting your guzzler? I'm trying to remember things."

Alison didn't dare with her *Sorry*.

She returned the burner to Alison and said, "Deliver the gift bag to that address and tell 'em Rodrigo says, 'happy birthday.' And 'sorry he couldn't make it.'"

"Rodrigo or Goliat?"

"ROD-RI-GO."

"Who am I telling this to?"

"The person at the address I just typed into your phone." The woman shook her head in disgust. "*Shit.*"

"I'm so—" A smile and reset. "I think we got off on the wrong foot. I'm Alison."

"You think I got amnesia?"

"No, of course not. I was just … what's your name?"

"Mamacita."

That couldn't possibly be her name.

"Why you looking at me like that?" Mamacita seemed angry again. "What you think my name was? What he say about me?"

"Nothing … I mean … are you Rodrigo's girlfriend?"

"I suck his dick!" she snapped.

"Oh …"

"*You* suck his dick?"

"No! Of course not."

"I ain't mad if you do," Mamacita assured her. "Nobody wanna be smiling like a donut all day long, and you know how Rodrigo always be—"

"I don't know anything about Rodrigo's … personal life."

"I know plenty. Ask me anything."

"That's okay." Alison looked down through the window, wondering if she was being rude. If maybe she should open the door and get out. Or maybe it was better to get on with things, and out of here. She held up the gift bag. "So I give this to the person at the address you texted me. Anything else? Am I supposed to bring something back?"

"You get something, give it to Miguel. He coming by your place sometime tonight. Say he be checking up on your daughter when he really be checking on you."

"What do you know about my daughter?" Alison asked, suddenly on edge.

"Relax, mama. Rodrigo ain't gonna do nothing to her if you don't give him no reason."

Technically, that meant that Rodrigo *would* hurt Sarah without cause, but Alison wasn't about to explain double negatives to … Mamacita … or whatever her name really was.

"You need anything else?" Mamacita was waiting with her hands on her hips.

Probably. Alison had no idea. "I'm good."

"You got this, girl!" Now they were on the same team.

She gave Alison a nod of solidarity, then turned around and started back toward her Mini Cooper. Only then could Alison see the lone word loudly bedazzled cross the back of her denim jacket: *MAMACITA*.

She rolled up her window and started the car, wanting to laugh at the series of absurd turns her life had suddenly taken. She plugged the address from her burner into the GPS and started driving south toward San Diego, cycling through every song on her first, second, and third favorite playlists before reaching the border to Mexico three hours later. She tried to keep her mind on the music, but couldn't shed her festering paranoia, at least halfway certain throughout her entire ride that she was being watched by the DEA, or Rodrigo's men, probably both as she approached the border, passed through from one country to the other, then navigated another ninety minutes of wide-open road before she finally arrived in a tiny town that would have been ramshackle by American standards, but managed to look quaint to her eyes.

Alison hadn't seen another moving vehicle for a while, but that didn't mean there hadn't been a drone (or drones) overhead that she couldn't see. Rodrigo's guys might catch sight of the DEA agents (they had to be somewhere around here), or it might happen the other way around.

She turned off the radio as her GPS announced Alison's arrival at her final destination. An old house that would have for sure been rickety enough to fall right over if it wasn't so clearly being well cared for.

She grabbed the gift bag, got out of the SUV, and walked to the front door.

She knocked, waited, knocked louder and kept waiting, then knocked hard enough to feel a bit of light blunt force trauma on her knuckles.

The door finally opened to an old woman giving Alison a curious smile. Her gaze found the bag and she beamed like an angel.

"Rodrigo must have sent you! I knew my grandson wouldn't forget me today." Her English was as crisp as Goliat's.

Then she opened her door all the way and invited Alison inside.

"Rodrigo says happy birthday," she said, entering the house and handing her the bag. "He's sorry he was unable to make it."

"My grandson is a very busy man," she explained, closing the door and pulling her gift from the bag. "Do you know what it is?"

Alison shook her head. "I have no idea."

"Why don't I get you a glass of limonada." It didn't sound like a question. "And then I'll open my regalo."

"That would be wonderful."

"Make yourself at home," she said on her way out of the room.

Alison's eyes swept over the small, humble house

festooned with a ton of framed photos on the wall and various religious paintings and statues.

Rodrigo's abuela came back a few minutes later carrying two glasses of lemonade, and beaming even wider than before.

The lemonade was delicious. Not too sweet, and not too tart. Alison had taken a pair of tentative sips (what if she was being poisoned?) before her first long swallow.

Grandma was already unwrapping her box.

Alison knew what it was the second she saw the first shred of paper torn enough to reveal the box, but Abuela seemed to know what it was at the same time. She squealed with delight as she ripped the remaining paper away.

She looked at Alison and raised her new iPad in triumph. "Perfect timing. My last one just stopped working." Then, without any preamble or pause: "Would you mind helping me to set it up?"

Abuela handed her the box.

"Of course," Alison said as she took it.

The setup was easy enough, and Alison got the distinct impression that the old woman really just needed a reason to request her company for a little longer. Alison was happy to stay the extra minutes, feeling less danger in this little cottage than she had on the road, or would once back on it. But there was something heartbreaking in their exchange, the way Goliat's grandmother was so proud of her youngest grandson, without having any idea who he really was, or of the countless atrocities he had surely committed on his way to the top.

Including what he was doing to Alison right now by having her deliver this present.

"I'm so proud of my nieto. Rodrigo is so enterprising. He sends everyone money. Takes care of his whole family down here, not just his abuela. You should see how many branches we have on our tree!" Grandma laughed, shaking her head and seeming grateful that she had someone to share in her pride. "And Rodrigo paid all of my medical bills. He is a big businessman in America, though I guess I don't have to tell you, seeing as you work for him."

Alison bit her tongue, unwilling or perhaps even unable to tell Abuela the truth. That her grandson was a drug dealer. A common criminal, and very likely a killer.

"Did you want me to give him a message?" Alison asked, after the iPad was all set up and it seemed that Abuela's pride had been at least momentarily exhausted.

"There is nothing I can say to Rodrigo that he does not already know. But please, give him this."

She handed Alison a small silver box.

Alison took it with a nod, wondering if there was more going on here then she realized.

But after saying goodbye, getting a mile down the road, then finally lifting the unlatched lid of that box, Alison found herself laughing out loud while all alone in her Cayenne.

The box was filled with cookies. Good old-fashioned chocolate chip by the look of things.

It was surreal, waking up this morning thinking she would spend a good part of it as a drug mule, when she had spent it drinking lemonade — *limonada* — with a sweet old lady, before playing coyote to a box of cookies on her way home.

This was clearly a test. To see if she could be trusted.

But that truth made her angry. Rodrigo had forced her to go through this charade, believing that she was smuggling a brick of cocaine and was about to get caught any second. Or worse, killed in the crossfire between rival gangs shooting it out. Maybe one of the gangs against the

DEA. A possible melee that somehow blended every one of those terrible options together.

She grew angrier and angrier as she drove. By the time she was trading Orange County for Los Angeles County, and crossing into Las Orillas, Alison was fuming.

Fuck going home.

She would be giving Goliat the cookies herself.

Chapter Thirty-Two

ALISON DROVE the final few miles on her way to Goliat's Victorian in a fugue. The world went blurry somewhere around Studebaker and Spring. That's when she started to see stars. That's when she noticed that her knuckles where bone white on the steering wheel. And that's when the reality that Alison wasn't in control of a single damned thing in her life became so readily apparent. Correcting that glaring injustice was suddenly the only thing in the universe that mattered to her.

She swung onto Chestnut, fast enough to squeal through the turn. Two men loitering across the street, both with tattoos covering their shaved heads, looked over in unison.

She parked in front of the Victorian on the corner, grabbed Rodrigo's box of cookies, got out of the car, and made it just past the gate before Miguel raised an urgent hand to stop her.

"Alison! Wait!" He grabbed her by the arm as she passed him, gently at first, but when she tried to keep going he had to yank her back. "You don't want to do that."

"Do what?"

"Whatever it is you're thinking of doing."

She showed him the box of cookies. "I have a delivery from his grandmother."

"That I'm supposed to pick up at your house tonight."

"Maybe I want to give them to Goliat myself." She shook herself out of his grip.

"Did his grandmother tell you to do that?"

"She didn't—"

"Do you have an appointment?"

"That's not—"

"I'm trying to help you, not boss you around." Miguel waited a second for her to settle before he continued. "This isn't just about protecting you, it's about looking out for my own ass, too. In case you forgot, I brought you here the last time, and I'm not sure Goliat isn't still pissed at me for doing it. I'd rather stay in his good—"

"It's not your fault that I'm here, Miguel."

"Why *are* you here?"

"I told you." She shook the box again. "I'm bringing Rodrigo his cookies."

"Don't call him that. It's Goliat."

"He told me his name!" Alison snapped. "Remember? He said we're *family*."

"Why are you really here?"

"To give him a piece of my mind for sending me out on that bullshit errand, for toying with me like that!" Alison snapped, the righteous anger still surprising her.

"Even if that wasn't a terrible idea, this isn't the time. So why don't you—"

But Alison pushed past him, ignoring whatever Miguel was going to say.

He reached out to grab her by the arm again. She shook out of his grip and kept marching toward the shack.

She burst through the door, but then froze once inside. She could feel the mood a moment before it hit her, and felt zero doubt once all the guns were drawn and pointed at her.

What the hell did I just walk into?

It was still Gustavo and Company, but this time none of the men were sitting. And a newcomer filled her with dread on sight. The tension was thick enough to part like a curtain, but Goliat still smiled.

"Welcome." He nodded at Alison, then turned his gaze to the newcomer, a large man with a tattoo on his actual face — a spiderweb running down the right side from just over his eyebrow to the edge of his chin. "This is my good friend, Julio."

"Nice to meet you," she said.

Her other words were all gone. Alison had gone from righteous fury to sudden fear that Rodrigo really would deliver on his prior threat about him calling her instead of the other way around. But oddly, and in a most unsettling way, he looked happy to see her.

"He will be your good friend, too," Goliat added.

Alison swallowed. "How's that?"

"I have a job for you."

"What kind of job?" Alison asked, wondering if she could get back to her SUV before one of these extremely dangerous men could put a bullet in the back of her head, or whether Miguel would even try to help her after she ignored his warnings.

"A big job." Goliat smiled and filled her with chills. "Big enough to repay your debt to me."

"What do I have to do?" Alison tried to ask again.

But the big boss still didn't answer. "Something you will do for me while Miguel keeps an eye on your daughter. Just to make sure that everything goes as planned."

She turned to look at him, but Miguel averted his eyes.

"Just give me the details," she said to Goliat in defeat.

He gave the room a nod and everyone holstered their guns.

Then he told Alison exactly what she would have to do.

Chapter Thirty-Three

This was stupid.

What had she been thinking?

Surely, Alison had made the biggest, dumbest, most careless mistake of her life.

She needed to stop driving this stupid SUV. Right now. The Cayenne represented everything that had been wrong with Alison's prior life, populated by a mess of idiotic non-priorities that had taken precedent over everything that actually mattered.

Fuck this Porsche. Fuck it in its … fuck hole!

She punched the steering wheel, determined to get better at this swearing thing.

Three blocks from home and the anxiety inside her still refused to die. Instead it kept swelling, getting bigger and bigger like a boil slowly filling with pus.

Because as much as Alison wanted to tell herself she was being paranoid, it really did feel like she had finally crossed the Rubicon. Sarah might be safe once this was all over, and if so, then it would all surely be worth the sacrifice. But Alison's death was imminent. She was willing to break the law for Goliat, even more than she already had, but in the end he would probably kill her anyway.

Fine by Alison, so long as Sarah stayed safe.

She turned onto Cedar, noting that it was the Tahoe's turn to live outside her house. They weren't the only officers of the law on her property. Alison had no idea which car belonged to him, but Ellis was on her porch, standing in a swath of shadows cast by all the wisteria crawling the wall.

"So?" Ellis said, expectantly.

"So: *You scared me*," she said, barely managing to swallow her yelp.

"We have a lot to catch up on." Then, in case he wasn't clear enough: "I want to know everything that happened in Mexico. And then I want to know what you dropped off at his place just now—"

"Can I please go inside my house first? It's been a long day." She opened the door without waiting for Ellis to answer.

But he nodded and gestured toward the open door. "After you."

Inside the house she managed to score almost five minutes alone. He granted her permission use the restroom and grab a glass of water. But he acted like Alison was applying for a license to hunt orphans. She wanted to call Sarah's cell to make sure she was okay, but figured it was best not to worry her daughter. Besides, when she'd called to check on her last night, Sarah was still in her pissiest mood.

"You hiding anything from me?" Ellis asked, once she was back in the living room with a freshly filled glass, after having already drained the first one.

She sat in the armchair and let him have the entire couch to himself.

"No, I'm not hiding anything from you."

"Tell me everything."

"Where do you want me to start?" Alison asked.

"How about why you were at the corner of Lampson and Candlewood this morning."

"I was meeting Goliat's … contact."

"Why are you saying it like that? Were you meeting a contact or not?"

"Yes." She nodded. "I was."

"Did this contact give you a name?"

"She said her name was Mamacita."

"What?"

"Her jacket said *MAMACITA*," Alison explained. "So it might have been legit."

Same as she had earlier that morning, Mamacita got Alison off to an awkward start. Her explanations were smoother after that. Ellis grew more and more excited, interrogating her about every little detail, drawing things from Alison's memory that she hadn't even realized she'd seen, like the picture on the woman's wall that included a bald fat man with a young Rodrigo, and another photo with the same men and an old thin man in a suit with a pencil mustache and thick glasses.

Ellis seemed interested in the thin man, making a note in his little book.

"And you're one hundred percent sure it was just cookies?" Ellis asked when she got to that part.

"I couldn't be surer."

Alison finished the rest of her story, telling the agent about how upset she had been, and how that rage had propelled her from Mexico to Las Orillas, then all the way back to Ninth and Chestnut, where she had every intention of giving Goliat a piece of her mind but left with a potential escape hatch instead.

"So what's the plan?" Ellis asked when she finished.

"Goliat has fake-surrendered to Rottweiler, and has agreed to broker a meeting with some guy named Priest—"

"I know Priest." Ellis nodded with a smile. "Goliat wants to negotiate a new arrangement between Priest and Rottweiler, right?"

"Exactly," Alison nodded.

Ellis stood and started to pace her living room, making his first circuit in silence and the second muttering to himself and leaving Alison out of the exchange entirely. But by the third circle all the way around her couch, words were finally coming out of his mouth loud enough for her to hear them.

"This would be great for Rottweiler, because it means he can get his drugs cheaper, and more conveniently. He pulls it off, the turf war is over, and with no more unnecessary bloodshed. Body counts are always bad for business, no matter whose side they're on."

He finally stopped pacing and looked at her. "Tell me what you're supposed to do. *Exactly*."

"Goliat wants me to deliver a big bag of cash to Priest."

"And what's Priest supposed to give you in return?"

"Nothing." She shook her head. "He's supposed to make sure that Rottweiler never returns from the meeting."

Ellis was nodding. "He'll end up in a hole somewhere in the Mexican desert, then Goliat will have doubled his territory overnight."

"It's hardly overnight," Alison said, then immediately wished that she hadn't.

"Where are you delivering the bag?"

"Somewhere in Mexico."

"Do you know where in Mexico?" Ellis asked.

"Not yet. But I'm supposed to act like I'm this guy's girlfriend."

"What guy?"

"Priest's right-hand man."

"What does he look like?" Ellis asked, his frown thoughtful.

"Even taller than you. But with a face tattoo. Giant spiderweb. It's empty, but when he blinks there's a spider."

Ellis nodded, his smile making her uncomfortable considering that danger seemed to naturally widen it, and this was her life on the line. "Julio."

"Right," Alison confirmed with a churning stomach. "*Julio.*"

"So the two of you are crossing the border together?"

"We're supposed to be visiting his family to announce our engagement."

Ellis laughed.

"What's so funny?"

"Be glad. That right there is a happy laugh."

"Fine. Then what are you happy about?"

"I'm just thinking how lucky it is for both of us that Goliat is using you for what sounds like a big deal operation."

"You look like it's Christmas morning," Alison said.

"I don't celebrate Christmas."

"Fine. Kwanzaa, then."

"Is that because I'm Black?" Ellis asked, sounding insulted for a long second before he burst into manic laughter.

"Has anyone ever suggested that you might be bipolar?" Alison asked.

"This is what it looks like when one of the good guys knows he's about to get one of the baddest of the bad guys off the street. We're about to bring down Goliat *and* Priest?

Two of the biggest players in the game ...” He shook his head, laughing louder. “*Legendary.* This is Christmas, Kwanzaa, and Chanukah all rolled into one!”

“I’m glad that you’re so happy. But this all sounds dangerous.”

“It’s not that dangerous.”

“You just used the word *legendary.* You referred to these men as ‘two of the biggest players in the game.’ And you don’t think I should be worried?”

“We’ve got you.”

“How have you ‘got me’?” Alison asked, feeling more rather than less anxious. “What if I don’t want to do this?”

“You don’t get to decide that.”

“Of course I can—”

“Unless I’m mistaken, you are in dire need of an escape of your rather substantial mess. Would you rather stretch this out? Haven’t you been wanting a way to be done with it?”

“Why is he called Priest?”

Ellis shook his head. His turn to not answer.

“Is he super religious or something?”

He sighed. “You really want to do this?”

“Yes.” It wasn’t like she was about to back down now.

“Priest crucified his predecessor, and all of his most loyal men.”

Alison felt herself blanch, wanting to melt down into the couch. She must have looked even whiter than usual.

Ellis sighed and took a seat on the couch two cushions away from her. “It’s going to be okay. Really. We do this kind of stuff all the time.”

“And you’re telling me that there are never any casualties?”

“I’m not saying anything like that.” His tone had finally softened. “Bad shit happens sometimes. But we’ve been watching this guy for a while, and you're a smart lady."

"I don't want to do this. Maybe—"

"You back out now and your life will never be yours again. You'll end up dead or in jail, and your daughter will for sure get taken away from you. Do this and you can end the nightmare with something better than what your asshole husband left you with."

"Do you believe me … that I didn't know about any of this before he died?"

"Of course I believe you."

"Then why won't you help me to—"

"Because that's not my job. My job is to bring down the baddest of the bad guys, and that's what you're going to help me do. You'll be in and out." He looked into her eyes with a reassuring nod. "Not like you'll have to spend the weekend with a murdering psychopath. You hand him a bag of cash, and maybe give him a moment to start counting it, then we'll be right there with you."

"How will you know where I am?"

"Tracker in your car. Goliat needs you for this. Not just because you're an American citizen, but because you're a well-groomed middle-aged white lady. Customs is much less likely to closely examine your car. We'll be tailing you at a safe distance with a full team."

"How will you know when it's time?"

"We'll swoop in there once the deal is in progress. Just make sure you take cover once the shooting starts."

"How will you know when it's time?" Alison repeated. Maybe her questions were coming out upside down or something.

"We'll know."

Still not an answer. "Shouldn't I have a gun?"

"If Goliat gives you one. But I doubt that's going to happen."

"What about a bulletproof vest?"

"You want a bulletproof vest?" Ellis asked, then kept going without letting her answer. "Do you think bulletproof vests are invisible? Where are you planning to wear this bulletproof vest? Under or over your sleeveless blouse?"

"I'm not planning on wearing—"

"It doesn't matter what you wear. Goliat will know if you show up in Kevlar. Then even that won't help you because you'll end up with a bullet right between the eyes."

"This is very comforting."

"It should be," Ellis said. "Point is, we know what we're doing, assuming you do what we tell you."

"Goliat is keeping one of his men on Sarah until I get back. Will you make sure that she's okay?"

"That I can promise you." Ellis held her eyes. "You focus on doing everything you need to do, and I'll make sure nothing happens to your daughter. Deal?"

"Deal." Alison nodded and swallowed, suddenly knowing exactly what she had to do.

Chapter Thirty-Four

THURSDAY ...

ALISON WONDERED if she would need to get a new steering wheel.

The Cayenne was durable, but she had been gripping the thing hard enough to break it. Not just now, but every time she had driven everywhere for the last few days. Her fingers were wrapped so tightly around it right now, she could feel the pressure pulsing from knuckles to temples.

Maybe she could finally relax, once that text from Jake finally came in.

She kept glancing over at her phone, sitting in the center console with the dark screen facing her. Every time she moved her eyes from the road to her phone Alison hoped it would finally go bright with his communique. But Orange County was now long behind them. They were nearing San Diego, so soon they would be waiting in line to cross the border.

And still, Julio kept pretending to sleep in the passenger

seat beside her. At least Alison thought he was faking it. His eyes were closed, but the He-Man barely seemed to be breathing.

Still, Alison really needed to stop worrying. Everything was going according to plan. Not just Goliat's, but the secret little scheme she had hatched with Jake to help her and Sarah escape this mess and make their way to a much better life. Something safer, something far away from all the danger Tom had invited into their world.

Even with the windows rolled up Alison could smell the salty air and—

Her phone finally buzzed with a text. She casually glanced over before it disappeared. Four simple words in coded message that relaxed her grip on the wheel.

Same Order Next Week.

She could finally exhale. A deep gust of heavy breath left her lungs, but Julio still didn't look over. Jake's message gave her faith, but she couldn't stop worrying about Miguel, wondering if the kid could really be trusted. If not, then Sarah was still very much in danger, and Alison was setting herself up for a life of bottomless regret.

How could she ever live with herself if something terrible happened to Sarah, just because she decided to play cowgirl? Alison had to keep convincing herself that any action was better than no action. And yet, in reality inaction might have kept them both alive.

Her thoughts looped for fifty miles. Julio finally started to stir, or at least he quit pretending to sleep, as the SUV slowed on their approach to the border.

Julio looked over, surely noted the gallon of sweat that had appeared on her face despite the AC cranked to full blast, and gave her a decisive shake of his head.

"Worrying only lengthens the shadow."

Those were the first words Julio had spoken since he

climbed into the SUV and closed the door with a grunted *Good morning.* His husky voice was like thunder through the Cayenne.

She looked over at him and he finished his thought.

"Worry makes you tired. It weakens your decisions." He shook his head. "So don't worry."

"Easy for *you* to say."

"You keep doing the hard things until the hard things become the easy things," Julio said, pressing his back hard into the seat.

A bit fortune cookie, but his words did make sense. So Alison repeated them to herself, alongside the reminder that *all was well.* She had a plan, and she had Jake helping her with that plan. Everything was under control.

"Do you think they're going to stop us?" Alison checked to make sure they were in the right lane, even though she had checked several times already. Yep, her SUV was still in the *nothing to declare* line, still waiting for a green light to the other side of a border that was right now radiating a skin-boiling danger.

"They stop everyone." Julio nodded toward the line in front of them. Each of the cars had to roll down their window and trade at least a few words with the customs agent before getting waved forward.

"But do you think they'll ... you know, ask us a lot of questions? Or want to search our vehicle?"

"Sounds to me like you're asking a question you already know the answer to, but wish you didn't."

Great. So she was sitting next to a brute *and* a philosopher.

Her heart kept pounding. And her palms were now slick on the wheel. One more car to go.

"Calm your breathing," Julio said.

"I'm trying."

"Try harder. You've done this once before, right?"

"I was alone … and all I had was the gift bag … I didn't even know what was in it. I thought I might be picking something up to take back to the States."

Julio didn't answer. Two minutes later it was finally their turn.

She slowly drove forward, lowered her window, and leaned out toward the customs agent with her most American smile. "Good morning!"

"Ma'am." The agent nodded, peering right into her. "Nothing to declare?"

"That's right." Alison smiled. "Nada que declarar."

Her smile wasn't returned.

"Are you an American citizen?"

"I am. Would you like to see my paperwork?" Alison didn't wait for an answer, already handing the agent her passport and registration.

But instead of taking it, she looked past Alison to her passenger. A long hard look, then the agent pointed to a second lane and said, "I need you to pull up over there."

"Is everything—"

"Over there." The agent stabbed the air with her finger, aiming it to the precise spot she wanted Alison to go, then she turned away from the Cayenne and waved the next vehicle forward.

"What do you think is happening right now?" Alison asked, pulling into the secondary lane while trying not to flip out.

"I think they're going to question us. Pretty white lady like you and Mexican John Cena like me, especially with all of this …" He gestured to the giant spiderweb. "It's natural that they'd have a few questions. Just stay cool and don't lose your shit."

"But what if—"

"That means stop talking."

Then he started laughing like Alison had just said something funny as another agent approached her window. This one with a mean-looking mustache that dipped over the top of his lip enough that the agent must surely be tasting it.

He leaned in and spoke with no expression. "Please exit the vehicle and stand in the clearly-marked area."

"Yes, sir. Of course. But may I ask what's happening right now?" Alison could feel Julio judging her, trying to will her mouth closed.

"We're going to search your vehicle."

"But I don't have anything to declare …" Her expression turned thoughtful. Alison was barely aware of what she was doing until she was already doing it, and wondering if her words were a shortcut to ruining everything. "This isn't because of what my fiancé looks like … is it?"

"Please step out of the car, ma'am."

And again she felt the heat of Julio's punishing assessment.

They walked over to the assigned area and stood there together, waiting.

"Do you think—"

"Not now," Julio cut Alison off, his words sharp but his smile wide, still looking like his half of a happy couple.

Two agents started searching the SUV, while another came over to them holding a clipboard.

Alison should be looking at the agent in front of her, but it was hard to ignore the pair now combing her Cayenne for something illegal.

"What brings you to Mexico?" he asked.

"We're going to visit my fiancé's family," Alison answered, beaming at Julio.

She wasn't sure what she was scared of more — the agent's next question, or the cash that could be discovered inside a vehicle registered to her … any second now.

Could the agent hear her heart pounding?

Because she sure as hell could.

Julio was answering the agent, but Alison couldn't hear his reply and had missed the question entirely. It required all of her focus to keep the panic from gurgling up from the growing ball in her chest.

"—with me?" The agent seemed to have just finished a thought and was now looking at Alison.

Julio was walking behind a second female agent that had appeared without her noticing, and now Alison found herself following the male who had greeted her with the simplest of questions:

What brings you to Mexico.

Muling cash for a drug lord.

Playing spy for Ellis Munk and the DEA.

Doing whatever she needed to make sure that Sarah stayed safe.

All possible answers, but none that the agent was looking for.

He opened a door and gestured for Alison to enter a small room — the kind she had seen so many versions of, always on television except for one time.

The questions started out easy enough. Alison had been coached on the answers so they were mostly right there on the tip of her tongue. But the agent inquired without expression, running through line-item queries in a way that in no way resembled conversation.

He wanted to know Julio's first and last names, where his family lived, how long they would be staying, if Alison had ever been to Nogales before, if she knew anyone else in the city, if she knew anyone else in the country, and how long she and Julio had known each other.

She managed to answer every one of the questions with an impressive degree of automaticity. Until he asked something that handed her tongue to the cat.

"How did the two of you meet?"

Alison laughed to buy herself time. "That's quite a story."

"I'd love to hear it."

Did they have one? Was she forgetting? If Alison and Julio were supposedly getting married, they really should have prepared themselves with a story for their meet-cute.

"I'd rather not." She tried to make herself blush, not knowing if that was even possible. "It's … rather embarrassing."

"I can think of a few things that might embarrass you a lot more," the agent pressed.

But still he spoke with no inflection, like the threat was yet another line on his list he'd read countless times before. This was not a man to be charmed.

She did her best to think about the story Julio would be telling on his side of their forced separation. "We met at a bar."

"What was the name of the bar?"

"You think I remember the *name of the bar*?" Alison laughed. "I was *sooo* drunk." She laughed again.

"And how did you meet at the bar you don't remember?"

"Well, Julio's not really my type. *At all.*" Every great lie had some truth in it, or so her late husband had taught her. "But there was just something about him. He wouldn't take no for an answer. He just kept coming back for more, even after I'd given him an insistent *No* a half-dozen times."

"So, he was aggressive?"

"Wonderfully so." She smiled, feeling icky inside and out.

The agent asked several more questions, but in less of a monotone which Alison chose to see as light in the tunnel. A few minutes later he ordered her to stay put. Then he left the little room. Alison sat alone with her thoughts for another ten minutes or so, until that same agent came in with his sad little mustache to collect her.

The Cayenne had come up clean, and their stories apparently matched enough to let the odd couple pass from one nation and into the arms of its southern neighbor.

"Did they ask you how we met?" Alison asked in Mexico, once she was back to breathing again.

"They did." Julio nodded.

"What did you say?"

"That I hit on you and you slapped me. So I knew you were a respectable woman."

"That's … kind of sweet."

He shrugged. "My embarrassing story gives you a reason to lie about yours."

Julio almost seemed like he might be willing to talk.

So she decided to give it a try. "What's Priest like?"

"You'll see when you meet him." Julio reclined and closed his eyes.

Again she was alone, this time cycling through the same old thoughts for more than an hour while driving south to Nogales.

Even if this little trip was exactly what it was supposed to be, everything about it was dangerous. And there was a good chance that it could be something more. Goliat might have been holding a grudge, and had determined that the best revenge on Tom would be to have Priest slaughter and bury her along with Rottweiler — a dumb dog who didn't know when to stop barking.

Or what if Goliat was trying to recoup his loss by selling Alison into slavery? Stealing a kidney? Something worse? Something too terrible for her to have ever seen on TV?

She swallowed and drove, her thoughts turning to Miguel again, hoping from her core that he had done what she'd asked. And that Sarah would stay safe, no matter what happened to her mother.

Chapter Thirty-Five

THE VIEW WAS *ALMOST* enough to put Alison at ease.

"It'll be just a few minutes," Francisco had told them, after answering the door and introducing himself, but before leaving to prepare their beverages.

Now they were in the living room waiting for those drinks, and for Priest to join them.

Alison had no idea how large the place was. Only that Priest had this tucked-away villa in Nogales Sonora. Her GPS led the way, and she hopefully left a trail for the DEA. But the property was designed for a full-frontal viewing, and the address directed her to what was essentially a driveway leading up to a gorgeous faux adobe wall fronted by a gate.

Julio gave her a code. She punched it into the keypad and the gate swung open to another small road leading directly into what felt like a large garage, despite its total lack of cars. There were several stacks of big plastic bins, all of them either black or red, but nothing else.

Then through a door and into a staggering living room. High rafters and warm Spanish tile, clearly hand-made judging by the variations. Dark wood served as a backdrop for vibrant splashes of color, every hue. Plush cushions lined four separate couches, all in shades of chocolate. The blades of wide-brimmed ceiling fans stirred a current through the room.

A glass wall opened onto a veranda overlooking the city. One rocky staircase down from the veranda Alison saw the reason there weren't any cars in the garage. What appeared to be a rotating platform had a half-dozen luxury vehicles.

Alison had no idea how many other rooms sprawled behind the four closed doors, not including the glass one inside the wall leading out to the veranda, but the living room alone was warm enough to feel like home sweet home if not for the pungency of murder brewing.

Francisco returned with their drinks — two bottles of Topo Chico — a beat before the man she presumed to be Priest entered the living room from one of the four closed doors with a trio of men in formation behind him.

Alison was picturing Scarface, but this man was Stanley Tucci. He had his mostly bald head working for instead of against him, his face covered in evenly sprinkled salt and pepper, from just over his ears to just under his chin. His crewneck was so crisp it looked sheen, and his jacket had the sharpest of edges.

"Thank you for driving all this way," he said by way of introduction. "They call me Priest, whether I like it or not." A warm little laugh. "Please. Sit."

He gestured toward the nearest couch, then sat himself. His three men stayed standing.

Alison sat on the couch across from him.

But Julio didn't join her.

Priest gestured to his men. "You'll have to forgive their

looming presence. I am relaxed because they never are. Thank you again for coming all this way."

"It was a beautiful drive." This was weird.

"Shall we get the unpleasantries out of the way first?"

"Unpleasantries?" Alison swallowed.

"I believe you have something for me?"

"It's in the garage. Look inside the hood insulation," Julio said from behind Alison. When she turned to look at him, he added, "Best place to hide shit in a Cayenne."

One of Priest's three men started toward the door leading to the garage.

"Is that what you meant by unpleasantries?" Alison asked, desperately wanting a *yes*.

"Money is the machine that makes this all work ..." Priest waved an idle hand about the room. "But it is still accounting, and numbers are my least favorite part of any job. This enterprise requires large sums of money to run, and to provide the lifestyle I have earned for myself and those people in this world I love most. With David now on his way to collect the money, we can focus on what excites me most."

Something terrible was about to happen.

"What excites you most?" Alison swallowed again, wondering if she looked as scared as she felt.

"Conversation." He smiled.

"What do you want to talk about?" His perfect manners were making her more nervous than the grounds of a thug.

"How did a woman like you come to be working for Goliat?"

"What kind of a woman am I?"

"The kind who does not ever work for a man like him." Priest pointed to her unopened bottle of Topo Chico. "You are not thirsty?"

"I'm fine." She smiled.

"You are nervous." Priest leaned forward. "There's nothing to be nervous about. Right now I am someone who is curious about you. There are no wrong answers. Oh," he shook his head, almost violently, "not true: if you lie to me I will kill you. But there are no wrong answers if you tell me the truth."

His voice was still so gentle, and his eyes so very kind.

"Thank you," Alison was surprised, or perhaps even horrified to hear herself say.

"Let's start over." Priest gave her a patient smile. "How did you come to work for Goliat?"

"I fell into it."

"You fell? Or were you pushed?"

"I guess pushed is more like it."

"Shoved?" he asked, still smiling.

"Maybe." Alison laughed, but only barely. "What is it you actually want to know? Of course 'someone like me' isn't the type of person who usually works with someone like Goliat. But I'm a single mother who's fallen on hard times. And I'll do anything to protect my daughter."

"*Anything?*" His smile widened. "Now this is interesting to me."

"I don't think I said that right—"

"You said it perfectly. I can always use an attractive white woman as a mule. They might stop you at the border if they see a man like Julio riding shotgun, but even then there is a halo around you. It isn't like they searched the hood insulation. Isn't that right?"

David returned with a stack of vacuum-sealed bags full of cash. He nodded at the two men still standing behind Priest, then the three of them went over to a table together, presumably to open the bags and count their spoils. Julio stayed standing behind her.

"Perhaps you would care for a different drink?" Priest suggested, instead of diving back into their prior conversation. "Something with spice? An habanero margarita perhaps? Xolo's are the best. He can stop counting and make you one."

"No thanks. I'm good. Still not thirsty."

"Perhaps that is the problem."

"I'm sorry?" Alison squinted at Priest, not understanding.

"Tell me what you want in this life. I bet that reality could be closer than you are making it. The underground economy is twelve percent of your country's GDP. Why not dip your finger into that stream?" He smiled again, but this one was Cheshire. "Come on in, the margins are warm."

"I appreciate the opportunity, really I do, but I'm looking to get out of the situation I'm in, not deeper into it … no offense."

"None taken. But do you mind if I ask you a question?"

"Not at all." Of course she did.

"What if Walgreens offered you a job, would you take it?"

"I already get where this was going, but—"

"Would you take it?" Priest cut her off, still sounding like a butler but now with an edge to his voice.

"I don't know what kind of job Walgreens could possibly offer me."

"A good one. You are a single mother. You have a daughter you will do anything to protect. And you are in a desperate situation you are dying to get out of. Do you take the job?"

"That would have to be one hell of a job."

He shrugged. "I imagine the pay would start somewhere around a quarter of a million dollars a year, tax free. But with this kind of position …" He shrugged again. "I think it could eventually end up paying just about anything you want."

"Like my life."

"This is what you are afraid of?" asked Priest.

"I'm terrified of plenty right now."

"Honesty." He gave Alison an approving smile. "I like that."

"A quarter million dollars is a lot of money, but how am I supposed to spend it if I don't even have a job? There will be eyeballs all over me. And that's not even the point. I could lose my life or go to jail at any time. Either thing would destroy my daughter, not protect her."

"You could take a part-time job. We could arrange an inheritance. Rare art could be discovered in your attic. Things have a way of happening, you know? Agree to participate and the business takes care of you."

"Just like Walgreens, right?" Alison laughed, but this wasn't funny.

But Priest agreed with a nod. "Just like Walgreens."

And Alison dared: "Except Walgreens isn't illegal."

Priest shook his head with what looked like pity, or perhaps embarrassment for Alison and her lack of understanding. "Why are you concerned about what is legal instead of what is wrong?"

"Isn't it usually the same thing?"

"The 'legal' pharmaceutical industry spends more than any other industry on influencing politicians." Priest paused to see if Alison had anything to say, then continued when she didn't. "Two lobbyists for every member of Congress. Nine out of ten House members and all but three of your current senators have taken campaign contributions from Big Pharma. What kind of a difference do you think that makes to this little war on drugs?"

Alison kept looking at Priest, mostly ignoring Julio standing behind her, and the three man-beasts finishing their tally over at the table. But she still didn't answer.

"Have you ever heard of a company called Truistic Pharma?" Priest asked.

"No." She shook her head.

"They are responsible for America's most loved 'legal' drug. Do you know what that is?"

"Succontin?" Alison guessed.

"That is correct." Priest gave her a smile. "Truistic bankrolled a campaign to change the prescription habits of doctors who became wary of the drug's highly addictive properties. Do you know one of the ways they did that?"

"No." Again she shook her head.

"By sending doctors on all-expense-paid trips to pain-management seminars."

"I don't see how—"

"The family that started it all is worth some $15 billion today. One legal company was responsible for distributing more than a hundred million opioid pills. Do you still think we're the bad guys here?"

Yes. Absolutely.

But, of course, Alison couldn't say that.

"Please … speak your mind. I would enjoy hearing your most honest response." Priest repeated his question.

Alison answered, despite her terror. "You're the ones holding the guns."

This seemed to insult him. "I am unarmed." Then he patted his body to prove it. "And my men carry weapons because they have been forced to. Don't you think I would prefer it another way?" He shook his head to show Alison the depth of his regret. "I am fighting this 'war' the only way I can. What else am I supposed to do?"

Priest shrugged, then started ticking off points on his right hand, raising fingers in time with his words. "Five companies contributed more than nine million dollars to interest groups for things like promoting their drugs for chronic pain and lobbying to defeat state limits on prescribing opioids, while also preventing legislation that would help to curb opioid use."

His second finger went up. "Sensein Therapeutics, a company whose founder was indicted for allegedly bribing doctors to write prescriptions for fentanyl spent a half-billon dollars to stop marijuana legalization. Fentanyl, my dear, is fifty times stronger than heroin."

And then his third. "It is clear who the true profiteers of the opioid epidemic are. Men like me only exist because of a system that has both created and supported me. How do you feel about what I am saying, Alison? At the very least can we agree that the truth of my arguments is making you uncomfortable?"

Alison didn't reply. Maybe she couldn't.

"I would like you to feel better about us working together, but alas, shall I categorize that want as yet another pipe dream?"

Alison stayed paralyzed, trapped between her fear of refusing him and the mounting fear that accompanied her silence.

"I understand … you need time to think." Priest offered her a nod. "How did Julio treat you?"

An abrupt change of subject, but she rolled with it. "Julio was great."

"All here," boomed the biggest of the three men counting all the money, which was now being transferred to the first of two large black duffel bags.

Priest smiled, nodding in satisfaction. "Do you know what the money is for?"

"None of my business. My knowledge starts and ends with me bringing it to you."

He nodded. Perhaps Priest believed her, but probably not.

"Tell me what you really want. Por favor. Or you can answer my original question: why is someone like you working for Goliat?"

"I wasn't working for him. But my husband was, not that I knew it at the time. He was murdered by Rottweiler." Rage swelled her insides like liquid into a balloon. "Goliat promised me revenge."

"This I also understand …" Priest nodded appreciatively. "Your silence is not a weakness, but the beginning of your vengeance."

Whatever that meant.

"I would like you to join me for dinner." Priest waved a hand toward one of the doors, presumably leading toward a kitchen or dining room, probably both.

"I really need to be going." Surely this was dangerous, refusing the man without flinching.

"We will be having a feast. Real Mexican food. Not like what you are used to up in Las Orillas."

"We have great Mexican food," Alison said, defending Las Orillas and Southern California in general.

"You will not think so much after leaving my house tonight. The sun sets beautifully over the city. And as I told you before, Xolo makes an excellent margarita. Have you ever had Kobe steak, Baja style?"

He smacked his lips. "Would you like to taste the most delicious guacamole of your life, made from avocados grown here on this property? Chile rellenos made with eggs from the chickens outside? Cesar salad prepared tableside, with anchovies smashed in front of you? All the sides … flan and deep-fried ice cream for dessert. Shall I continue?"

"That really does sound delicious. But I need to get home and make sure that my daughter is safe."

"This I understand." Priest offered Alison his warmest smile so far. "For dessert my men will be extinguishing the life of the man who murdered your husband. Are you sure you wouldn't like to see that?"

No. She didn't want to see that at all. Again she said, "I have to get home to my daughter."

Priest addressed Julio, still standing behind her. "Please make sure our new friend gets home safely. Her part of this arrangement has been completed."

Then he found her eyes again. "Thank you for your time. I am sure the longer you are away from Nogales, the more you will realize the value of my offer." He dipped his head. "I do look forward to seeing you again."

Alison felt the deepest flush of relief as she followed Julio to the garage.

She closed the Cayenne door a second before Julio slammed his, then loudly exhaled before starting the car.

"You did good in there," Julio said.

"Thanks." Her heart was still pounding, for some reason expecting worse.

They barely made it to the other side of the gate before her paranoia was proven right.

"Shit," Julio muttered in defeat.

But it was already too late.

Chapter Thirty-Six

A PAIR of SUVs was waiting on either side of the gate, just out of the security camera's view. Alison registered the danger, but without any time to react. She saw the first vehicle, then turned toward the second one, where in addition to the SUV she could see a broad-shouldered man holding a crossbow, but his bolt had already been shot — or so she realized along with the THWAP of it hitting her tire, followed by a menacing hiss of air.

"Just sit tight," Julio said as the gate rolled closed behind them.

"Why aren't you drawing your gun?" Alison asked, half frantic but doing her damnedest to sound calm.

"Because I'd prefer we both leave this situation alive."

The passenger door on the SUV to her left swung open and a man dropped with a thud to the ground. A cloud of dirt swirled like pigpen around him as he started walking toward the Cayenne. Medium height, buzzed head in need of another buzzing; stubble that somehow looked angry. He had a manic, wild-eyed swagger, and by the time he was at Alison's window he'd drawn a weapon seemingly from nowhere and was banging the butt of his gun against the glass.

"That's Rottweiler," Julio whispered.

"That's the universal sign for roll your fucking window down before I shoot it along with any dumb bitch who happens to be sitting there acting like that shit's a concrete wall." Rottweiler banged on the glass even harder.

"What do I do?" Alison asked Julio, fully frantic now a hiccup away.

"Lower your window and stay cool."

"Good girl," Rottweiler said once there was no longer a window between them. He used his gun to point at the gate. "Priest's guests are early for dinner, bitches. So you're going to pull this limping horsey over there," he nodded toward the right-side SUV, "then you're going to open this gate so we can all go back inside together."

"Gonna have to shoot us both. Ain't no way I'm letting you back inside."

Shoot us both? What the hell, Julio?

"What makes you think I don't like shooting people?" Rottweiler asked.

"Oh, I know you like shooting people. But you like getting what you want even more. And right now, that's getting inside. Unfortunately, I can't do that for you since you're here for no good. Several hours early and with as many as a dozen men divided between those two vehicles."

"Helps to know folks on both sides of the border, eh?" Rottweiler proudly waved his gun. "Look, I ain't bringing no trouble. I'm bringing Priest a proposition to consider while we're sipping margaritas."

"The deal is done," Julio said. "Just like you and Goliat discussed. Dinner is a celebration."

"See, though, that's the problem." Rottweiler scratched his head with the butt of his gun. "I don't trust neither

Goliat nor Priest. So I figured it was the worth the time to drive down here with a few of my men and negotiate my own deal."

"A few, huh?"

"A few," Rottweiler told Julio with a grin.

The DEA should be swooping in right now. Why weren't they here? Were they observing the entire situation from overhead with a drone … or was Alison really all on her own? Ellis said she would need to be in there long enough for them to count the money. Her cavalry was overdue.

"You'll never get inside if you shoot us," Julio said.

"I'd beg to differ, but I ain't ever begged for nothing in my life." Rottweiler lowered his gun. "Look. Good men are my best assets and I don't want to lose any of the ten I got with me. What benefit is there in my leaving here right now without a deal? Nada. So open the gate and everyone is happy."

When Julio didn't immediately answer, Rottweiler shoved his gun against Alison's temple.

"Five … four …"

"JULIO!"

"Fine." Julio drew a breath, then ordered Alison to pull the Cayenne over to the side. Then he got out, marched over to the gate, and entered the code.

"Gracias." Rottweiler gave the word three distinct and very American-sounding syllables.

Two minutes later Julio was walking with Alison, the two of them just behind Francisco, heading back inside with the mad dog and his small army of snarling mongrels. After she dared to throw a fit about not leaving her purse in the car. Rottweiler seemed to think this was funny, and laughed his ass off while Alison went for her purse.

Francisco greeted them with a smile. Rottweiler greeted him back with that manic laugh and a gun in his face.

Unlike last time, Priest was already sitting in his living room with the three man-beasts still standing like sentries behind him. He looked up at his visitors, and though Priest might have been surprised, he managed to hide that truth from his eyes.

"Rottweiler, I presume?"

"Priest." Rottweiler smirked. "Ain't we all got funny names?"

"How can I help you?" Priest asked, now giving his uninvited guest an unsettling smile. "And please, before we get started with whatever it is you would like to insistently discuss, might I kindly request that you holster your weapon and make sure your men all do the same. We do not need the claustrophobia of firearms."

Rottweiler gave Priest a dirty nod, but he didn't argue, instead pointing at Alison with his gun before putting it away as instructed. "Who is she and why is she here?"

"Didn't you know?" Priest replied with a laugh. "She is Julio's mistress. He brought her down to Nogales because his wife would like to meet her."

Rottweiler turned to Alison. "That right?"

She nodded, just as scared of the mad dog as she would have been if he were still holding a gun.

"Tell me … how did you two meet?"

Alison spun the same little yarn as she had for the customs agent, but with a tighter knit thanks to her time with it, delivering a new ending the original narrative hadn't required.

"—so she's fine with it all, but only if she gets to meet me. Julio had some business here, and said that—"

"Stop talking," Rottweiler commanded Alison before returning his attention to Priest and the three men still behind him. The entire room felt poised to strike, and the situation had painted her body in sweat. "Imma let you know how things are gonna be."

"Please." Priest held his smile. "I would very much like for you to tell me. How are things going to be?"

"First off, I'm taking over the Fish's territory. *All of it.* And second, you're going to keep me supplied with whatever I need for a reasonable price."

"Why would I do that?" Priest asked, as if actually considering Rottweiler's nonsense.

"Because Imma sell twice as much as the Fish ever did, and turn this here into a win-win for everyone."

Priest laughed, lightly at first, but then uproariously.

"Wanna tell me what's so funny?" Rottweiler looked like he was longing for his just-holstered gun.

"It is amusing to me …" Priest finally stood and approached his intruder without fear. "You coming into my home and attempting to dictate 'how things are going to be.' Do you not understand that more than anything else, we are in the relationship business?" He shook his head in disappointment. "This is not the best way to start a new relationship."

"Proving I can get things done?" Rottweiler smirked as he nodded. "I beg to differ."

"How do you plan on staying ahead of the cops?" asked Priest.

"I'm always ahead of the cops."

"That is not an answer. Allow me to rephrase: *How do I know that working with you will not open my operation to the DEA?*"

"You think the DEA don't know about your business already?"

"I am quite sure that they do. But there is a big difference between *knowledge* and *vulnerability.* Unfortunately,"

Priest waved a hand at Rottweiler, "everything about you strikes me as a liability."

"You know, I tortured some of Goliat's men ... but I didn't want to." Rottweiler shook his head, lamenting like he actually meant it. "They were asking for it, you know?"

He looked at Priest as if the well-mannered drug lord might genuinely sympathize with him. "I always give people a chance to work with me. You think my head would look like this if I wasn't a practical man?"

He laughed while running a hand over his stubbled head. "This little back-and-forth all started when I had to take care of some business with one'a his men. Preppie little bitch moving product to the country club set. I ask for a piece, preppie refuses, I give the guy a second chance, then another one after that. But preppie ain't been learned in the laws of threes and he done struck out like a bitch. I'm a daring fellow, but we weren't in a place where I felt brazen enough to use the old pistola, so I had to jab my knife into his throat to keep him from screaming, before I stabbed him another twelve times all over his body. I left the little bitch in a shopping cart at Target because it struck me as funny ... you know why I stabbed him thirteen times?"

"I do," answered Priest, displaying impressive poise in the wake of Rottweiler's monologue.

"You do?" Rottweiler raised his eyebrows.

He nodded. "You have a big mouth. And I have heard stories. Like the one about how generous you are when it comes to murder."

"That ain't how it goes." Rottweiler shook his head. "It's 'necessary sacrifices get one free stab with every dozen.' Way you just said it lost the punch. Maybe—"

Rottweiler stopped, his mouth still open, suddenly staring at Alison. It might have been the insane levels of rage wafting out of her soul and rolling toward him. He started laughing. "Julio, right?"

Julio nodded.

"Apologies. Looks like I upset your bitch." Rottweiler turned to Alison. "And apologies for calling you a bitch, but you know ..."

She clenched her fists, doing the same to her toes while biting her tongue. Alison wished that her anger wasn't so obvious, but it was better than doing what she really wanted to do.

There was a good chance that Alison wouldn't be leaving here alive. And if that was true, then she wanted to strangle Rottweiler dead before leaving this life behind.

"Don't worry." Julio put his large arm around her. "I won't let him hurt you."

Alison was grateful for Julio covering her reaction, but now she had a new goal: Kill that motherfucker before she attempted her escape. And if she died while trying either thing, so be it.

"I have a counter offer," said Priest to Rottweiler.

"Oh yeah? What's that?"

Priest opened his mouth and—

Chapter Thirty-Seven

THE GUNSHOT EXPLODED inside the living room.

Alison had no idea which side shot first and hadn't seen anyone draw a gun. She heard the noise and made a swan dive behind the couch, cowering as more weapons were drawn and a volley of shots whizzed through the living room before punching into walls and furniture.

Alison was sure she had heard at least two people landing hard on the floor.

Glass shattered. Bullets zinged by and sent stuffing flying out from both pillows and couches as two sides scurried about, with everyone either bellowing nonsense or cursing in one of two languages.

David took a bullet to his shoulder and a second one to his chest before falling face first a few feet from Alison. His jaw hit the hard tile with an audible CRACK and his gun skittered past her.

She flopped like a fish on the floor, flipping her body around while minimizing her exposure to the crossfire.

She got close to the pistol's handle, but even stretching all the way out she couldn't quite reach.

Alison would have to leave her barely-safe harbor if she wanted to retrieve the weapon, despite all the flying bullets, but without some way to protect herself she'd end up dead anyway.

She lunged forward, but a large hand yanked her back.

Alison yelped and scrambled away from her attacker, enough to grab the gun.

Then that big hand grabbed her by the wrist, gentle but firm as it dragged her back behind the couch. Alison turned around and aimed her new gun at the attacker.

"Quédate jodidamente abajo, estúpida mujer blanca," Julio said.

"Sorry."

"You're going to get yourself killed." He nodded at the weapon. "Do you know how to use that thing?"

Kind of. Sort of. Not really.

Tom had taken her and Sarah to the shooting range a few years ago. He had suddenly insisted that they 'learn to handle a firearm' seemingly out of nowhere, and Alison had in turn thought that her husband was losing his mind. They had fought for more than a month about him keeping a gun in the house, until Tom finally backed down and bought some fake jewelry to pretend he was sorry.

Only now did Alison understand that *a few years ago* was probably right around the time he started planting the seeds of his family's destruction.

Why had she fertilized the dirt by allowing him to pile his bullshit so high? Seeing it in retrospect, there was no excuse for those years Alison had spent letting him walk all over her.

Chaos kept exploding around them.

"Do you know how to use that thing?" Julio repeated.

Alison looked down at the gun, then back at Julio. It had been a while. She had never practiced beyond the basic lessons Tom had insisted on. The weapon felt leaden and awkward in her hand. She could see the safety, but didn't know if it was on or off. This gun didn't look or feel like the one Tom had forced her to hold at home, or any of the three she had tried at the range.

Alison would get straight-A serious about learning to shoot if she got out of this alive, but right now she had no idea what she was doing. Maybe she should have been watching Discovery Channel instead of all those thrillers.

"No." She shook her head at Julio. "Not really."

"Here." Julio held out his hand.

But then in no discernible order: thunder, her face drenched in blood, Julio falling to the floor with a THUD to reveal a mad dog barreling toward her.

Rottweiler had been hit in the thigh and he was smearing a puddle of blood as he dragged himself across the floor toward Alison with one hand while holding his gun with the other.

She aimed at Rottweiler and pulled the trigger.

But the safety was on. So the mad dog just laughed.

And now Alison was breathing so hard she was practically panting, the trembling weapon threatening to slip from her sweaty hands.

He was just a few feet away from her,

So she flipped off the safety, pulled the trigger a second time, and wildly missed her shot.

Rottweiler kept laughing at Alison, even more manic-sounding before as he stopped crawling and raised his gun, level to her face.

She remembered the instructor at the range, eyeing her impatiently before attempting to tell her the same thing again:

You have to breathe. Inhale and exhale. Breathe out when you're firing and squeeze slowly.

So in the two seconds she had, that's exactly what she did.

Inhale. Exhale.

And for the third time she pulled the trigger, squeezing it slowly.

This shot grazed his temple. Rottweiler bellowed in rage but held onto his weapon.

A hair to the left and he'd be on his way to hell.

Instead the mad dog was going to kill her.

"You ain't got me so far and your odds don't look good now. You drop that thing and I'll let you keep living." The dangerous gleam in his eyes and the barrel of his gun were enough to make Alison drop it.

"Good girl." Rottweiler grinned. "But big mistake."

He aimed the barrel right between her eyes and grinned even wider.

"Adios," he said.

Chapter Thirty-Eight

But then ... pure silence.

The sudden quiet seemed to unsettle her executioner. Alison had been expecting the end of everything. Instead she looked up to see him glancing around.

"What now, Dog?" asked as one of Rottweiler's men broke the silence of a ceasefire that had instantly yet unquestionably settled into the room.

"Come over here and help me up." Rottweiler gestured past Alison to someone behind her.

Gustavo scurried over and helped the jefe to his feet. Blood kept gushing from the wound on his thigh. She could see bone and fat peeking through all that shredded fabric and blood.

Rottweiler looked around the room and started to laugh. Then he shot his gun into the ceiling three times. "How do you say yeehaw in Español? Is it *arriba arriba*? Or *andale andale?* Like that little Mexican rat was always saying?"

Priest entered her view, and for the first time it looked

to Alison like he wasn't sitting on the perfect answer. His men were all lying dead on the floor, as was Jose.

"Imma ask you this simple." Rottweiler pointed his barrel at Priest. "You got any more of your men in this place?"

Priest shook his head.

"How'm I supposed to believe you? Could be a bunch of pussies don't wanna get fucked, so they waitin' for shit to dry up in here." Rottweiler shrugged. "Or maybe a bunch of dicks expecting to fuck us like pussies soon as we ain't paying attention."

Priest answered him calmly. "Antonio will be here shortly. He is my chef, and he has a staff of three. I have some associates joining me for dinner, along with some professional company. But alas, I did not expect some of those guests to show up early and double-cross me. I was prepared for a much simpler transaction this afternoon. For that, my three men were plenty. Plus Julio." Priest shook his head while glancing down at the body.

"Your mistake."

"Yes," Priest agreed. "And yours."

Rottweiler looked around the room, pointing at each of the standing men with the barrel of his gun, counting as he went. "—four and that makes five. Plus me. Sure, I lost a few guys, but I'll be leaving with the deal, because what else are you going to do, now that it's just you and her."

Then he moved his gun back on Alison with a laugh.

"Their names were David, Xolo, and Marco," said Priest, still speaking calmly while holding his enemy's eyes. "Francisco deserved to die least of all. He would have made you a drink if only—"

"They're gone and I'm not. Doesn't sound like I made much of a mistake."

"Did you come here hoping to conduct business with me?" Priest asked.

"More like I came here to make sure you did some with me." Rottweiler turned his gun back on Priest.

"Then you have failed."

"You'd rather die?"

"Then conduct business with a man like you?" Priest nodded. "Absolutely. Because it is only a matter of time before you will cross me."

Alison understood: Rottweiler was nothing without a supply to sell. Which meant there was little if any chance he'd put a bullet into what was probably his only — or at the very least his *best* — pipeline.

"We'll start with her."

Gustavo needed no further instruction. He walked over to Alison, grabbed her roughly by the arm, and dragged her over to his boss.

"Let me go!" she yelled.

Gustavo shoved her down to the floor and she landed at Rottweiler's feet. Then he laughed and said, "There you go."

"Be nice," said Rottweiler to Gustavo. "You're bruising the merchandise."

The surviving members of the mad dog's crew joined him in laughter. Their menacing chorus rolled through the living room as Rottweiler holstered his gun like a cowboy and then used his newly free hand to slap her.

Alison's head was violently smacked to the side with a sudden force that shook her body. Then he did it again, this time slapping her even harder from the opposite side.

He spit on her head when she crumpled to the floor in a pile of glass. "Now you're going to pay for making me bleed." Another glob of spit landed on the back of her head, then she turned her body in time to see Rottweiler pulling back his foot for a kick.

But he paused before letting it go, his attention perking to some commotion outside.

"What was that?" Rottweiler turned to Priest.

Nothing from Priest.

More noises, louder now, including what had to be the crunching of tires on gravel.

"You know what it is!" Rottweiler bellowed, looking down on Alison, infuriated by her expression. "Why the fuck are you smiling?"

Because the DEA is here to take you down, dirtbag!

"Remember his chef is supposed to be coming," Gustavo reminded the boss.

"How many people did you say he would be bringing with him?" Rottweiler asked Priest.

But still he said nothing.

At least for now no one was paying attention to Alison, so she used the distraction to grab the longest shard of glass she could find as a voice brayed from a megaphone outside.

"Come out with your hands up! Sal con las manos en alto!"

"Who is that?" Rottweiler asked Alison.

"How am I supposed to know?"

"Why are you smiling?" Rottweiler screamed, his raining spit now seeming accidental.

Alison snarled up at him. "Because whoever it is, they're here to take you down."

He shoved the gun into her ribs. "Good thing I got me a hostage, then."

"This is the DEA! You have five minutes to—"

"We'll see about that," Rottweiler roared over the announcement. Then to his men: "Take care of our visitors while I keep our host and hostess company. Gustavo, get your ass over here and help me first."

Rottweiler's men headed for the garage, except for Gustavo who came over to help get his boss into a secure spot in the corner of the living room, then ushered Alison and Priest over to a prone position at his feet.

She tried not to imagine Rottweiler opening her throat the second he discovered that she had a piece of glass hidden away, waiting to drag its tip across his throat.

But once the mad dog was alone with Priest, Alison, and all those fallen bodies, he rattled a laugh and asked if anyone wanted to play Monopoly. Then he sat there expectantly, as if waiting for his two prisoners to join his guffawing.

She stared back at him placidly, wondering if she could execute either attack before Rottweiler shoved her back to the floor and filled her with bullets.

Or thirteen stabs if he used a blade on her instead.

Priest would probably watch it all happen, still frozen like a statue.

"What are you staring at?" Rottweiler asked her.

Alison could feel the end coming. She tightened her grip on the glass. Her palm was suddenly wet and sticky and warm. If he looked down she was done for.

"I said—"

The first shot rang out, then was instantly followed by a second, third, and fourth.

Rottweiler turned his attention toward the garage door, despite there being nothing to see.

Then Alison lurched up and jabbed the shard into his thigh.

Rottweiler screamed like someone had punched through his stomach to grab a handful of intestines. He doubled over, clutching his leg. Alison had meant to stab him where the bullet was already embedded. She might have hit her target, but it looked like she'd struck an artery as well.

The gunshots were a constant outside, with no way of knowing which side was firing at any given time. But the DEA had come prepared to handle this. So maybe the mad dog's men were mostly gone.

Rottweiler tried to compose himself, muttering curses while pressing down on his thigh.

Priest nodded to himself as he calmly stood, retrieved Rottweiler's gun from where it had fallen on the floor, then leveled the barrel with his enemy's head and casually pulled the trigger.

"N—"

More blood all over Alison.

"If you'll pardon me, I have business outside." Priest pointed to one of the closed doors. "There is a bedroom at the end of that hallway. Lock yourself inside. My apologies, but that is the best I can do."

Then he turned around and headed for the garage.

Alison appreciated the offer, but she wanted to get the hell out of here, not hide. So she grabbed her purse from the counter, went to the wall console and yanked the fob with a Mercedes sign off of its hook, then dashed toward the glass wall.

But she couldn't leave. Not yet. Not without all that money.

Alison had every intention of taking the bags, but even one was much heavier than she expected and required both of her hands.

The skirmish had dwindled to the occasional shot, each one sounding more like the battle's dying gasp. And terror that the door would burst open at any moment turned that one duffel into plenty.

Alison headed for the veranda. The DEA, Priest, or anyone from Team Rottweiler — she needed to escape all of them.

She ignored all the bodies littering that gorgeous tile floor — now smeared and spotted in blood — and made it outside. Down the veranda stairs and onto the rotating plinth of luxury vehicles.

She pressed the fob and saw a smoke-colored Mercedes that looked like a bullet. Half of the cars had American plates. Fortunately, the Mercedes was one of the three.

She tossed the duffel into the trunk, then opened the driver's side door, climbed into the seat, dropped her purse in the seat beside her, and started the engine.

But then Alison realized that she couldn't leave without rotating the platform, and that she had no idea how to do that. There must be some sort of remote ... an app ... something.

She got out of the car, terrified of the silence.

The gunshots had completely stopped. The DEA was probably already in the house. She needed to leave NOW. She glanced around and spotted a control box. Alison went over and saw that — mercifully — there was a single bigger button in addition to several smaller dials.

She pushed the button, then the platform loudly hummed and started to turn.

She ran back to the car, got inside, and wished that she had known how to stop it from turning at the right spot.

This would have to do.

The second its nose was aimed at open road she floored the gas.

Tears soaked her cheeks before she was a mile away from the chaos. The adrenaline of imminent death was still lighting sparklers inside her, making her more than just grateful to still be alive.

She was on her way home to Sarah … and the mother-fucker who had murdered her husband was now lying dead on the floor.

And for the first time since Tom's death, Alison finally felt competent. In control. Like she could take care of herself and Sarah just fine.

As she drove along an endless stretch of road, she rolled down her window, and tossed her burner phone into some dry brush.

Now she just needed to get back across the border.

Chapter Thirty-Nine

ALISON HAD SPENT her entire drive from Nogales drenched in paranoia and trying not to cry.

Her tears weren't a constant, but she was always just starting, just stopping, or working her way toward one or the other. She was in a foreign country, driving a stolen car, with a bag full of drug money in the trunk. Danger would be omnipresent until she reached the border, then made it to the other side.

She wondered if Ellis got his man, or men as it were. She wondered if Priest had survived. She wondered if it was bad of her that she sort of hoped that he had.

Fresh doubt kept creeping up on her, peaking not as she pulled into the line of cars waiting to cross back into America, but when she was midway through that line with nowhere to go.

She was still in a stolen Mercedes, still suffering from an acute case of paranoia, and still with a face that had recently been plastered with tears and blood despite her wiping the evidence mostly away.

It got worse and worse as she inched forward. With

only one car left in front of her, Alison felt a hundred percent sure that she would end up in prison. Somehow Eleanor would find out what had happened to her, figure *good riddance to poor white trash*, then do everything in her power to make sure that Alison rotted in her Mexican jail forever.

But as she pulled up to the border patrol agent and lowered her window, she realized that all that time crying had been like power-charging a secret weapon.

"Oh, honey, are you okay?" asked the female border agent.

"No!" Hilariously, Alison started to cry. And not just a little drizzle of weeping, she really let it all out. Deep and heaving, all the emotions that had been plaguing her since Nogales escaped in a flood. There was no exaggeration in her performance, and by the end she was working to reel it in, but after the emotional squall had blown mostly away the border agent was willing to hear anything Alison had to say.

So she sputtered a story in sorrow soaked bursts:

He was so gorgeous … I'm so stupid for believing him … Nogales is beautiful, you'll love it … HOW WAS I SUPPOSED TO KNOW THAT THE ASSHOLE WAS MARRIED? … I'm so sorry about this … I don't know if I've ever cried this hard … I just really, really, REALLY want to go home.

Alison was very aware of all the vehicles behind her, and that the curtain would have to close on her performance soon. So she did her best to stop crying, wrestle control of her breathing, then look the border agent right in her eyes.

"I apologize … I had no idea how upset I really was until …" She shook her head. "I'm so sorry."

"Nothing to be sorry about, honey." She looked at

Alison with sympathetic eyes. "Men are bastards. Every single one of them. You have your passport, darling?"

Alison nodded, grabbed her purse from the passenger side footwell, and dug inside until she found it, starting another round of light, performative sobbing as she handed her passport over to the agent.

Maybe she felt so sorry for Alison that nothing else mattered. Or perhaps she was simply trying to move the line along after the hysterical woman in her Mercedes finally stopped having her little tantrum. Either way, the agent barely glanced at the passport before handing it back to Alison and waving her along with another *All men are bastards* in her eyes and a "Good luck" from her mouth.

The Mercedes rolled forward, slowly at first, Alison still unreasonably afraid that if she went too fast sirens would flash and blurt behind her. The jig would be up for sure.

She exhaled with her acceleration, and was steadily breathing along with a humming engine by the time the Mercedes hit sixty. Alison was far from home free — she had 124 miles left to Las Orillas, then a long drive to her final destination after that — but at least she was back on her side of the border. Headed north, according to plan.

Alison pulled into the parking lot just before leaving San Diego. Jake had told her she'd see a bowling alley, a Sloppy's, and a 'beat to shit' Big Lots. But she also saw a Thai Charcoal Pit, and even though the place looked like a dump, even a hint of spicy Thai food made her stomach rumble. And with all that money in her trunk, she could order a thousand of everything on the menu.

Instead she ignored the rumble and traded her race car for the twenty-year-old hunter green Subaru that Jake had left for her, parked between the bowling alley and the Big Lots, exactly as promised. Also waiting, as promised, hidden beneath the front seat, was a new burner phone she was supposed to use to contact Jake and confirm she'd made it.

But when she went to turn it on, its battery was dead.

She plugged the phone in to charge it and keyed the ignition hoping that she wasn't dealing with two dead batteries.

Another mighty exhale as the car started with a rattle and hum. The Outback was battered to hell, but Alison already liked it better than her old Cayenne.

Despite the odds, Alison had made it.

But now, on her long drive north to Humboldt, she couldn't stop wondering: *had Sarah?*

Chapter Forty

ALISON PASSED APPROXIMATELY ten thousand places to eat while trekking eight hundred miles in a Subaru, from San Diego to Humboldt, California.

While the phone said it was charging, it refused to turn on every time she checked it, making her uneasy, and she wondered if she should stop somewhere and get another burner. But this one had been programmed with all the numbers she needed — Sarah's, Jake's, and Miguel's.

And while she thought she'd committed Sarah's and Jake's to memory, after everything that had happened in Mexico, she could barely remember her own phone number. So she had to just keep hoping that Jake and Miguel had done their parts.

She was driving the twelve-hour journey on faith and hope alone, two resources that had been in limited supply the past couple of weeks.

She was determined to make as few stops as necessary, just to get gas and use the bathroom, but hunger was making it hard to focus. She ignored the first Thai Charcoal Pit she saw off the highway, and barely considered the second, but that third one finally did her in.

A gobbled order of fried spaghetti later, and Alison was back on the road, justifying the stop since she was at a quarter tank anyway. One more tank of gas and she was in Humboldt County, though there were still quite a few miles of meandering road before she finally pulled into an artery of dirt, directing the Subaru to a barn that might have been red, though it looked black even beneath a moon that was long past its midnight, and a series of buildings behind it.

Despite the hour, everyone was waiting for her: Sarah, Jake, and Miguel.

"MOM!" Sarah ran out of the barn and into her mother's waiting embrace.

"I'm so glad you're safe! Why didn't you call?"

"I'm sorry. The phone wasn't turning on. I thought about getting another one, but … I'm sorry."

"We were so worried!" Sarah said, wiping tears from her eyes as Jake and Miguel joined them outside.

"I'm here now," she said, hugging her daughter tight, never wanting to let her go.

"Hungry?" Jake asked, with his calming smile.

A full order of fried spaghetti — meant to serve four — churned in her stomach. She might never be hungry again. "Starving. What are we eating?"

"All the barbecue you could want."

"What kind of meat?"

"Every kind." Jake smiled.

"Buffalo?" Alison asked.

Sarah laughed — the first time Alison had heard the sound directed at her in too long.

Miguel took her hand and she let him. So clearly the two of them had patched things up.

"Okay, no buffalo," Jake said. "But there's brisket and chicken and ribs and steak, plus burgers and dogs if you want them."

"Why so much meat?"

"Because Uncle Chip won't be back until the weekend," Sarah said.

Then Jake clarified. "My buddy Chip is a vegan. I figured we could all use some protein, so we should maybe get that out of the way now. It's just rude to cook it in front of him."

Sarah laughed again. She seemed so happy. Even happier when Miguel squeezed her hand.

Jake led them all back to the barn. Up close, it was red, and handsome. The inside was even more gorgeous. Nothing at all like Alison had expected. A cavernous space with a few partitioned-off areas. A stunning kitchen area with a gourmet stove, adjacent to a sturdy dining table that was already long and looked like it could be expanded into something much longer. There was a spacious living room with several comfortable-looking couches, a cornered-off spot that was likely the downstairs bathroom, and a spiral staircase leading to a second-floor loft that likely harbored bedrooms and a bathroom with — it seemed so obvious — a clawfoot tub.

The meat smelled delicious. A wallop to the nostrils as Alison entered the barn.

Jake must have seen it on her face. He laughed and said, "It'll air out before Chip gets back."

Chip: this was his barn, his farm, his good graces that got her here. Jake had owed Tom a favor, and Chip was indebted to Jake. So now here they were with a place for her and Sarah to stay, plus the fresh start Alison could have never had otherwise.

Sarah and Miguel went to grab plates. Alison had no

idea whether they were really hungry, or pretending in celebration. She watched them go, sensing that Jake wanted her to stay behind.

He handed her an envelope once they left. "It's all in there."

She opened it and peeked inside.

"Chip got you and Sarah both new driver's licenses and social security cards. You're also welcome to stick around here on the farm, long as you want to if you're willing to work. That goes for both of you. But beyond that, me and Chip are now square."

She shook her head in disbelief. "I can't believe we get to start over."

"Chip's also offered you a gig as a budtender if you want."

"Is that what I think it is?" Alison asked.

"Sure is." He grinned. "Chip owns some dispensaries. California, Colorado, and Oklahoma. You wouldn't even have to live in Humboldt. He could train you here and you could move to any one of those places."

"What does a budtender do … exactly? Is that basically being a cashier in a weed store?"

"More like being a bartender who knows everything there is to know about all the beers on tap."

"I have to tell you something," Alison whispered.

He raised his eyebrows: *Yeah?*

First she told him everything that had happened from when they arrived at Priest's to when she cried her ass off to get back into the country. Then she leaned in and whispered the best part.

"I have the money. It's in the Subaru. Well, one bag of it, but it feels like *a lot*. What do you think I should do?"

"Keep it and tell no one."

"Do you want—"

"Absolutely not." He shook his head, cutting her off. "I'm glad you have it. But you should still get a job doing something."

"Why?"

"So it appears to anyone looking that you have a normal life. And it's best to keep that cash around in case Goliat comes looking for you. Maybe wait a few years until the coast is clear."

"How many?"

He shrugged. "Two. Ten. Hard to say."

"I doubt I can send my daughter to college working as a budtender."

"But you can send her to college by working for Chip. He's a smart guy. And best of all, you can trust him. Nothing illegal about his business, it's all above board … nothing to make you uncomfortable."

"I'm not uncomfortable."

"Okay." He smiled.

"Will I have to live with a go-bag for the rest of my life?"

"Probably." He nodded. "But at least you have a life to live. Hopefully a long one. And you'll always have a friend in me. Chip too, I'm sure. You'll love the guy once you meet him."

"Will you please take some of … what I have."

"Absolutely not." Jake shook his head. "What's yours is yours."

"But I wouldn't have what's mine if you hadn't helped me."

"I was happy to do it, and would've been even had I not been obligated to Tom. I owed my old buddy a favor, and now that favor's paid. The wheel of karma keeps right on turning and the moon outside keeps on holding her smile. Everything is sweet, and sweeter if you stop trying to repay a debt you don't owe me so I can delight in doing the right thing."

"Do you always talk like that?" Alison might not have asked, if all those words hadn't dripped out of his mouth like he'd dipped them in honey.

"Only after I take a ride on the unicorn. You wanna gallop?" He pulled a small silver box from his pocket and flipped it open in offering.

"You only have two left." The citrusy lavender and something or other aroma of the Unicorn hit her nose as the words left her mouth.

"This farm here," Jake looked all around the barn, "this is where Green Unicorn was born. I got two in my pocket, but we've got acres of the stuff. Here."

He handed her the box and she took it with a smile.

"Want me to light you?"

She shook her head. "Not in front of Sarah."

"It's better to be——"

"I know," Alison said, cutting him off. "You're right. I'm just not ready for that. It's been a long day."

"That it has." Jake nodded and gave her a grin.

"You really won't tell me why you owed Tom?"

"I'll just say that I got the better end of the deal, and that a weight has finally been lifted off of my shoulders."

"Not even a hint?"

"Okay, you know how you took the rap for Tom's weed when you were kids? Well, when we were stationed in the Middle East, I got into a spot of trouble, and Tom took the heat for me. I didn't ask him to. But he insisted. I might not be here if not for him saving my ass. Whatever he did to put you in this awful situation, I'm sure it wasn't his intention. He was a good man, but even good people make bad choices."

"And the wheel of karma keeps turning," Alison said

with a half-hearted smile. She wasn't ready to forgive Tom yet, but maybe in time she could hate him a little less and remember the good man she'd fallen in love with.

Then they grabbed their plates, piled their meat, and walked over to the table together.

Sarah and Miguel were eating. And judging by the remnants, they had definitely not filled their plates to be polite.

"More news," Miguel said, looking up from his phone as they sat.

"What's happening now?" Jake asked, with the tone of a continuing conversation.

"The story is breaking here, but it's huge news in Mexico already. This might go down as the biggest bust in recent history. The DEA took down Rottweiler and Priest. Goliat is rumored to have been in Nogales to meet with the other two, so there's a manhunt for him now."

"Why did they let me cross at the border?" Alison asked, finally voicing something she had been wondering ever since her flight from Mexico.

"You said you were crying and—" Jake started.

"I know why that border agent didn't stop me, but why wasn't she on the lookout? The DEA had to know that I'd been there, and that I had taken a car. Why didn't they stop me?"

"Maybe that Ellis guy was letting you go," Jake suggested.

"Maybe ..." Alison mumbled to herself.

"Hard to believe that Dad really started all of this," Sarah said.

She looked older. But more, a blush of appreciation had colored her cheeks with a hue her mother could both see and feel, like sun lighting a new day for the both of them.

"Half the time I still can't believe it," Alison agreed. "But then the other half I think, *Of course.*"

"I know what you mean," Sarah said.

"I guess I always knew." Miguel ventured a laugh.

"Ditto." Jake raised his hand.

"Maybe we could toast him," Sarah suggested, raising her glass of water. "Even though he did some stuff that he shouldn't have, I'll still miss him every day for the rest of my life."

Everyone else raised their glasses.

And Alison said, "Here's to remembering all the good stuff he did, and learning from all of the bad."

"Here's to that," Sarah agreed.

Then everyone toasted and ate.

Alison was sleeping soon after that. She barely remembered being led to bed, where she crashed hard until it was deep into the next afternoon.

Epilogue

ONE YEAR LATER ...

AFTER A LONG DAY OF WORK, Alison and Chip were sitting on the sloped roof of the barn, looking out at the setting sun as it painted the horizon in a melange of ochre and violet.

"*Riiiiiiiighht?*" Chip finished his story with a long laugh and a matching nod, stopping only to take a massive drag from what were affectionately referred to as "Chip Joints" around the farm. They were rolled with regular papers, but each roll somehow managed to pack what seemed like five times the usual amount of flower into it. Alison loved them.

He finished his hit and handed her the Unicorn.

She put it to her lips and inhaled with a smile.

"Have I ever told you about the doobie toss?" Chip asked Alison, already onto another story.

"I don't think so." Definitely not. She would remember something called a doobie toss.

Alison passed the current Unicorn doobie back his way. Chip accepted the gift, but then held it with a smoking tip while telling his story.

"So … me and a bunch of buddies would sneak as many pre-rolls into a concert as we could, then we'd get up high and toss 'em down to the crowd. *Doobie toss.*" Another laugh, another nod, another long inhale and exhale of smoke.

Chip was a good time, and Alison always enjoyed his company.

Even more, she enjoyed *working* for his company. Chip Off the Old Farm grew premium flower, and despite his outlaw roots, Chip now played a cannabis game that was a hundred percent legal. Alison took to her new job like flower to sunlight. She started out as a budtender like Chip had suggested, but soon enough she wanted to know everything. Just like when she was first learning to cook.

Soon enough Alison was blending her passions like ingredients in a bowl, mixing an old culinary love with her newfound affection for cannabis. Starting tomorrow, she and Chip were working on a recipe book.

"You sure about this?" Alison asked him again.

"Stop it. Or you can't smoke any more of my weed." He took a puff. Then a medium hold with a mighty exhale. "Just kidding. You can always smoke my weed."

"Isn't it smarter to do this with a celebrity chef?"

"Who says I'm not also working with a celebrity chef? There's room for both. I bet there's more moms like you than Gordon Ramsay realizes, *riiiiiigggghhht?*"

Chip tried to pass her the Unicorn, but she wasn't sure if she could take any more.

"Right." She laughed, shaking her head with a smile while raising her palm in refusal.

He took another puff, then leaned back and really held

it this time. Once the smoke was like a halo over his head he resurrected a question he couldn't seem to let die. "You sure you don't want an advance on the project? Wouldn't be nothing."

She shook her head. "I'm happy with the budtender money, and fifty-fifty if this book takes off."

"*When*," Chip corrected her with a nod.

"When," she repeated, both his word and the gesture. "And it's good for Sarah. We're in a really great place right now. I like who I am, and I like who she is. Most of all, I like who she's becoming."

"You don't miss all the bells and whistles of that old life?"

"Not a single one of them." Alison sighed — it felt so good to say this out loud. "I don't have a Cayenne or a big house, but I also don't have a mother-in-law breathing down my neck, or the pressure of an overpriced mortgage. I'm *relieved* that I'll never have to go back to that ... that *place*. Ugh — even thinking about the Rolling Knolls Country Club makes me want to throw up in my mouth. So, no, I don't have a lot of things that I used to enjoy, but I also don't have a lot of things that I used to." She laughed. "Sarah and I are closer than ever, and I don't have to put up with other people's bullshit. What else could I possibly want?"

Before Chip could respond, Alison added a thought.

"It's funny. I spent most of my life chasing some dream of what I thought I wanted without ever really stopping to wonder where that dream came from. Was it my dream? Was it planted there by childhood experiences? Was it what society, the media, and my peers told me to dream? And it wasn't until the nightmare Tom sent us into that I truly woke up to find out who I really am, and what *I* really want. And how none of it has anything to do with fancy cars, nice houses, or that life. All I really need is family, a few *real* friends, and to feel like I'm making a difference to someone."

Chip nodded, "Amen, sister," then handed her the Green Unicorn.

She took another hit and handed it back. "And as a wise man said, the wheel of karma keeps right on turning."

Natalie hasn't thought about her sorority sister, Olivia, since she slept with — then married — the love of Olivia's life. Now Olivia is back with information that pulls the rug out from under Natalie's comfortable suburban life. She also has a proposal…

Get Tell Me No Lies Today

A Quick Favor

Thank you for reading *Blown*.

If you enjoyed this book would you please consider writing a review of it on your favorite bookselling site so other readers might enjoy it too. Just a couple of sentences. That would mean a lot to me.

Thank you!

Sean and Dave

About the Author

Nolon King writes fast-paced psychological thrillers set in the glitzy world of entertainment's power players with a bold, insightful voice. He's not afraid to explore the darker side of human nature through stories featuring families torn apart by secrets and lies.

Nolon loves to write about big questions and moral quandaries. How far would you go to cover up an honest mistake? Would you destroy your career to protect your family? How much of your soul would you sell to get the life of your dreams? Would you cheat on your husband to keep your children safe? Would you give in to a stalker's demands to save your marriage?

www.ingramcontent.com/pod-product-compliance
Lightning Source LLC
Chambersburg PA
CBHW060622100726
47907CB00006B/1727